A Cloud of Outrageous Blue

ALSO BY VESPER STAMPER

What the Night Sings

A Cloud of Outrageous Blue

Vesper Stamper

ALFRED A. KNOPF
New York

THIS IS A BORZOI BOOK PUBLISHED BY ALFRED A. KNOPF

This is a work of fiction. Names, characters, places, and incidents either are the product of the author's imagination or are used fictitiously. Any resemblance to actual persons, living or dead, events, or locales is entirely coincidental.

Copyright © 2020 by Vesper Stamper

All rights reserved. Published in the United States by Alfred A. Knopf, an imprint of Random House Children's Books, a division of Penguin Random House LLC, New York.

Knopf, Borzoi Books, and the colophon are registered trademarks of Penguin Random House LLC.

Visit us on the Web! GetUnderlined.com

Educators and librarians, for a variety of teaching tools, visit us at RHTeachersLibrarians.com

Library of Congress Cataloging-in-Publication Data is available upon request.
ISBN 978-1-5247-0041-6 (trade) — ISBN 978-1-5247-0042-3 (lib. bdg.) — ISBN 978-1-5247-0043-0 (ebook)

The text of this book is set in 12-point Adobe Jenson.
The illustrations were created using acrylic ink, watercolor, and black colored pencil, enhanced digitally.
Book design by Trish Parcell

MANUFACTURED IN ITALY
August 2020
10 9 8 7 6 5 4 3 2 1

First Edition

Dedicated to Notre-Dame de Paris
and the memory of Carl Titolo

It did not really matter what we expected from life,
but rather what life expected from us.
—VIKTOR FRANKL

synesthesia

(sih-nuss-THEE-zhuh)

n. A condition in which one type of stimulation
evokes the sensation of another, as when the hearing
of a sound produces the visualization of a color.

THE QUARTER DAYS

Lady Day, March 25

Saint John's Day, June 24

Michaelmas, September 29

Christmas, December 25

THE DAILY OFFICES

Matins, Midnight Prayer, *midnight*

Lauds, Dawn Prayer, 3:00 a.m.

Prime, Early-Morning Prayer, 6:00 a.m.

Terce, Midmorning Prayer, 9:00 a.m.

Sext, Midday Prayer, *noon*

Nones, Midafternoon Prayer, 3:00 p.m.

Vespers, Evening Prayer, 6:00 p.m.

Compline, Night Prayer, 9:00 p.m.

Prologue

The Legend of the Spring

When the earth was newborn and the waters were being gathered together around the dry land, when no bird flew above or fish swam below, a fissure opened in the ground, and a spring emerged, heated by the fiery cauldrons beneath.

It bubbled there happily, effervescent and warm, and when the first wanderers arrived in that place, they drank its sweet waters and were refreshed. They planted a sacred yew seedling at its edge and called the place holy.

Now, once every generation, a bright ball of fire appeared in the sky, and shortly after, a disaster would follow—famine, pestilence or war. But though all the peoples around them fell, those who drank from the spring were spared. They venerated the spring, building it around with stone.

Over time, attitudes changed. Hearts grew proud, and the spring was abandoned. The stones sank back into the earth, and the yew's roots thickened over the spring. The ball of fire would flash as it always had, though few noticed. Fewer still grasped its significance. Countless thousands were lost.

But a stream needs only one stone to change its course, just as a generation needs only one person to take notice of a warning, and avail herself of the remedy.

This is the story of one.

Winter
1348

— 1 —

Everyone in the canvas-covered cart is asleep. Four other travelers nestle into the deep straw of the wagon bed—strangers, all of us, except for a father and his son of maybe nine or ten years. The old monk there's a snorer, and it takes him the whole trip to get his bones comfortable. When I got into this cart, the only space had been next to the woman with the gray hair, the pink fleshy face, the gentle-eyed, reticent smile. She made as much room as she could, but someone's knee or elbow is always in my side—

—like the proverbial thorn. That's what Mam would have said.

"Tusmore village," says the driver. "Everyone out who needs a piss."

The monk needs help getting out, so I lend him a hand. From the gap in the cart cover, the white winter sun blinds me, and when my eyes adjust, it's like I haven't left Hartley Cross after all. They look the same, these villages, and each one makes me hurt for home.

I don't dare leave my satchel in the cart for curious eyes or fingers. It wouldn't be right to say that *all* of my worldly possessions are here in my stitched-up bag. Most things I had to leave behind. The blankets. The cooking kettle. Pounce barking me home, and Juniper winding around my ankles with that deep purr. The sheep, the trees, the forest trail.

Don't forget the fort you built with Henry against that uprooted oak.

Don't forget the scent of the fields in the rain.

Don't forget the crack on the daub wall that looked like a fawn's face.

Don't.

Forget.

I reach into the satchel and run my fingers over each item until I feel the drawings I made of my parents. What's left is barely discernible, the fine lines made with the brass stylus on fire-browned parchment, burned in a moment of anger.

Don't forget Da's face. And don't forget Mam's face. And don't forget baby sis's face.

Nor even your brother Henry's.

I would have stuffed the entire house into the satchel if I could. But I only took what fit—Mam's cloak and dark woad-blue gown, the small clay honey pot Henry gave me, my best willow charcoal twigs, rolled in a piece of linen, to draw with.

I hold the stone cross from Mason and sense his impact on it, his hands shaping and smoothing it. *And don't forget Mason's hands.*

I may have to surrender all these things when I get to the priory, but it's a risk worth taking—they're all I have left of everyone I love.

It was only yesterday, midmorning, when everything changed.

"Edie?" Henry's voice was alarmed. He shook me. Shook and shook. "Edie, wake up!"

I stirred, shoved his hand off my shoulder and looked sideways at my big brother. Suddenly everything came rushing back like a tempest:

Da's murder.

Mam's death, birthing little baby sis.

Mason avoiding me, just like the rest of the villagers.

The fear of starvation.

The intensifying fights with Henry as we got more and more desperate.

Death and loss and fury and hunger.

"Get away from me," I grunted, rolling back over.

"You weren't waking up," he said. "Are you all right?"

"No."

Henry ignored me, grinning, almost dancing with excitement. I sat up slowly, suspicion gnawing at my belly.

"Edie, I know where you're going to go!"

"Henry, we talked about this," I reminded him. "You said we were leaving together. In the spring. You said that Lord Geoffrey would wait until then to evict us. Remember?"

"I know, but this is better. Brother Robert's got a prioress friend up north, and she said she'd take you in. Lord Geoffrey agreed. It's Saint Christopher's Priory, in Thornchester. It's all sorted. They normally only take noblewomen, but out of charity they'll take you as a conversa!"

A priory?

The word felt like a fresh, icy slap to the side of my head. And a conversa—a lay sister, a servant? So instead of being a wooler's daughter with at least some dignity, I'd be cleaning the latrines of prissy nuns? How was that better?

"What do you mean, it's all sorted?" I pressed him. "Who put you in charge of me?"

Henry looked stunned. "Da did, Edie. When they murdered him."

Of course it was Henry's decision; I knew that. The moment Da died, Henry became head of house, but that didn't really give him options. He still had to answer to Lord Geoffrey Caxton, the very man who killed our father. We were bound to Lord Geoffrey, and I was bound to Henry. But I didn't want to accept it. Henry was only two years older than me—my brother, not my lord.

"But don't you understand?" he coaxed. "It's better than we could have hoped! You and I would have been lucky to find a house half this size to let, in some strange place, scraping by on someone else's land—we could have been beggars!"

I tried to be calm, but I just couldn't. "This is it, then, Henry? Sixteen years old, and the best thing I can hope for is to rot away in some convent? Where they send the old hags and toady girls? And I should be grateful? Go to hell!"

The words singed my mouth as I spat them, and Henry flinched, all the optimism drained from his face in a moment.

He set his jaw and spoke with an unnerving softness. "Fine, Edyth. I tried to do my best by you. If this is your thanks . . . then we'll say goodbye now. The wagon will be here for you at dawn."

He opened the cupboard and grabbed half a loaf and filled his waterskin with ale. I had never been angry with my big brother before, my best friend, my hero—but desperation lit one last flaming arrow on my tongue.

"Traitor! It's you and me, Edie," I mocked his childhood promise. "What a lie! You don't care about anyone but yourself! It's Henry and Henry, and to hell with little sister! Edyth, Edyth, Round and Red, might as well be left for dead!"

Henry turned and gave me a look I'd never seen. Something about the muscles in his face made him look much older than eighteen, like fate had cornered and caged him. He clenched his teeth and his muscles pulsed; he sniffed hard, walked quickly out of the house and slammed the door to my enraged scream.

I sank to the floor, skirts in a pool around me, and cried.

The day darkened early. A raindrop hung pregnant from the edge of the windowsill, all silvers except for a thin strip of rainbow edging its metal belly, and I could feel those colors on my tongue, like the time when I tried licking the edge of the cold kettle, just to see if it tasted like I thought it would: yes, like blood and ash, like the dark brown stripes that appeared at the outsides of my eyes. That was when Mam could stir things in the kettle, the green alexanders with the fresh spring butter. She could stir things in a kettle, because she was alive.

That was when Da was alive, too, and he would dip the hardest edges of the brown bread and sop up the iron-tinged butter, and it would drop in his beard and glisten there for a bit, until he'd grab the corner of Mam's apron and wipe his mouth proper, like a gentleman.

But my father was no gentleman, much as Mam would have liked him to be. He was stout and red-bearded and loud and butter-drippy. Da, with a belly like the raindrop, with a belly rivaling Mam's, carrying the child that would end her life.

Nothing can be done about it now. Come spring, Lord Caxton will turn Henry out, and someone else will be living in that house where I was born. Someone else will make their pottage on our fire, rise their bread dough in our proofing pot. But before the next family moves in, they'll bring the priest to cleanse the house of the evil that once resided there, the scourge that caused a whole family to fail.

— 2 —

Somewhere in Derbyshire, the road beneath us changes suddenly from packed dirt to bumpy stone and jostles everyone awake to a harmony of groans. Little lightning bolts shoot at my vision with every crash of the wheels. The stones of the old Roman way are at odd angles, and the driver eventually moves off to the grass just to avoid them. Days upon days have passed, and we are all road-sore.

"Stopping," says the driver, pulling in through a town gate. "I'll go find a tavern. Wait here."

He's taking a while, so I jump out and stretch my legs. The town's not a large one. But it's eerily quiet, except for some skinny horses and sheep in the streets. The driver comes back with a distant look on his face.

"Strange," he says. "Town's empty. Old man told me to stay out—everyone's dead. Some kind of illness . . . he's the only one left."

Dead. That's a word I've heard too often this year. I tuck my face into the hood of Mam's cloak and will her to be alive for me, just for this moment, while we shake the dust of the town off our feet.

After Henry left that last day, the wattle gate crackled open and a pair of shoes shuffled on the flagstone. I was afraid of being alone in the house like that. No one could be trusted, and no one was asking for my trust, anyway. Henry and Edyth le Sherman were poison people, not to be pitied, only shunned.

Once I was sure the stranger was gone, I rose slowly from the hearth and cracked the door open. On the threshold, placed on a thin layer of fresh snow, was a wooden box. Inside was a kettle of just-made porridge, steaming hot. A loaf of bread, some dried apples and a cheese. A thick woolen blanket, a little moth-eaten. Two pairs of old knit mittens. A palm-sized cross carved from stone.

Mason.

Is that sort of kindness even possible now, where I'm headed? I've heard about priories, vast and cold, where women go to hollow out and shrivel until their skin's like the parchment of their prayer books.

A place where I've got to hear day and night about God.

After He took every good thing from me, to make me go to the very place I can't escape Him? It's like giving vinegar to someone dying of thirst.

At the edge of town, by a bend in the river, Mason and his da lived in a house smaller than mine. Mason's mam died when he was very young, and not one to stand on ceremony or comfort, Old John chopped off a third of their house and burned the walls as fuel. Piles of different kinds of stone lay in the yard. A small barn barely held a horse and its tack. Mason's people weren't crofters like us; they earned wages or were paid in kind, so there was a meager kitchen garden but not much land. Besides, stonemasons travel where the work is, so home was *a relative concept.*

Just as I lifted my fist to knock on the door, Mason came out of the barn, clapping dust and straw off his hands.

"Edyth!" He started. "What are you doing here?"

I pulled my hood back a little; I couldn't hide the despair in my eyes. "Could we go somewhere?" I asked flatly. "I need to tell you something."

He searched my face with apprehension. "Let me tell my father."

Mason came out of the house a few minutes later. We walked to Saint Andrew's churchyard and sat beneath the yew tree, where we had talked for the first time in May.

"I made you something, Mason. Here . . . I'm your Saint Nicholas." I placed the square of parchment in his palm, smiling to conceal the way my heart was being sliced in half. It was a miniature drawing of this yew tree, our tree, cut away to show two doves inside, with the tips of their beaks touching.

"It's beautiful," he said. "Did you draw this?"

"Yes."

He quietly traced the thin lines with his finger. "There's so much I wanted to—" His voice caught, and he didn't finish.

"Mason, I don't hold it against you. Since Da was killed, I know you've had to dodge me, just like everyone else. But I wanted to tell you myself—I have to leave Hartley Cross."

"What do you mean, leave?"

"Henry's sending me away," I said. "We can't run the croft ourselves. We barely met Lord Geoffrey's wool and grain quotas, just for the right to stay in our house for the winter."

"What? Why would he—" Mason's eyes narrowed. "Where is he sending you?"

"To some priory in Yorkshire . . . Saint Christopher's."

"A priory?" He turned his head in disbelief. "You're going to be a nun?"

"No. No. I could never be a nun." I shook my head. "Just a laborer. There's a wagon coming tomorrow at dawn."

"Tomorrow?" He unwittingly began to crumple the drawing in his hand. "He couldn't give you more time?"

"No," I said. "It's my only chance to avoid begging or . . . or worse."

Mason rubbed his eyes in frustration. I decided to risk an idea, one I'd been thinking of but never dared to say out loud.

"Mason, what if . . . I . . . stayed with you? And your da, I mean. I could help you take care of him—"

"What?"

I pressed on. "Or we could leave together, like we always dreamed about. Go where no one knows us. You're a freeman, and a stonemason. You can find work anywhere—"

"It's not that simple, Edyth!"

His shout rang in my ears, reverberating like white-hot coils in front of me, and I shut my eyes tight against the assault of noise and color.

"Of course." I got up quickly and gathered my skirts to run home, away from the growing seed of shame. "You can't be with an orphan from a cursed family. I'm sorry."

Mason grabbed my hand. "Edyth, wait. I'm sorry. Please sit, please." He turned my hand over. "I have something for you, too." He opened my palm and placed there another stone cross, as smooth as glass, carved with a trail of oak leaves. Its color was just like the one in the box on our doorstep.

"You're the one who's been leaving us meals, aren't you?"

"You don't deserve all that cruelty," he said. "But I couldn't come see you. Not because of these stupid Hartley Cross folks. Who cares about them? " He drew a long breath and blinked, hard. "My father is dying."

"Oh . . . Mason . . . I don't know what to say."

The snow clouds cleared away, and the early moon reflected glittering crystals off the white, like the ground was twilight.

"So you see why," he said.

I nodded and hung my head, wanting to fall forward into the earth.

"Everything's changing, Mason. Everything's fading away."

He opened his cloak and wrapped it around both of us. We grew quiet, holding each other's gifts. There was the comfort of Mason and the loss of him, and I craved to keep feeling this moment, willing tomorrow never to come.

— 3 —

*H*enry and I arrived home at the same time that night, not speaking, and we lay down to sleep in the single bed. Pounce whined at our feet, his brow wrinkled above his big fire-lit dog eyes. Rain began to crackle on the thatch.

My brother and I had slept on the same pallet together since I was a toddler, and after our parents died, Henry was there in the night to get a new rag to dry my tears when the last one was soaked through. He was my closest companion, the one who stood up for me against the cruelty of the other village children. But I guess this is what happens to orphans: life turns you the wrong way round like magnets and forces you apart.

Just then, the frost came so sudden, it slid under the door and crawled into bed with us. And, I knew, anything green outside was now dead. That was that. I blew out the rushlight.

But cold as it was, I got out of bed, walked away from my brother and lay down on the hard floor where our parents' bed had been. And that night it was Henry who shed tears, silently, and alone.

The packed earth radiated cold up through my body as I woke alone in the still-dark house. Pounce lay pressed against me—Henry must have left him and gone to feed the animals. Embers glowed on the hearth, bits of wood seizing and popping, though the fire was pretty far gone.

I sat on the stool, stoking what remained, and let thoughts fill my head.

In one long thread they came, spinning themselves before my eyes:

I have to leave this house today and go to a place where I don't know anyone. I will bring Mam's blue wool dress, and her pale green linen one. And the little pack of parchments Da gave me. And the drawings I did of the family. Henry'll take Pounce, and Juniper will have to live on field mice. And I will be utterly alone. Henry can force me to go to some priory, but maybe I'll show him and die early, and then I will be free. I will be with Mam and Da, and I will be free.

And Henry will be sorry he sent me away. He'll be sorry he broke up what was left of us.

I shook myself and tried to resurrect the fire, blowing on the glowing embers. Once winter finally settled upon the house, the only thing for Henry to do would be to endure.

I rummaged through the rough-hewn wooden chest, and at the bottom was my father's old rucksack with the drawstring top. I ran my fingers over the rough, waxed weave, then went around the house, packing things into it.

Suddenly I felt how red I was getting, how hard I was shoving my belongings into the sack. Soon I was punching the bag, punching and screaming, and explosions of hot colors mixed with my steaming tears. I threw the bag across the room. It hit the stool, and both tumbled into the fire. Startled, I opened my swollen eyes: the corner of the bag had caught alight. Pounce cowered and Juniper puffed up. I jumped and grabbed the sack, rolling it over to put out the flame. The scorched corner of the bag revealed a singed dress hem and an unfortunate knitted stocking—nothing that couldn't be mended.

But the drawings—the drawings were badly burned. I held them to my gut and folded over, laid my head on the rucksack and waited for dawn.

Well, this is it, *I thought. I strapped on my pattens, shouldered Da's satchel and trudged outside into the darkness, waiting for the wagon to come. Clouds pulled apart* like carded wool, and a bright moon, just shy of full, peeked through the torn sky to shine blue on the whiteness. Across the field, a cloud squalled, and powdery snow rolled and dissipated, falling like a thin veil. I flinched at the sight of a mouse—no, a leaf skimming the surface of the snow.

The stillness was killing me, so I walked to the sheep pen, took off my mittens and ran my hands over the warm, growing fleeces, pressing into the wool and letting the heat swirl around my cold fingers. And the voices of Mam and Da were so present in my ears that the agony of their missingness made my knees buckle under, and I was grateful the sheep were there to lean on. Just then, the dawn light emerged, streaked with the dull sound of a horse's hooves, and of cartwheels rolling up to the market cross.

— 4 —

"This'll be Thornchester," says the driver. "The rest of us'll get out here and seek the guesthouse, but you two, monk and young maid, see the gatekeeper on your own."

The passengers begin packing up. The father breaks off some bread and cheese for his son, who offers me a few dried Spanish apricots. My knitted brow softens; my pressed-white lips part and I thank the boy. The tart sweetness of the apricots tickles the inside of my nose like little blue sparks. I take a deep breath and chew as slowly as I can.

The old monk lifts the wagon covering up front. On a hilltop ahead, the Priory of Saint Christopher rises white-limed and clean from the encircling town. In Hartley Cross, it wasn't unusual for houses to be raised and fall back into the soil within one generation. The only two stone structures we had were little Saint Andrew's church and the river wall.

The huge priory church looms in the moonlight, its heavy base tapering upward to twin quill points laced with tracery that defies its material, like two arms reaching to be picked up by a parent, a rock child learning to walk.

We ride over the stone bridge and under the massive arch of the gatehouse. I'm surprised to feel solid pavement beneath my feet.

When I jump out of the cart, the monk gets out, too, helped by the father and greeted by a tall priest. While the driver hands a note to the gatekeeper, I stand in the vestibule, staring back at the river encircling the priory, torchlight rippling reflections in its current.

The town spreads out on the other side of the river, its two-storied row houses, some timber-framed, some limestone, winding along the streets. Every now and then the flutter of candlelight punctures the darkened windows. There must be *glass* in those windows; no sane person would keep their shutters open on a wintry night like this.

After a few minutes, I'm ushered forward by a dark female figure and led through the vestibule into a wide, open space. The moon makes the pale buildings glow and the shadows utterly black. In front of me towers the enormous church. *Oh, that stone could fly like this, weightless, above the earth!* I think, in spite of myself. We turn in to a doorway and wind through tangled passages, the middle-of-the-night quiet punctuated by loud snoring. That awake-but-am-I-dreaming feeling governs my feet as I follow the silent form to a little room.

In the light of my guide's candle, there isn't much I can see of the tiny, stuffy cell. A hundred questions fill my head, but I think better of asking, since this woman does not speak one word to me. She puts my satchel in a chest at the foot of the bed, lights a candle on a shelf, and leaves me.

I don't know what to do. Sleep? Unpack? I stand in the shaft of moonlight and stare blankly, with nothing but an unformed question turning over again and again in my mind, until I begin to wobble on the balls of my feet. I lie down on the bed in my cloak and shoes, too exhausted to cry.

The light dims, and freezing rain begins, with a different sound than I've always known, the soft *patter-tap* on thatch above and mud below. This roof is timber, and the drops echo on the inside of this wood-and-stone box that is now home. A different rhythm, a different peace, a different color—pale yellow pops of powder on the insides of my eyes.

Where is the earthen floor beneath me, the animals burrowing holes for their beds beneath my straw pallet? I'm on a second story, lifted from the floor on a bed frame, floating in the air, unconnected to anything I know.

Pahhh goes the powdery sound, falling and falling, like a game of volleyed wool puffs. On nights like this, Da would sit at the trestle table and watch his family sleep by rushlight, singing to his Heloise a tune he learned in Flanders—

> *Car tant vous aim—sans mentir—*
> *Qu'on porroit avant tarir*
> *La haute mer*
> *Et ses ondes retenir*
> *Que me peüsse alentir*
> *De vous amer.*

> *For I love you so much—it's no lie!—*
> *That one could dry up*
> *The high seas*
> *And hold back their waves*
> *Before I could hold back*
> *From loving you.*

The memory makes my heart ache. I fumble in the satchel for the bundle of little parchments and sit at the desk. Da's face in the burnt drawing is only fractionally recognizable. In the half-light, I try to re-create, on a fresh sheet, what I can remember of him, and stare at the ghost of his image.

I'm sorry, Da. I'm sorry our last words were quarrels about Mason. I'm sorry I never got to say goodbye.

I lie down on the warm floor, kiss the brass-point lips and hum his song, falling asleep with the drawing under my cheek.

I wake a little to a change in the atmosphere of my priory cell. At home, I could always tell it was snowing by the color of the light, the way the world became muffled and the Sound grew brighter and wider.

At night, even when my whole family was asleep, without even the rustle of my wool blanket on the bedsheet, there was always the Sound.

It's like the drone of a bow on a psaltery string being played across a field. And it vibrates in a thin green line just out of the corner of my left eye. It's only disappeared a few times in my life, so it usually blends into the background. But I've learned the hard way that no one else hears it or sees these colors except me.

There are a thousand sounds that make up silence. There's the wind blowing snow past your ears, right to left and back again. There's tree branches clacking together like drum beaters. And there's what surely must be women's cries for help—until you realize it's the boughs of a half-fallen tree squeaking against its neighbors' bark.

But you can't *know* the loudness of silence, can you—unless you've known what it is to be truly alone.

— 5 —

I wake to a blinding beam of sunlight falling across me through an arched slit of a window set high in the plastered wall, like a bright keyhole. A shadow interrupts the light, and I become aware of a lavender voice repeating—

"*Good morning, miss. Good morning. You must rise now.*"

Finally I focus on two figures standing above me: a plump, middle-aged woman with her hands folded low, and the girl who's trying to wake me—all smiles and energy, a little older than I am.

"There she is!" the girl chortles. "Thought you might never wake!"

"I . . . uh . . ." I try to speak through a pang of embarrassment at being found sleeping on the floor when something as luxurious as a *bed* has been provided me.

"We'll be waiting outside your door, then," says the older woman, with more measure. "Be dressed in five minutes, and we'll tour the priory." She looks at my mass of curly dark hair. "You'll veil your head, please. And bring your psalter for terce prayers."

I get up and stretch the cricks in my back. I hadn't even covered myself last night, but though there's no fire, it's warmer in this room than it ever was at home. I open the chest at the foot of the bed. There's a gray habit inside, folded neatly, with a veil on top and a set of paternoster beads. I put on Mam's heavy blue dress instead, the thick wool still smelling of her, even months after her death. There's no reason to put on any *nun's* uniform. I'm only here to work.

Across from the bed is a kneeler and, on it, a prayer book, opened to a picture of the Nativity, and another, thinner book, Saint Benedict's *Rule*. *Two actual books.* Maybe there's a mistake. Maybe they forgot that I'm a peasant.

The pitcher of water and towel cloth in a niche in the wall make up the rest of the furnishings. The room is simple, but clean—so much cleaner than anywhere I've been before. I splash my face with the water, pat my cheeks dry and unpack the few other things in my bag.

I slip a couple of sheets of parchment into the psalter and put my brass stylus in my fitchet pocket, in case I get a chance to draw. But my chaperones are waiting, and they tap once more on the door to hurry me. I grab my wrap and go out to join them, pinning the veil over my tangled braids.

"She let you sleep late this once, miss, since you've had a long journey," whispers the girl as we fall in step behind the older woman. "But tomorrow, you must be up with the prime bell." No one's ever called me *miss* before. Me, a shepherd's daughter with dirty fingernails.

"I am Sub-Prioress Agnes de Guile," the woman says over her shoulder. "Welcome to our beloved Priory of Saint Christopher. This is Alice Palmer. She is a novice and a promising scholar, aren't you, Alice? She will be your guide."

Alice shifts the attention from herself. "What's your name?" she asks.

"Edyth. Le Sherman. Of H-Hartley Cross," I stammer. "I'm here to work—not to be a scholar."

"*Conversae* usually stay in servants' quarters," says the sub-prioress. "You must have had . . . connections."

I'm not sure how to take that.

But something dawns on me, and I turn to Alice. "Wait, you're a *palmer?* You've been to the Holy Land?"

"Yes, with my parents," she says wistfully as the bell peals for midmorning prayer. "Before I came here."

Someone who's been all the way to Jerusalem and back—*the things she must have seen!*

Alice wears the same kind of gray habit that was in my wooden chest, and a simple white veil that goes past her shoulders. I guess from the color of her eyebrows that she's probably ash-blond under there. She has green, wide-set eyes and a kind face—and a *lot* of freckles. We walk the long hallway and down the staircase to stand in a large, open room that spans the entire length of the dormitory building.

"Well then, Alice," says the sub-prioress, "after prayers, you may show our new *conversa* the whole of our home. We will have our lessons here after the midday meal. Welcome, Edyth. I hope you'll find your place here quickly."

"Thank you, Sub-Prioress," says Alice with a bow of the head.

I manage a shy smile. "Thank you, ma'am."

No great fire roars in the middle of this vast hall, yet it's hot as summer. The clear leaded windows are fogged with steam. A forest of columns lines the room, and vaulted ceilings radiate the wavy heat downward. It feels good.

"Now I know why my room was so blessed warm," I say. "But where's the hearth?"

Alice laughs. "Don't need one," she says, pointing to the floor. "It's under there. This is a warming room. It's called the calefactory. We have classes here in winter, because there's no heat in the church, as you'll soon find out!"

I smile. "Well, I could get used to this. I don't think I've ever been this toasty in December."

"I'll show you the rest of the priory after terce. There's a creepy old chapel that burned down a long time ago. It's even got saplings growing up through the floor."

I like Alice. She doesn't act like a typical nun, noble and aloof.

Sisters file out of the calefactory with Agnes, and Alice and I fall to the back. We exit into a covered cloister surrounding a large courtyard. A blast of cold smacks me, and I long to go back inside. Alice talks and moves very fast, pointing out every door along the cloister, every carving . . . and every person of interest.

"You want to think that holy places make holy people," she says under her breath.

"But you learn fast here. Whatever was going on at home to make their families dump them at a priory, well, they brought those things with them. We all did."

I wince. "My family wasn't like that."

"Well, I can tell you didn't *choose* this," she says. "It's written all over your face."

I feel my cheeks go red, and my heart drops, thinking of Henry's decision to send me here. "Did you choose? Why are you here instead of some exotic country?"

"I could go places with Father when I was younger, but things change."

"What happened?"

"Well, Edyth, I'm the tithe," she sighs. "The tenth child. There were six sisters ahead of me in line to get married. But you know what? I would have joined a convent anyway, really. Especially this one. I came for the library—it's the largest collection of books in Yorkshire. It's the best-kept secret for a scholar in a dress."

"I'm glad it's going your way," I laugh.

"I like it here. You will, too. You'll see. Keep an open mind."

"I'll try." The thought of *liking* it here hadn't occurred to me.

We walk the arcade around the cloister, past the brushy heads of spent flowers, stalks of frosted rosemary, stone saints wearing powdery shawls of snow.

"So you're a *conversa*." Alice adjusts her veil. "What is it, then? Were you born in a brothel or something?"

I blink away the cold on my eyelids. Where would I begin?

The outside walls of the church crouch above us like a hulking troll. Before coming here, I'd only seen one building so large—Saint Gabriel's Abbey, which governs Hartley Cross—and that from a distance. We enter through a dim side vestibule, and the church's interior reveals itself, as when the dark peel is pared off an apple. My sight is instantly drawn heavenward. Golden spines of stone splash up into peaks on the ceiling, pouring back down pointed arches between impossibly tall windows of colored glass.

Never have I seen light *do* this. Colors dance like spirits on the surfaces of the gleaming lime-washed stone, embellished with vivid paintings of ancient stories. I want to grab Alice Palmer and say, *Are you seeing this?* but I'm afraid it's just in my head, as always. No, this is different—this is their everyday miracle; in here, the nuns can almost see as I do.

Alice shows me to a bench with some other simply dressed women who must be *conversae* like me. I look to the eastern end of this cold, bright forest. The ornately carved rood screen casts a shadow of open doors on the floor, pouring more rainbows through the spaces. I feel it in my skin. I reach into my pocket and touch the stylus. This space is begging to be drawn.

The nuns are already seated in their facing rows, ready to begin the daily office.

Gloria, sings one side, and my own colors flit and spark against the others.

Et nunc et semper, sings the opposite side, and they continue, one row breathing the song into the other.

Inhale, exhale.

This is nothing like the plain-folk attempts at song I grew up with in the parish church, nothing like singing around the fire, when Brother Robert would come over from Saint Gabriel's with his hurdy-gurdy, and we'd dance in circles with the pallets flipped up against the wall.

Gloria, sings one side.

Et nunc et semper, sings the other.

"It's like another world," I whisper. And something in me begins to stir.

— 6 —

"*Ora et labora*," Agnes de Guile begins our afternoon lesson. "Pray and work. It's the same thing, after all. Work is prayer, and prayer is work."

Alice and I and several other girls cluster around Agnes in the calefactory for our class. I'm trying to focus, but I don't really understand what she's talking about; it's not about wool or woad or anything I'm familiar with. And the room is so warm, my stomach so full from the morning meal, my first night's sleep so spotty. I drowse to the cadence of the magicky Latin.

"Edyth le Sherman," Agnes says, sharp but short. I jolt awake and slurp the small reservoir of drool at the corner of my mouth.

"I've been told that you can read. Please, my dear, the first chapter of the *Rule*."

"I, um . . . I don't understand Latin." The other girls stare at me with comical looks on their noble faces. Only Alice seems to see how mortified I am.

"That's fine," says the sub-prioress. "*To be expected.* Just do the best you can, and I will interpret."

I look at the writing. I look at Agnes, and Alice, and the other girls, and sweat erupts on the back of my neck. The letters run together and look almost identical to each other, but I have to try.

"*Caput Primum: De gen-er-ibus mona-cho-rum*," I stumble. "*Mona-chorum quattuor esse genera, ma-ni-fes-tum est. Primum c-coeno . . .*"

"*Coenobitarum,*" Agnes corrects me.

". . . *coenobitarum, hoc est mo-na-ster-i-a-le, militans sub reg-u-la—*"

"Would anyone else like to try?"

Several hands go up, and the girls take turns reading in fair perfection. I sit and look at my hands, notice a hangnail, pick at it. A tiny trickle of blood comes out.

"What does this passage tell us?" Agnes asks. "Alice Palmer?"

"That the best way to live as a consecrated vessel is under the strict guidance of an abbot," says Alice. "Or in our case, a prioress."

"Well done, daughter," says the sub-prioress. "Mercy has decreed that you will all live out your days here in our priory, serving this community with all of your strength, under our strict and careful oversight."

The blessed bell rings for the next office. I am the first to stand to leave, and everyone stares at me again—apparently, this is the wrong thing to do. The others rise slowly.

"This is Edyth le Sherman," Agnes introduces me. "Everyone, please make her feel at home. Thank you, girls. Edyth, may I speak with you privately?"

"Yes, Sub—Your Holi—ma'am?"

"My dear," she begins lovingly, "it's all right if it takes a while. You'll only be learning the basics. You are not a novice, like the other girls. You are a *conversa*, a lay sister. Your life here will be rather more about *labora* than *ora*. Do you remember what those words mean?"

"More about . . . working than praying?"

"Yes, that's right." She clasps her hands, tips her head to the side and smiles, revealing a row of gleaming teeth with a single yellow tooth in front. "It's not as though you have Alice's bright prospects. Do your best and keep at your reading. Now you may go."

Her words pinch my skin. She *may* have been calling me stupid. But what do I know?

Alice has been waiting for me, and we file into the side door of the church. She sits in a choir stall with the other novices. We *conversae* sit in the back row.

The prayers are long and opaque, and I wish the bench had a back, like the nuns get. It's better than Saint Andrew's, though. There were no seats at all there, except for the priest's.

I sit at the very end and let my eyes wander, getting lost in this beauty. All the forms, the people carved in stone, the teardrop shapes of their drapery echoing the pointed arches of windows and doors—my fingers itch to draw everything, but I'm nervous to risk taking out my parchment and stylus. I'll have to memorize it and draw it back in my cell.

One Sunday, Lady Caxton came to see Mam at the house after Mass. They were worlds apart in rank—Mam had grown up at her manor as a servant—but Lady Caxton still knew how to be a friend.

"I brought something for you to see, Edyth," she said. "Lord Geoffrey just bought this in Flanders. You may look at it while I visit with your mother."

Lady Caxton stretched out her velvet-sleeved arms, and my eyes went wild. It was a book, a leather-covered one. I'd never touched a book before.

"This is a bestiary," she said, "a book of animals. Some are familiar, but some are from Elsewhere." She widened her eyes with a sly smile of intrigue.

"Thank you, Lady Caxton," I whispered, bowing. I received the book reverently and sat on the threshold. Inside were wolves and boar, hares and beaver and mice and deer. And creatures from the faraway lands—unicorns and two-headed serpents. I traced the animals with my finger. I couldn't read then, but the animals told me their own stories. I'd never seen colors like that before—except when they came with sounds.

Whoever painted those animals must have seen colors like I did.

When Lady Caxton took that book home with her, I stood in the doorway and wept. Mam shut the wattle gate and caught sight of me wiping my eyes.

"It was so beautiful, Mam," I declared. "If I had a book of my own, I'd never put it down."

Mam was pensive as she cleared the table from the visit. "Come here, Edyth." She beckoned, gesturing for me to sit, then took up a piece of charcoal from the ashes and began to draw on the table.

"I'm sorry I never taught you how to read," she said, with that sad look she got when she realized her daughter was growing up. "I took it for granted that I learned in the Caxton household. Maybe I thought you wouldn't need to if you were a weaver, like me. But time got away from us, I guess.

"This is B, for bird," she began. She wrote the letter and made its sound, then added short, triangle wings, a beak and feet—and the B became a puffy little robin. She made a lopsided vessel for V, and for girl, a circle-faced G with strands of hair like garlic scapes.

"Now you try, Edie," said my mother. "This is D. It's the first letter of dragon."

I made the D into the coiled dragon from the animal book. L became a gaping lion's mouth.

"Yes, you have it," Mam said, surprised at how quickly I grasped it, and how effortlessly I could draw. "Has that been in there this whole time?"

"I draw things, sometimes," I said.

Truth was, I'd been hiding my drawings from Mam for years. When I was little, Da brought home a load of salvaged wood, and we all helped unload it. In the cart was a smooth-planed board, long and wide. I sneaked the board into the barn and hid it behind the cow manger. After my chores were done, I'd grab a cold charcoal nub from the fire's edge and go out to the barn. I started drawing pictures on the board, and soon I brought life to the images that came to me from daydreams or night dreams.

Mam borrowed a small prayer book from Lady Caxton. Day after day, she took time from her work to teach me to read. I loved the feeling of the words jumping from the page into my mouth. After we'd been at it a few weeks, Mam had me demonstrate my skills for Lady Caxton.

"Your reading needs work, but your letters are quite good," she said. "You should encourage her, Heloise. Reading and writing can help her secure a position in a manor house."

"That's my girl," said Mam. But before Da came home, she rubbed the drawings off the table when I wasn't looking.

Little by little, I filled my drawing board with a world of impossible and imaginary creatures. I discovered that if I made my charcoal from a twig and scuffed the end into a point, I could get finer details. I drew fantastic scenes from my head—battles and horses, stories I heard in church, huge hands coming down from the sky or up from the earth. I drew my family and my dog and cat and the sheep and the fruit trees growing by my house.

But the black charcoal on the brown board didn't show up the way I saw in my head. I tried rubbing in the green juice of leaves, but it absorbed and turned brown. The best I could do was draw the shapes of color—concentric circles, starbursts, jelly-like blobs with points of light.

If only I could make the colors I saw.

— 7 —

I don't want to admit it, but I am starting to like it here. It's warm and clean, and in a way it feels like a fresh start. I don't have anything left to lose; there's a kind of comforting blankness about each predictable day.

But what if all this beauty, all this routine—what if it's just making me sedated, like daily doses of theriac? Is that how these women make it for decades without losing their minds—by numbing themselves with minutiae? I may like it now, but a lifetime feels awfully long. There's nothing for me in Hartley Cross, of course, but I still long for it. I want to sit by a real *fire*, not just waves of invisible heat. I want to smell fresh-cut hazelwood, dig my hands into oily fleeces. Want to feel Mason's whiskers on my cheek and inhale the scent of his skin. Saint Christopher's is nice . . . but safe.

The bell rings for the morning meeting. I choose a seat in the farthest corner of the chapter house, the back row, by the door. The novices chatter about the goings-on down in Thornchester. Most of them are from here, and they know city words and city ways. They know how to navigate a town and its alleys. Hartley Cross has no alleys, only one L-shaped street made of muck, and beyond that, fields—and beyond that, the river I was never going to cross, with its mist rising like feathered spirits in a warning dance: *It's all right, it's all right not to venture past here; we will possess and devour you if you do. You belong here, where it's small. Here, where you won't dare to expect more.*

The more I think, the higher the water rises in my eyes. So I take out a piece of parchment from my psalter and draw what I remember of my little village. It's not that I could ever go back there, but if I'm to be part of this priory, someone will have to pull me in, will have to tell me how it's supposed to work here, how to never yearn for home. How to forget, for the rest of my life.

I made the mistake—once—of opening my mind to the other children in Hartley Cross. I was eleven years old. We were playing blindman's buff in the market square, me and my best friend, Methilde. I was it—I was always it—blindfolded and bucktoothed, stumbling about like an idiot with my hands waving in the air. That's when I saw one of my favorite colors. It was so delicious, I stopped in the middle of the game and grinned.

"Mmm . . . Do you see it?" I said. "Coming from Lord Geoffrey's house—it's bacon cooking, all violet and scratchy!"

"What?!" cried Methilde. "Purple bacon!"

"Bacon's green, stupid, didn't you know?" taunted Emma. "With orange spots!"

"And scratchy, too?" said puny Will. "Maybe the way your mam makes it, with the pig hair still on it!"

"Edie's mam makes hairy purple bacon!" Methilde jeered. I blushed, my cheeks like round fireballs, and pulled off the blindfold. My best friend was standing there pointing at me, laughing. They all surrounded me, mocking me and slapping the back of my head and my shoulders and chanting—

Edyth, Edyth, Round and Red,
Something's broken in your head!

They hit me, harder and harder, until one of them smacked me right in the face and cut my lip. It was like they all smelled blood, and then they were on top of me, and kicking me, too. Not Methilde, though. I could make out the hem of her dress, her bony ankles. At least she wasn't beating me. But she wasn't stopping it, either.

Through the pounding, another hand grabbed mine and lifted me out of the pile. Henry set me on my feet and walked me home, his arm around my shoulder, the cruel laughter of the others disorienting me more than the blows.

"What was that about, Edie?"

"I don't want to talk about it," I said through swollen lips.

"Was it the colors?"

I didn't answer. There was a violence going on inside my ribs.

"I'll tell Da. They can't treat you like that. You can't help it."

"No, Henry, don't tell. Please. It'll only make it worse."

"Well then, if they give you trouble, you tell me. It's you and me, Edie. I'm always looking out for you."

It's you and me, Edie. Those words make my heart ache now.

That was the day I knew, really knew. It wasn't just how the sounds and smells brought on the colors. I was different in every way possible: my dark frizzy hair that wouldn't stay put; my stupid overbite and apple cheeks; the way I had to draw all the time, on everything. The games the others played, their awful jokes, how the Other Girls talked about boys in that way—that's what I was supposed to do. That's who I was supposed to be. I just couldn't sort out how.

In Hartley Cross, at least I knew what I was dealing with. But what if the sisters here at Saint Christopher's are just like the Other Girls at home, only with different faces, different names?

My face flushes and sweat pools in my armpits, every sound too loud, too loud. I'll sit on the outside like always, sweating through the linen, sweating through the wool.

But someone comes into the empty space between: Alice sits down next to me as Agnes dismisses the chapter meeting.

"I'll help you with your Latin," she says.

"Oh." I blush. "Thanks, Alice, but you don't have to do that. The sub-prioress said I'm not going to need it, since I'm just a worker."

"But even the *conversae* go to the offices and Mass. Don't you want to understand what you're praying?"

A thousand nights of bedtime prayers with Mam swirl into my memory. The night she died was the last time I prayed. The last time I tried to *understand*.

"Why?"

"So you can . . . you know, talk to God?" Alice makes it sound so obvious.

I feign nonchalance. "Why would I want to do that?"

"That's what prayer is . . ."

"No, I know *that*. I'm not that stupid." I smirk. "I mean, *why* would I want to talk to Him? We don't have anything to say to each other anymore."

"Oh," says Alice, disappointed. "Well . . . all the same, it's Latin, Latin everywhere. And it'll keep the sub-prioress off your back if you just *know* it, that's all."

That's as good a reason as any, I suppose. "All right."

She's a good teacher, Alice is. She knows—really knows—the language. Not just the translations of the words, but the meaning behind the passages. For some reason, Sub-Prioress Agnes's teaching muddles my mind, and I usually leave class feeling dumber. But Saint Benedict's instructions make sense coming from Alice. After a few weeks of her tutelage, I follow along pretty well in class, and I think Agnes is even a little impressed.

— 8 —

It's a warm day for winter; little puffs of cloud hang around everyone's faces, but outside's warmer than the church, so we have class in the cloister. The courtyard flits like the inside of a beehive. Sisters swish down the corridors or poke at patches of bare soil in hopes of seeing some early green.

We recite from after terce until sext, memorize from after the midday meal until nones. The endless rote memorization helps me brace against the grief that comes when I least expect it. I welcome the constant interruption of the day. The moment I begin to drift into thoughts about my family, or Mason, the warning bell rings, and I drop everything and go to the daily office—and forget again, at least for a while.

Forget Da's body swinging above the river.

Or Mam lying lifeless, the baby suckling at her anyway.

Every now and then I see a man, usually a workman, inside the cloister, which is jarring after days upon days of being solely in the company of women. There's Father Johannes, the priest who performs the daily Mass, leaving the church and returning to his own house by the gatehouse. And there's the old monk from my journey here, but other than the church or the refectory, I don't know where he comes from or where he goes.

Alice and I sit on the ledge in a corner of the cloister and quiz each other. I can't imagine anyone more knowledgeable than Alice—her flawless recitation, her insights, just how *many* things she knows about. It's not limited to books, either. There are girls and women here for all kinds of reasons, and Alice seems to have the dirt on every one of them.

"I've had a revelation, Edyth," she says, looking down at her book and pretending to recite. "You've basically got three categories of people here: I call them the Pious, the Privileged and the Pitiful."

"So how can you tell who's who?"

"Oh, you can spot the Privileged easily. They're just like whatever priggish girls you knew back home, always judging you but always changing the rules. And the Pious, they keep to themselves, like Mary over there." She points to a girl daintily turning the pages of her *Rule* with her pinky up. "As for the Pitiful, well, you'd never guess, but Beatrice there, they say she's got a baby back home by a baron. He gave a big donation to put her away here. Poor thing."

"Lord, that's awful." I cringe.

"They're the unmarriageable daughters, the ones no one else wants."

"I guess I'm kind of in the Pitiful category myself."

"Oh, come on," she chides. "Give yourself a chance."

I shrug it off. "What about you?"

"Let's do our recitation," she dodges with a wink.

We turn to today's lesson and I read the Latin, still halting, but better.

"*Decimus humilitatis gradus est, si non sit facilis ac promptus in risu.*"

Alice looks up and smiles. "*The tenth step to humility is to avoid laughter,*" she translates in a whisper. She nudges me mischievously. "I'll never last."

Suddenly a great cry goes up in the cloister, and we all go running down the corridor. The sub-prioress herself is on the ground, holding a young nun in her arms.

"He crouches there in the shadows," the girl pants, gesturing above her head. "The dragon . . . fire glowing in his iron belly . . . spitting hot coals at me!"

The colors of her voice shake like shimmering flame. I could almost believe her—some nuns keep vigils and stay awake for days until they begin to see things. Creatures. Beings from another realm.

That kind of orange-sparked fury has appeared to me once before, on the day I fought with Da—the day everything began to unravel.

The sun was well past noon. All morning I had vacillated between tears and growls—Da had said there was no future with Mason. Now that Da had been named reeve, he said it was our chance to raise our prospects.

"I won't allow this family to go backward," he'd said. "He's a wanderer, Edyth. All stonemasons are. If we were still just a family of sheep shearers, he would be a fine choice. But I'm telling you that we must wait and find someone more appropriate. I won't have you leaving Hartley Cross. Your mam needs you here when the baby comes. Put him out of your mind. Forget about the Mason boy."

That afternoon, I sat on the threshold, furiously carding wool, my body hot with anger. Then I heard a little sound, like the distant scurrying of a mouse at first, padding and scratching down the garden path. The noise rapidly changed and grew voices: a celebration? A wedding?

Well, now I know that'll never be me, *I thought.*

Shouts and hollers exploded from the roar of a crowd, an orange-sparked cloud of men's voices rolling up the hill. The ground beneath my feet popped with the energy, not of reveling, but of rage, and it lit into me and I bolted out of the wattle gate. As I ran, I saw more sparks, pocks of flame rising from a mob rushing down the high street.

Thief!

Liar!

Traitor!

In their midst, the gray eye in the firestorm, was the hooded and roped victim of their fury.

My mind went crazy with the cacophony of crowd color. I hated public hangings; I'd seen a dozen criminals hung from this bridge over the years. But I ran toward the growing throng anyway. I jumped along the fringe of the crowd, trying to get a glimpse as they willed themselves, one throbbing entity, onto the wooden bridge. The men were all from Hartley Cross. The miller wrapped a noose of heavy rope and handed it to Lord Geoffrey, who shoved it down over the hooded head and tied the other end to the rail. There was no chance the victim could break free of his bonds; down was the only way out of this.

I ran around the bridge to the riverbank and stood shin-deep in the water, my skirts waving in the current like fish tails. Just as the men hoisted the condemned man up onto the bridge rail, I saw something flash in the sun: a familiar bronze belt buckle under a round belly.

The mob pushed the man from the railing, and he dropped into the frothing river, flailing there, wet only to the knees, until the violent splashing gave way to a gentler wake, and finally stillness, as the water ebbed against the unresisting body. Lord Geoffrey reached over the railing and pulled off the sackcloth hood. Red hair and beard tumbled over the scarlet, bulging face.

Da.

Currents of green life lapped at my ankles and surged up my body: the last of my father's life, washing out into the river soil.

"See there, men?" spat Lord Geoffrey. "There's justice yet! Reeve Edgar le Sherman, honest and fair," he mocked, "defrauding his own fellows for gain. Funneling my money to a Flemish woolers' uprising! Remember this: anyone who steals from a lord steals bread from your own table. Today you did your duty and caught the thief!"

A righteous cry went up from the mob.

The sting of the cold water waved up into my feet and I froze to the spot in the muck.

"From this point on, shun his family!" With that, Lord Geoffrey shot a look directly at me. I hadn't been aware of how conspicuous I was. "Let no one come to their aid—let them beg or starve!"

"But my mam . . . the baby—" I didn't know where the words were coming from, since I was outside my body.

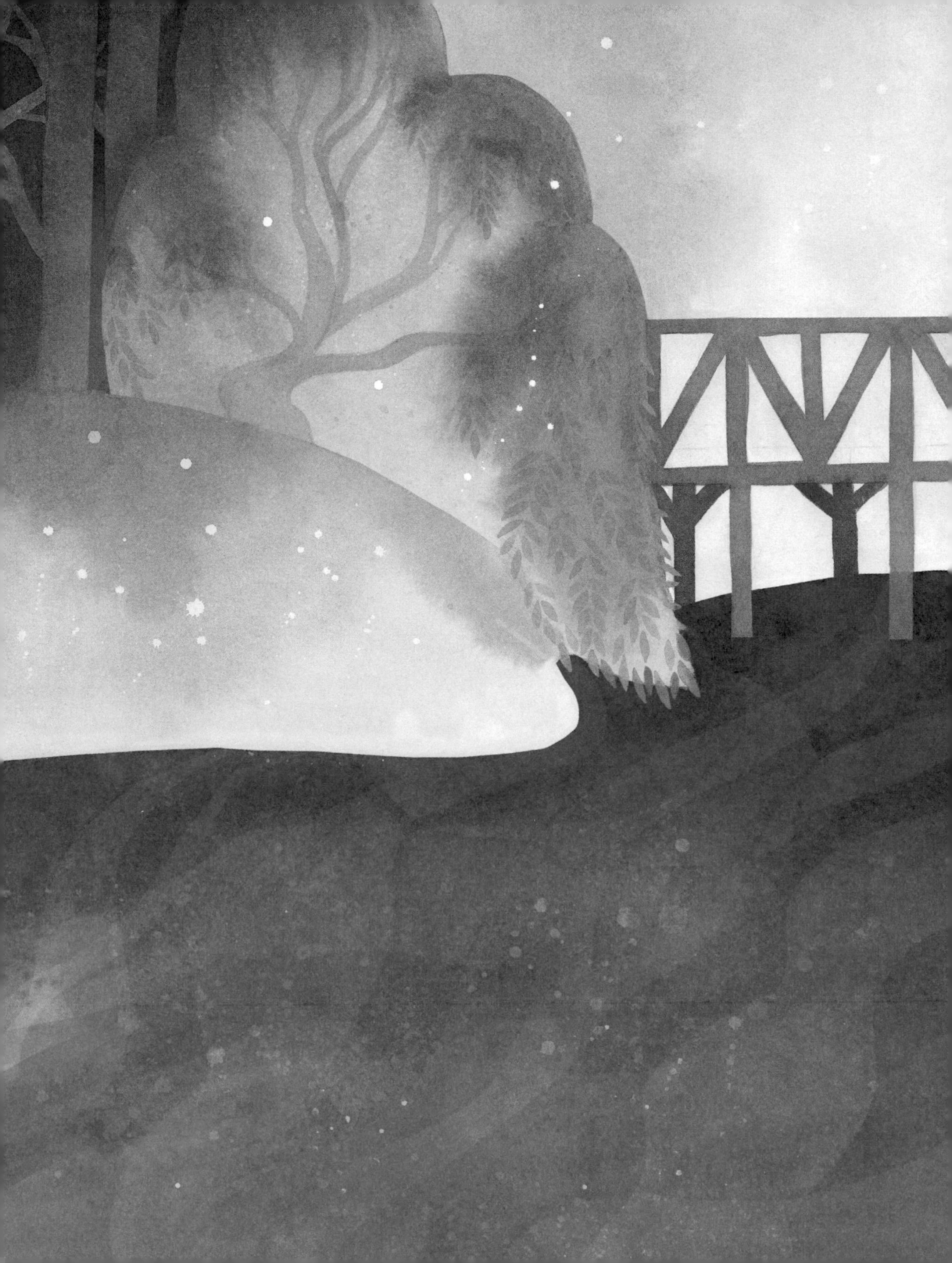

What was happening?

Just then, a woman's wail threaded through the venomous cheers. Mam. My mother was coming, her legs buckling as she leaned the full weight of herself and her unborn baby on Henry's arm. The crowd dispersed at the appearance of the pregnant widow they'd just made, shame turning their heads this way and that.

Two figures stood alone on the bridge: Mam and Henry, looking over the rail at the eddying body below them. Henry rushed into the water and grabbed our father around the waist, trying to sort out a way to get him down. He spotted me on the other side of the river.

"Edyth!" he called. "Help me!"

Like a statue coming to life, I took a step toward Henry, but the riverbed dropped, too deep to wade across.

"Go up and cut the rope!" Henry shouted. I took my knife from my belt, ran up to the bridge and hacked at the rope. My face burned and I could barely breathe. The damn thing was too thick. I sawed and sawed, cursing the rope, tears and snot and spit everywhere, the sparks so furious I couldn't see past them. Mam sat on the ground, her huge stomach resting on her outspread legs, hands helplessly at her sides, howling and howling.

At last the rope's inner core snapped, and the current jerked Henry and Da forward.

"Edyth! Get down here!" Henry hollered.

I ran back around and plunged into the water. Together we lugged our father's body to the bank. We sat stunned and soaked and panting.

"Wait here," said my brother. "I'll go home and get the cart."

I stayed under the bridge with my father's body, my mother above, watching the frayed rope flap in the wind. Two women alone, as alone as could be, the water flowing on as ever before.

Henry and Mason dug the grave under an oak tree, with Da's own sleeping sheep the only other witnesses to his funeral. Brother Robert did his ministrations, sprinkling the body and the rest of us with hyssop and holy water. We all helped slide the home-made coffin off the cart. Then I saw it.

One of the planks of Da's coffin had been cut from my drawing board. Right there, by his head, was a drawing of me and Mason sitting on the church wall.

"No," I cried out loud.

Mason came and put his arm around me, but I shrugged it away. All I could think was that my last words with Da had been a fight over this boy. He nodded sadly and joined Henry instead. They lowered the open coffin into the grave, and the clouds parted, barely, to reveal a sliver of moon.

The sparks of the memory settle like fiery snow and disappear into the stone pavement of the cloister. My heart pounds in pain.

Sub-Prioress Agnes holds the terrified girl until she calms, then rises and sends her on her way with a kiss of peace. I've absently drawn a dragon on the parchment sheet in my psalter. Alice takes it from me before I can stop her.

"Pitiful," whispers Alice.

"What?"

"I guess you'd act that way, too, if you'd gone through what Felisia did," she says, examining the drawing.

"Who?" My ears are still ringing.

"That . . . dragon girl," she says, waving her name away. Before Alice can say more, Agnes approaches us, and Alice shoves the drawing under her book.

"I'm sorry you had to see that, girls," says the sub-prioress. "Felisia has a tendency toward the dramatic. People like her have a long journey of penance ahead of them." She excuses herself and goes on her way.

"I can't sort it," says Alice, gazing again at the drawing.

"Sort what? It's a dragon. See? That's the head—"

"No, I mean the sub-prioress. She changes like the weather. I mean—one minute, she's praising you, the next, she's cracking the whip. Who *is* she?"

"I think she's all right," I suggest. "Strict, maybe, but she's in charge, after all."

"But everybody gets quiet when she comes in the room, waits for her to speak, hangs on her every word. And she loves it; you can tell. I don't trust people like that."

"Well, what I want to know is, where is the *actual* prioress? Isn't she supposed to be running things?"

"Prioress Margaret? She's never here," says Alice. "But it would be nice if she'd come home once in a while."

"Although you know what they say," I counter. "Better the devil you know than the devil you don't."

— 9 —

The new year comes, and with it I turn seventeen. My birthday's right on the feast of the Epiphany, and there are dried figs at breakfast, left over from Twelfth Eve. I slip one into my sleeve for later. Make that two.

After breakfast, Agnes de Guile announces a meeting for the novices and *conversae*, and we all gather at the lectern. The rest of the community files out to begin their work.

"Girls," she says, "we've been watching each of you since you arrived to identify your unique gifts and where you will serve best. I am happy to announce your work assignments." We all grin and some of the girls bounce on their toes. I'm curious to know where Agnes sees me fitting in here.

"Right," she begins, "we'll start with the sacristy. To work there is a great privilege. Not only will this person care for the holy vessels and vestments, but she will be in the presence of the Body and Blood themselves. This is entrusted to . . . Beatrice." Agnes hands the girl a small parchment sealed with a linen tassel.

"Next: working in the library means being trustworthy with knowledge, and not leading seekers astray. Mary, this honor is yours. You'll report to the *armaria*, the head librarian, in the scriptorium tower.

"Felisia," she continues, "you will be my assistant. I will personally teach you penance and help you through your troubles." We all smile with pity at Felisia, whose eyes brim with grateful tears.

"The care of the medicine garden requires encyclopedic knowledge, and responsibility for life and death. Alice Palmer, you will apprentice to Joan, our physician." I'm happy for Alice; this is perfect for her. She beams with satisfaction.

All the girls smile at the honors they've been given, the way they've been noticed, the parchments with their names written on them. In Hartley Cross, women might be masters, like Mam with her weaving, but no one was going to give Mam a parchment with her *name* on it.

I wonder what mine will say.

"Edyth le Sherman, such an . . . earthy girl deserves a commensurate assignment. You'll be in the scriptorium, preparing pigments," the sub-prioress declares, that yellow tooth peeking through her smile. She makes the sign of the cross over us. "Thank you. You may all go to your work now." The girls practically skip to their respective jobs.

"Come, Edyth, Felisia. We mustn't be late."

The *scriptorium*. The word rolls around in my mouth delightfully. It sounds like someplace distinguished, like a manor hall or a bishop's house. I trip over my skirts trying to follow Agnes's brisk pace. We wind through a labyrinthine succession of halls, and as well as I know my way around by now, I quickly lose my sense of space. We cut through winding halls, past other nuns and doorways hung with evergreens, across the nave of the wide church, and finally, panting slightly, Agnes whisks outside through the back church door, into the entryway of a three-story tower and up the dizzying steps of a spiral staircase. She pushes open the heavy door.

Instantly my tongue crackles.

The room smells of chalk and leather, smells I haven't conflated before. A cluster of large oaken desks are pitched at quarter angles, each one occupied by a scribe rapt at work. An entire floor-to-ceiling bookcase is filled with heavy leather- or wood-bound books—and through a passageway, I see what can only be the library, with the novice Mary already talking to the *armaria*. It's utterly quiet except for the scratches of quills and the swishes of brushes. No one raises their head.

"Sub-Prioress," someone greets her plainly.

"This is the *conversa* Edyth le Sherman," says Agnes. "Edyth, this is the scriptorium, where the priory produces very precious books. Do not touch anything, or disturb those at work. Remember that they also are at prayer."

"*Ora et labora*," someone else mutters. Felisia reaches out to touch a stack of pages on a shelf. Agnes slaps her hand away.

There are mostly women here, but a man, too—the wizened old monk I traveled with in the cart. Each desk has a side table with inks, jars of quills and a globe-shaped flask of water on a metal stand. There are bowls and seashell halves full of different-colored paint, corked jars of various liquids. Light streams in from the windows, aided by candles, and I even glimpse occasional glints of *gold* jumping off the pages.

"This is Muriel," says Agnes, leading me to the desk of a tall nun with a sharp nose. "She specializes in fine line work. See what she's working on here?" I hesitate, but Agnes urges me over. I lean forward until I can see all the detail clearly. The rich clothes of the painted figures hang in neat, sharp folds. The lines are web-thin. I think of my own drawings, so clumsy in comparison, and blush.

"Anne next," Agnes diverts me. "She came to us from York Minster. She doesn't paint, but she's the best scribe we have here. Just *look* at the control, each letter so perfectly *vertical*. I am always awed by you, Anne. What do you think, Edyth?"

"It's perfect" is all I can say. But how could I possibly express the sensations coming at me, through me, from everywhere? This room is full of artists.

"I'm experimenting with a *bastarda* of *Anglicana* and *Textualis*," the scribe says incomprehensibly. I can only give a polite nod.

The old monk is last. "I'm Brother Timothy," he says with a jocular, grandfatherly smile. "I'm pleased to meet you in more . . . comfortable circumstances, Edyth."

"Timothy is a fixture here," says the sub-prioress.

"He's been here since God was a boy," calls a thick Scottish voice from another room. Everyone laughs, except Agnes.

"Brother Timothy was a young monk here when this priory was a double monastery, men and women living together," Agnes resumes. "Joan the Physician has also been here since that time, and so have I. It's not as common now as it once was."

"I am working on a botanical for Joan, as a matter of fact," says Timothy. "I hear she will be assisted by a promising young sister named . . . ah . . . Palmer? A friend of yours?"

"Yes, Brother Timothy! That's Alice." My attention is drawn, however, to one empty desk by the window. "Who sits here?"

"Well, now . . . ," says Anne. "We don't really . . ."

"That was mine," says Agnes curtly, ending the conversation. "A long time ago. Thank you all. I know you will help Edyth to be *precise* in her training."

The sub-prioress ushers me into a side room. We go through two doors, with a muslin sheet hung between them. I sneeze in the intensely dusty air. A rainbow shines in the shaft of sunlight, made of colored particles, not light. Without this veil between rooms, the dust would cover all of the pristine parchments the scribes are laboring over.

A long, rough table occupies most of the room, scattered completely with bowls of different sizes. On the right-hand wall is a bureau full of small, labeled drawers: *Azurite. Minium. Lapis. Arabica.*

A woman is working there, her linen veil tied up and tucked under. She's not wearing a nun's habit, but a deep madder-red gown with a linen apron over it. Her sleeves are rolled past the elbow, her hands rainbows like the dust.

"Edyth," says Agnes, "this is Bridgit."

The woman turns and her eyes glint at me. "You're very welcome here, Edyth," she says in her brogue. "We're like a wee family up here, away from all the noise and fray."

"You will apprentice to Bridgit," Agnes instructs me. "She is a *conversa*, like you."

Agnes pulls Felisia's hand out of a bowl of colored powder, and the girl sticks her finger in her mouth, pigment spilling on her chin. Without another word, Agnes grabs her hand and exits the double doors with her assistant.

Bridgit shakes her head and beckons me over to the bureau.

"They're all in Latin," she says. "Do you read?"

"A little . . . ," I say sheepishly. "I'm learning."

"Sound this out, then." Bridgit points to a drawer.

"Terre Verte, Prason."

"Good, child. Open that one and see what you find."

It's nothing special, just a drawer full of brown, dust-covered rocks. Bridgit takes a small stone mortar and pestle down from a shelf and wipes them off with her apron. "Bring one here. I'm going to show you something."

I put the little egg-shaped rock into the bowl. Down Bridgit's pestle strikes, and the stone cracks in half. Inside is not the earthy color, but a bright olive green, and the taste of the oil that would have come from such a fruit floods over my tongue.

"What do you think of that?" asks Bridgit.

"That was inside the stone?"

"The earth yields its treasures if you know where to dig," says the woman. "These you find in the river, just a mile downstream."

A flood of awe rushes through me. Who could have guessed? The whole time I lived in Hartley Cross, I had wanted colors for my drawings, and they had probably been right under my feet.

Bridgit seems eager to have a protégé. She leans closer to me with a sparkle in her eye. "Now, the painters don't use this only for drab, green things. If their red is too bright, they'll tone it down with this. I've even seen them laying this underneath the color of flesh. Whoever heard of green flesh, eh? But it works."

"This is what they paint with in there?" I marvel. "Rocks?"

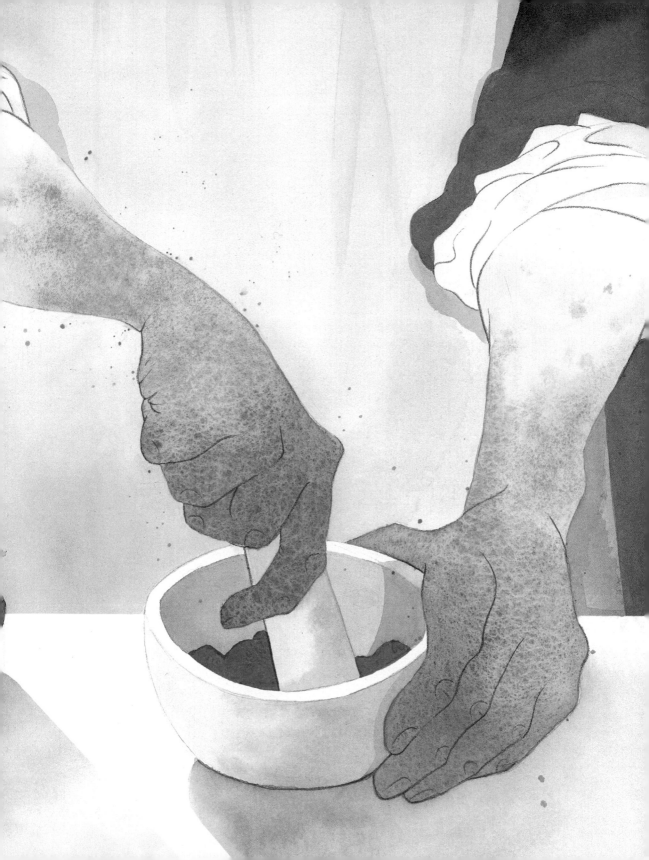

"Yes, Edyth. Watch." She pounds the rock into smaller and smaller bits. "Then you grind the pieces against the sides of the mortar. Do you see?" She dips her fingertip in the bowl and rubs the pigment between her fingers. Then she pounds again for a long time—it might be ten minutes. But at last, the powder is so fine, it no longer resembles sand crushed from a stone, but costly flour.

"How do you get it to . . . um . . . stick?" I ask.

"To the parchment? Good question. With a binder. That's next." She reaches into a basket full of eggs. She separates an egg into two bowls, yolk and white, picks up the yolk by its invisible membrane and breaks it into another bowl.

Bridgit pours the powder onto a slab of marble. She adds the yolk a drop at a time, and a little water, too, and keeps mixing with a glass muller until it's smooth, until it becomes *paint*, the consistency of fresh cream.

"It looks delicious," I say, the taste of olive oil still on my tongue.

"Don't try to eat this, child," Bridgit laughs. She keeps mixing, longer than seems reasonable. Under her breath, she mutters, "Beautiful poisons, the lot of them."

I think of the chilly reception Agnes got here in the scriptorium, and for a moment, I don't know whether Bridgit's talking about pigments or people.

Spring
1349

— 10 —

In the afternoons, I like to take the long way around from the refectory to the scriptorium. The river encircling the priory wall seizes, the sound of the water heaving underneath the ice. The cold squeezes my ribs, too, and I have to remind myself that it must come to an end someday.

The basic rhythms of the priory are ingrained by now. I've almost memorized the entire *Rule*, which seems to have mollified the sub-prioress, and I fairly well embody the order of the day. There isn't much else I need to know, now that I spend most of my time in the scriptorium.

Once upstairs, I settle at the table and review the list of pigments that the illuminators need prepared, nibble on a pilfered oatcake and attempt to study a bit of my *Rule* before everyone else arrives. Instead, I wind up with my head on my arm, drowsily doodling in the book with my brass stylus, embellishing the simple drop-capital letters at the beginning of each paragraph with flourishes. *If only you could see me now, Mam, reading Latin, surrounded by scribes and artists. This is more than "B is for bird."*

One day Da drew me aside and, without a word, pressed a small bundle into my hand. I unwrapped the cloth. Inside was a stack of small parchments and a brass stylus.

"You think I haven't seen you, Edie, your drawings on that board in the barn. But I do see." He winked at me, planted a big Da kiss on my cheek and went whistling back to his work. He called over his shoulder, a finger pointing in the air, "A real artist deserves some real tools!"

That was the night I sat my family down and drew their portraits, one by one. But this time, my drawings were as fine and precise as I saw them in my mind, and I could look each of my family members in the eye when I did it, without hiding a thing.

In the warm shaft of sunlight across my table, I jolt awake, my mouth open and dry, the last of a snore answering the sound that rouses me.

PING. Pt-*ping.* Pt-*ping.*

I didn't realize I'd fallen asleep. The terce bell rings. I rub my face, confused and annoyed at the disjointed, angular patterns of the sound—

Pt-*ping.* Pt-*ping.* Pt-*ping.*

I look out the window and see the source of the noise. On the side of the ruined chapel, a makeshift shelter's been erected. Some men are under the canvas roof, mixing yellow mortar, hammering wood. One's chiseling white limestone; another sledges a dark dull rock. The sound does not stop.

Pt-*ping.* Pt-*ping.* Pt-*ping.*

Red. Red. Red. Like the tip of a blade plunging downward between my eyes, unending, flashing. *Red. Red. Red.*

Once I'm in the church for terce, the pounding hushes to tiny red dots instead of daggers. I can deal with that. But even under the women's song, there's the sound of men's hammers.

After prayers, the novices exit through the back door of the church, trying their best to get a peek without turning their heads in the direction of the workers. Most of the builders are old geezers, but some are young, strong and broad, and the girls recite: *We must prepare our hearts and bodies for the battle of holy obedience.* I head back toward the grinding room. That's over for me, anyway. I can't care about stonemasons anymore.

But still, I know that's a lie. If it wasn't, Mason's stone cross wouldn't be in my pocket. I cradle it in my hand. Just thinking of him feels like someone's writing stories under my skin. I sit on the steps outside the scriptorium and draw columns and arches.

Pt-*ping*. Pt-*ping*. Pt-*ping*.

Red. Red. Red.

Next morning at the beginning of chapter, Agnes takes the floor for an announcement.

"Many of you will remember when the chapel of Saint Eustace was partially destroyed by fire. Its blight has always been an embarrassment to us. Unfortunately, we have had no choice but to keep the relics of Holy Eustace tightly locked in the church crypt, and we are unable to properly serve our pilgrims without them."

The older sisters murmur in agreement.

"Now, every year at Lent, as you know, our lord baron pledges a tenth of his estate to the rebuilding, but he has been late on his promise . . . these twenty years." Sardonic laughter rises from the nuns.

"Around Christmas, though," Agnes continues, "a surprise benefactor stepped in with a large donation. Saint Gabriel's Abbey in Dorsetshire has provided the funds for the project. No doubt you have seen—or heard—the laborers," she says with a chortle. "Please do not interfere with their work, nor let them interfere with yours. And let us pray for the new pilgrims who will come through our gates to worship in the restored chapel of Saint Eustace!"

The room reverberates with applause, clashing with the construction outside. I reach into my fitchet pocket and touch the little stone cross, its smoothness balancing the sharp red flashes of noise.

The next morning, Alice puts in a good word with the sub-prioress and asks for my help preparing seedlings for the medicine garden. After all, there's much to do getting ready for early planting in a few weeks. Thank God, I can put away my studies and get into the fresh air.

The garden shed's a three-sided stone extension on the back of the infirmary, with roll-down linen curtains to let in light and keep out frost. All sorts of baskets, spades, forks and rope hang on the wall, with clay pots stacked up tall, and a wooden bin of soil in the corner. Alice takes a shallow box off the windowsill. It's full of tangled seedlings, with sticks labeled in chalk.

"Prick out the seedlings by kind, and pot them on, Edyth. Like this." She scoops some loose dirt from the bin into a pot and makes a hole in the center with a sharp stick. Then she inserts the stick into the corner of the seedling box, lifts out a group of white-rooted shoots, separates them carefully and puts one seedling into the pot, packing it in tightly.

"Understand?"

"I think so." I nod, trying to conceal a smirk. I know how to pot seedlings, for goodness' sake. I'm not some soft-handed nobleman's daughter. Setting seeds is a toddler's job.

"And water them in when you're done," says Alice, taking off her apron. "I've got to go ask Joan what she wants planted next."

I'm at this for a long while, alone in the shed, when I sense someone come into the room behind me.

"Well, isn't this a surprise!" says a male voice, a swirl of golden ochre. I jump and turn to see a boy's form standing in the doorway.

"God be with you, sister," he says, bowing his head to me, the waves of messy, sandy hair tumbling over his hood. The arch of his upper lip. And the familiar flash of midnight-blue eyes . . .

"*Mason*—"

I have to keep myself from shouting it as I knock a pot on the bench, but right it just in time. I gawk at him, feeling the blush rise, my scalp tingle, this irresistible force pulling me to him. I want, like instinct, to throw my arms around him, to bury myself in him. I reach a hand toward him and just as quickly draw it back.

"What are you doing here?" I whisper, then, suddenly conscious of my over-bite, cover my mouth with both dirty hands. "*Here?* Of anywhere in the whole country?"

"It's . . . ah . . . a few reasons. . . ." He looks down and wipes the stone dust from his hands onto his leather apron. "Work in Hartley Cross slowed down, and Brother Robert said Saint Gabriel's was sending stoneworkers up north to rebuild an old chapel, and . . . here I am."

I simply can't believe it. This isn't a dream—I can see the color of his voice. He's got on the same green tunic covered in fine limestone powder. We just stare at each other, not speaking. I haven't looked another person in the eye in months, let alone *him.*

"Your da?" I manage, fingernailing a crease in my apron. "Is he well?"

"No," says Mason. "That's the other reason. I said goodbye when I left."

"God rest him," I offer, my heart falling.

And something unlocks in me. For months, since Mam and Da died, I've been stopping up my heart, like I might pour out of myself if I let go even a little bit, not wanting to admit that *people die,* and they don't come back. That my parents, and now Mason's father, aren't traveling somewhere, aren't on pilgrimage, but are in the ground; not growing like these seedlings, but decaying, back into soil, back into time. But here stands Mason, alive, familiar, like a pillow placed under that grief. It's all I can do not to grab onto him and never let go.

"It was that cough, you know, from the stone dust," he explains. He touches a pot of earth and runs his finger along its rim, a resigned smile revealing how sorrow has slightly aged his eyes. "We all knew it would come. I expect it will for me, too, the same way. Death comes for all of us sometime."

"Don't say that. You're *here.*" I look at his hands, callused and huge and full of cuts and scrapes, like they should be. Those hands, rough and gentle, the memory of their touch going through me even now.

"You're right. It's good to see you, Edie." His is a thinner smile, with a new sadness.

"This isn't what I expected," I say, biting my bottom lip.

Mason gingerly picks up a bunch of seedlings and teases them apart. I make holes in the soil and hand him the pots to plant in.

"No. Nor I," he says. "But I imagine *you're* not going anywhere for a while, and this chapel here will take a long time to rebuild, don't you think?"

I blush and try to hide my smile, looking down at my work. "I'm glad you're here," I say plainly.

"Me too." He inches his hand over to mine and brushes my dirty fingers.

"Edyth, it's your turn to— Oh! Hello!" Alice stops suddenly as she rounds the corner into the shed. Instant dizziness spins a web of blue around my vision, and Mason pulls his hand away in a flash.

"I'm sorry," he says to both of us with a polite smile. "I'll go."

"No, wait—Alice, this is my friend, John Mason. He's from Hartley Cross, can you believe it? I didn't know that he was on the chapel crew this whole time."

Alice draws breath to say something, but nods and smiles instead. "Alice Palmer," she introduces herself. "Edyth, it's time to wash up."

"God give you grace, sisters," say Mason humbly, exiting with a bow. I feel Alice's prying gaze, but I put the box of seedlings back on the windowsill and hang up my apron, backing out of the shed, trying not to burst.

— 11 —

I wash my hands and face in the fountain and retreat to the scriptorium, drunk on the waking dream of Mason's presence. The chalky smell of the room hits me first; that, and the faint goaty aroma of the parchment. It brings me back to earth—but I swear I can almost see angels reaching their hands right into the dirt of the world and pulling up spirit-stuff, hands filthy with these rough building blocks of holiness. The air whirls with rock dust and animal skins, planks of wood and beeswaxed linen thread.

My reverie is sharply interrupted.

"Huh?"

"I said, I need you to go to town for me, Edyth," says Bridgit as I enter the grinding room. "Alice is going as well, for Joan's medicines. Here's my list. Go see the druggist first for the mastic and gum, and then the jeweler for the stones. Be careful when you come out of the jeweler's—keep your wits. You don't want anyone following you, thinking you've got something to steal."

The list in my hands is simple, and going to town, what a relief—a long walk to shake out the thousand emotions coursing through my body.

"I can't believe we get to leave the priory," says Alice when we meet up at the gatehouse. "My world's shrunk to the size of a peach pit over the last few months."

"Don't I know it," I reply, distracted.

"Though it seems to me like yours is expanding," she says, an impish smile on her lips.

On the bridge, we stop to drop dried leaves into the river and see whose comes out on the other side first.

Footsteps on the wooden bridge make us stiffen. We lower our heads and wait for them to pass, but they pause, and a reflection appears next to mine in the water.

"Are you going into town?" Mason asks, smiling at our mirror image.

"We are! Shopping for stones, and, um, mastic, and"—*if only I could stop babbling*—"and, uh, resin! Those things."

"Funny, I'm going, too! Am I . . . allowed to join you?" he asks cautiously.

Oh, the delightful sickness pressing in my chest! I open my mouth to reply, but Alice cuts me off.

"We appreciate the escort," says Alice. "Don't we, Edyth?"

"We do." My cheeks burn. We all turn toward town, and Mason falls in step next to me.

"Cold today," he says.

If only he knew how *not* cold I felt just now. "It'll be warm soon enough."

"So what do they have you doing for work? I hope it's not too awful."

"I'm working in the scriptorium, as a matter of fact. Grinding pigments. Did you know there are *colors* inside rocks?" I squeeze my eyes shut. *God, I sound like a child.*

Mason doesn't seem fazed at all. "Who would've guessed we'd both be working with stone?" he chuckles. "You were always more of a wool girl."

Alice lets us talk—occasionally giving me a sly nudge. It's so good to speak freely, away from the eyes and ears at the priory.

We enter the town gates, and instantly all of my senses war. I've never seen so many people. The buildings look like tumbled boats in a moat of dreck, their second stories leaning toward each other, blocking out the sun. Children and animals are running, hawkers shouting, customers haggling. Beggars huddle in ragged, shapeless bundles; coughing and sneezing are everywhere. I'm reeling from the dissonant smells—incense and various animal excrements and baking bread and strong cheese. Shards of dark metallic hues clash and burn with smothering billows of green, and I can barely see, barely hear for the ringing in my ears.

Alice has been here before—Thornchester is her family's nearest town—and she weaves through the crowd, leading us, and thank God for that, or I'd fall in a faint, and I don't want to do that in front of Mason. Then I'd have to tell him about the colors—and maybe he'd think that I had a demon.

But I feel him close behind me. Then beside me. He slips a hand into my cloak and brushes mine.

Our fingers touch. Our hands clasp.

And we make it through the chaos, to the other end of the high street.

We separate to do our various errands, and Mason meets us at last outside the jeweler's. It's a good thing he came: as we head back through the crowd, I feel a thousand eyes searching for my purse, heavy with precious stones, waiting to pounce on a girl who's half blinded by conflicting, hurtling colors. Bristling with fright, I feel a hand on the small of my back and brace myself for a thief to make a grab.

It's Mason, thank goodness. "What's wrong?" he asks.

"It's—it's time to start back to the priory," I stammer.

"We can take our time," he says softly. "The day's not half spent."

It was two years ago at Michaelmas when I first saw Mason.

Services had ended and the congregation filed into Saint Andrew's churchyard, the little ones playing hide-and-seek among the tombs and trees, and the old ones gathering to gossip and talk harvest. Da was about to lead us in a paternoster at the graves of Mam's parents when Lord Geoffrey Caxton took him aside and made him an offer.

"We're starting a cloth trade right here in town, Edgar. We'll need weavers, full-ers, dyers. And all those workers will need a manager. Your name was put forward as reeve."

Reeve? That was almost like being in charge of the whole town! Was this really happening? To us?

"You're the man for the job," said Lord Geoffrey, playfully slapping Da's chest. They laughed and shook on it robustly. "It will mean being away sometimes . . . Flanders and such . . . but you'll be given a wage. Your wife will be happy about that, won't she?"

A wage! Mam and I grinned.

"We'll be rich," I whispered, grabbing her by the elbow. Mam and I were on our toes with anticipation. Da turned to us with a new straightness of spine, his red beard swinging.

Henry and I followed Mam and Da home along the copper-green river, gathering the last of the fallen walnuts. The larder was already full, because Da had a knack for getting to the walnuts first. That is, unless Old John Mason beat him to it.

"Looks like Old John's been here and about cleaned us out," said Henry, cracking a nut against the stone river wall.

"Oooh," I replied with a shudder. "Don't say his name, Henry!"

"How can he eat all them nuts with no teeth?" He mimicked the gumming mouth of an old man. We laughed and I hopped up onto the wall and balance-walked, leap-ing across each gap. My cheeks were flushed despite a bit of chill in the air, and my lungs felt pained, but I was having too much fun to care.

Old John wasn't really that old, and I felt guilty for poking fun. He was only about the same age as Da. When he'd reach up to shake the thick branch of the walnut tree, the lines in his forearms would carve the story of decades of stone pushing and sledgehammer swinging. But the stone dust got into his chest and threw his humors off balance; his twisting cough, huge hunched shoulders and gray skin made him a living gargoyle.

"Boo!" Henry suddenly jumped up in my way just as I was about to leap across to the next wall. I stopped short and wobbled, falling onto the soft, grassy bank, my ankle twisting as I rolled. I rubbed it—it wasn't sprained—and I heard Henry laughing at me, but further down the bank, someone else was looking our way.

A wooden punt was tied to the landing, and a boy was helping load it with baskets of river clay. His shaggy, dark blond hair waved out under his cap. He smiled at me, and I tasted honey.

"Boy!" a gruff voice threatened. "Boy, get these baskets loaded, or by 'is bones I'll give ye such a thrash—" It was Old John himself down in the boat, his menace dissolving into an awful cough.

Henry helped me up and left me, running over to the boat landing. "Mason!" he called to Old John's son. "Where have you been?"

"Henry, old friend!" The two clasped hands. "I had an apprenticeship, building the new spire at Christchurch. I'm glad to be home! At least until the next job."

"Well, come by for a bite later," said Henry. "We've got the goose roasted, and my father's just been named reeve! Things are looking up, I guess!"

Mason shot another look at me. "Looks that way." He smiled, and I felt the river flow right through me. "I'll see you around vespers."

Mason came every Sunday after. Mostly, he and Henry went off to help Mason's father get ready for winter. The old man's cough was getting worse. But always, as he left, Mason nodded and smiled at me—mocking me, I was sure, the way they all did—but my whole body filled red as cherries anyway. It took me three weeks, but I finally got the courage:

Right, I told myself. I may as well smile back.

It's just past noon, and the sun starts to drop toward the treetops up on the priory hill. Alice climbs a little ahead.

"Mason, you'll need to go separately from us," she calls over her shoulder. "Wait until we've gone in, and come later. If the guards see us all together, there will be talk, or worse."

"I'll *avoid all appearance of evil*," he pledges cheerfully. But as we approach the bridge, he suddenly takes my hand and leads me quickly down to the riverbank. He looks up to make sure Alice can't see—and wraps his arms around my waist completely, kissing me hard. Months of longing and grief fill our mouths, like we could resurrect everyone we loved with this kiss, like we're swaddled in blue velvet.

"I have to see you," he says. "Edyth."

"It won't be easy," I whisper, and kiss his cheek. "But we'll find ways. We just have to be careful."

"It's not an accident that we're both here."

"How could it possibly be?" Maybe I haven't been tossed to fate, after all. For the first time in months, true hope wells up in me.

I squeeze Mason's hand and run back up the hill to meet up with Alice.

Under her veil, she's grinning. "Not exactly one of the Pitiful now, are you?"

— 12 —

Can a room be alive, alert?

The scriptorium feels carved with eyes, in the walls, the books, the magnifying globes. Everything must know what happened under the bridge. The tingle of Mason's kiss still on my lips, my body all secrets, and that's how it must stay if he and I are to meet again.

I'll go straight to the grinding room, give Bridgit her wares and make some excuse to leave early and find Mason. Potato-peeling duty, something like that.

But no luck—Brother Timothy says hello and waves me over.

"Good morning, little sister!"

"Good morning, Brother Timothy!"

"Fine job on the paints yesterday." He leans in and whispers, "I like yours better than Bridgit's. Hers can be rather gritty."

"Let's not hurt her Scottish pride," I chuckle.

"She's had too much experience. There's the zeal of youth in you, little sister. You haven't yet learned where to cut corners."

"I can hear you, Timothy," Bridgit chides, emerging from the pigment room. I give her the bag from the marketplace, and she hands me a list of the afternoon's orders.

My hopes of leaving early are dashed. I just pray she can't see my annoyance, so I feign a good attitude. "Thanks. I'll get started right away."

Muriel: Terre verte and ochre, each 30 grains.
    Azurite, coarse dark, 12 grains.
Anne: Vermillion ink, 4 drams.
Timothy: Sinopia, 20 grains. Ultramarine, 2 grains.

"Bridgit, it says *ultramarine* on my list. I think you meant to put it on yours."

"No, it's no mistake. I was thinking to myself, *Now, that Edyth, she's a bright girl. What would happen if I gave her just a little bit more?* So today, I'm going to show you how to extract the lapis lazuli. You can do the other pigments afterward."

I gasp. *Lapis lazuli? Me?*

"But, Bridgit," I protest, "I shouldn't do it. I haven't even mastered the other recipes—"

"Oh, come on," she coaxes, a cheeky twinkle in her eyes. "You'll see. It's a bit of magic."

There's no debating her; Bridgit's already set up. She's got lapis stones in several stages of grinding: a little drawer of raw stones streaked grayish white; brighter little blue pebbles; a light blue powder the color of a summer sky.

"These are the raw lapis stones, very hard and worth their weight in gold. We'll leave off grinding them for another time, and just make the pigment with some I've already done." She melts beeswax and resin in a brazier and adds the powdered lapis. When it's done, she pours the grayish-blue slurry out on a slab.

"You make it into wax sticks and let it dry for three days. Here's a piece that's done, see? Soften it in that warm water there and knead it like bread dough. Go ahead.

"Now put the dough into this bowl of lye. Careful, don't touch the liquid or it'll burn your skin clear away. Take these wooden sticks, and pound the dough into the lye. There, do you see how the liquid turns blue? That's the pure pigment coming out. It'll settle at the bottom."

Bridgit taught me to say a prayer before I work on each pigment. Because lapis is used to paint Our Lady's clothes, Bridgit prefers the *Magnificat*. So we recite as I begin kneading—

Magnificat anima mea Dominum
Et exsultavit spiritus meus in Deo salutari meo
Quia respexit humilitatem ancillae suae.

My soul magnifies the Lord
And my spirit rejoices in God my Savior
For He has looked on the humble estate of His servant.

"Here's a bowl I did yesterday," says Bridgit. "Take a spoon to the bottom, and see what you pull up."

"My God," I gasp. A warm glow climbs the back of my neck as I draw up a spoonful of vivid violet-blue.

The color completely takes me over, like I'm living inside a memory.

Or kissing Mason. The same feeling.

I'm inside color itself, inside purity, inside nothing and everything at the same time.

Before I know what's happening, I hear Bridgit chiding me—

Wake up, girl, wake up! What's wrong with you?

—and she's patting my cheek. Hard.

The cloud of outrageous blue before my eyes dissipates into soft paleness and clears away. I've been staring at the ultramarine, frozen and holding the spoon, dripping vivid puddles of blue soup on the table around the bowl. A total waste.

"What . . . what happened?" The trance peels away from me and leaves me with goose bumps.

Bridgit clucks her tongue and gestures toward the table. "You were day-dreaming, or in some kind of stupor—I don't know! But look at this mess!"

I scrape what I can of the spilled pigment onto a piece of scrap paper.

"You can't use that now," Bridgit sighs. "It's tainted. You'll have to mark it as substandard. Maybe someone will use it for patch work. Good thing it was only a small bit."

My cheeks flush fire at Bridgit's scowl, at the pigment, like I've thrown pure gold into the rubbish pile.

"I don't know why that happened." I hang my head in my hands. "I knew I shouldn't have done the ultramarine. I'm sorry. I'm so *sorry*. . . . It's too much."

"What's too much?" she rebukes. "It's just a different process, Edyth. Why on earth—"

I'm paralyzed, mouth gaping, tears coming. *Can't tell her about the colors. She'll think I'm insane. She'll send me away from the scriptorium. But Bridgit's been good to me. Maybe—*

"The color—it took over," I confess. A shroud of shame covers my head.

"What do you mean, *took over*?" Her face is twisted in confusion.

"Almost like fainting," I try to explain. "I've never seen a color like that. It's beautiful when it's dry, but when it's wet like that . . . too much."

Bridgit lifts her hand and I flinch.

But instead of striking me, she puts her arm around my shoulder and gives me a little squeeze.

"Forgiven," she sighs. "It happens."

"It does? Really?"

"Well, no," she says. "But . . . you'll try again tomorrow."

A headache is beginning just behind my eyes. Bridgit cleans up the pigment, wrings a cloth in cool water and puts it on the back of my neck, then sits across from me and folds her hands, staring at me.

"Right," says Bridgit, finally. "Let's get you to bed. I'll say you've taken ill."

Bridgit walks me down the endless winding halls to my cell. I sleep through the bells and wake at dusk, staring at the shadows being thrown by the dying light, that space between, where I always seem to live.

After compline, Bridgit brings Joan the Physician to see me, with Alice assisting her. Joan asks me a string of questions.

"Bridgit said the color . . . took over? What color? What do you mean?" A suspicious glance passes between the women.

"I've never seen blue like that before," I say, shamefaced. "Doesn't it . . . do something to you?"

"What, lapis stone? Hardly," she chortles to Bridgit. "I use it for eye sores." She gives me tincture of hellebore in a brown bottle and a corked pitcher of water. "At any rate, I find nothing of concern. But keep this tincture here in your cell. If it happens again, four drops in this spring water, no more—or you will vomit all night."

"All right," I say, eyeing it warily.

"It probably won't kill you," she says dryly, "but give a holler if you see Saint Peter."

Alice looks at her boss sideways.

Joan packs up her medicine box. "Have Cook prepare her a curative supper, Alice, and bring it to her later. And you, Edyth, stay behind from the daily office for one more day. Eat here in your cell, and pray. I'll vouch for your absence. But try to pay attention next time to what brings it on."

Later, Alice returns with a bowl and bread, and pries my secret out of me.

"You don't think I'm out of my mind, then?" I ask.

"Give it a few more months here, and then we'll see if you still want to ask that question," she teases. "But come on, you really blanked out because you saw some *ultramarine?*"

"It's not only that," I admit. "I don't just *see* something, or *hear* something, or *smell* something. There's always color with it, sometimes a lot, sometimes a little. But this is the first time it's been that intense. There's something about that blue. It's . . . overwhelming."

"Joan said there was one other person this happened to—you know, trances, things like that."

I perk up, intrigued. "Here? At the priory? Who?"

"The Anti-Pri." She giggles. "Oops, I meant the *sub-prioress*. Agnes de Guile."

"What did you call her? *The Anti-Pri?*"

"Never mind, never mind. A little play on words."

"I like her just fine," I say.

Alice scoffs. "That's because she likes you."

"Seriously, Alice? I'm pretty sure she thinks I'm addled. You're the one she's always praising."

"Oh, no, trust me," says Alice. "It's all an act. She picks on you because she knows you're smarter than you let on. She *hates* me. There's a certain type who doesn't care for questioners."

"But isn't that what you're here for, to ask questions? *Alice Palmer, the promising young scholar?*"

"As long as my questions don't apply to the people in charge. Aristotle and Aquinas? Fine. Agnes de Guile? Pfff."

"Do you really think Agnes . . . sees things? The same way I do?"

"Well . . ." Alice ponders. "Didn't you say the Anti-Pri used to work in the scriptorium?"

"Sure. Muriel showed me a few folios of hers. They're gorgeous."

"Now, what would make her leave something she was so good at? Come on, Edyth. Guess. What would happen if people found out that she saw things that weren't there?"

"But don't *saints* see visions?" I suggest. "What about Blessed Francis? He *levitated*, and Eustace saw a cross in a stag's antlers, and—"

"Look, Edyth, usually those people die hideous deaths or get run out of town. Not everyone who sees weird things is saint material. Maybe Agnes preferred an easier path. You should think about that."

"But everyone knows what happened to me now! What do I do?"

"Trust me, the only ones who actually know are me, Joan and Bridgit. But the next time you feel one of these things coming on, take my advice: put down the pestle, fold your hands in your lap and shut your eyes until it passes. Don't risk it."

"I hope you're right. I hope no one else really knows. Swear you won't tell."

"I'm not supposed to swear, Edyth. But I promise. And I'm good for my word."

"Then, Alice," I say, cautiously changing the subject, "would you be willing to do something else for me?"

"What, get a message to your Mason?" she teases me.

My cheeks flush. "Is it that obvious?"

"You're not a nun, like me. Technically, you don't have to renounce the world. You'll have to be creative to keep it hidden, of course, but sure, I'll be your messenger."

"Oh, Alice, thank you!" I throw my arms around her. "You really are a true friend."

"That's fine," she says, hugging me back. "But I *will* be expecting details."

— 13 —

The white skeletons of trees reach up toward the sun, begging for warmth. A late-spring snow casts a pale shroud over everything, dusty and disintegrating, the wind peeling it away a layer at a time. But plump snowdrops are starting to push up from the frosty ground, and the hellebores' miraculous blooms hover over mounds of star-shaped leaves.

From the array of baskets on the shed wall, I choose a shallow one and lay down a damp cloth to wrap the stems in, take the shears and go out to collect the early flowers. Past the churchyard and stables, they grow thickest against the priory wall. I miss clipping garden flowers with Mam. I can't help thinking of how this could all have been so different.

Spring, when cows are in the early grass, is the best time for milk. It's rich and fat and even a little yellow from the field flowers. There's nothing slight about the butter it makes, or the thick cream, spread on warm bread.

I had finished the afternoon milking, and by the light of the late-evening candle, I took the cloth from the top of the clay pot and skimmed off the risen cream. Even in the almost-dark, the slow pull of spoon through milk rippled soft hues before me, the strong, round smell of it.

My father appeared, sudden but hushed, in the doorway of the cow barn.

"Come here, Edie," Da whispered. "Do you want to see something wonderful?"

I covered the milk and cream and followed him into the sheep shed. The last ewe was finally lambing in the dim light. We watched the late lamb tumble out, days after the other sheep had given birth.

"Isn't it a miracle?" he said, his eyes sparkling. "Think of her, waddling around the field like a ball, just a round ol' sheep, like, and you can forget there's a life in there."

"Like Mam." I smiled, pressing my cheek to his arm.

"Just like," Da said, pulling me close.

"Da? Will she be all right?"

"What—the ewe? She'll be fine."

"No, I mean Mam. After all the other babies she's lost—she's tired and . . . older. What if something happens?"

Da sighed. The mother sheep licked her baby clean. The little one trembled and fussed.

"Edie, you know I've never lied to you, don't you?"

"Yes, Da. Of course."

"Then I'm going to tell it to you true. You never knew me mam and da. They died in the famine when I was a boy. But me brothers and sisters and I, we went on. We took what they taught us, and the love they gave us, and it was enough for us to fight with. If anything happens to your mother, she'll have given you enough. You'll have what you need."

"But it's not about what I need. I couldn't live without her. She's the only one who understands—"

"It's not only the people who are like you who can understand you, Edie."

"I know, Da, but—"

"People die, Edyth," he said abruptly. "Parents, and children, and the lonely, the rich, the poor. It's never fair. It's never the right time."

"You're scaring me." I clung to him even harder.

"Now, I'm not going to sweeten this for you—your mam's good at saying those soothing things. But not me. It's a hard world, this. But one thing I know: you'll never be alone. Even if you go off and live among strangers in some far place, the right folks *will always be there. People who see you for you. Ones who are willing to try. You will have to look for them, and be willing to see them, too.*

"And you know, don't you? People don't really die. They're just changed, like seeds break into wheat. All right," he chuckled, "some change into weeds, too. But you, me girl, you must live so that when it's your time, your life counts like wheat, not weeds. And I'll do the same."

We watched as the lamb stood at last on its wobbling legs and immediately butted against its mother's belly for milk. Even minutes old, the little one somehow knew what to do.

Sunday night after compline, the moon above is full. Mason meets me, as we've arranged, in the shadows behind the chapel, and we sit against the outer wall. The branches wave over us; the clay is cool beneath. We can't be together long—Alice is ready with a few alibis just in case—but we hold hands, talk in whispers, kiss a lot. There's no mention of future plans; we simply wait here between layers of life and time.

"Mason." I make my voice casual and a little teasing, even though the question I'm about to ask is serious.

"Edyth."

"Why did you come here? Why did you seek me out?"

He grins. "What kind of question is that?"

"Is it because I'm familiar—*Edyth from the village?* You're *free.* You could have your choice. Shouldn't you be with someone who isn't bound in a priory . . . and"—I nervously fiddle with my messy braids—"someone . . . prettier?"

He reaches for my discarded veil and puts it back over my hair. "Edyth," he coos, smoothing the linen, "you're beautiful. You're . . . different."

"You don't have to remind me. I hate that word, *different.*"

"Why? Do you *want* to be like those girls in Hartley Cross, laughing at people behind their backs, never letting anyone else in on the joke?"

I suddenly see Mason with new eyes. "I never would have thought it."

"What?"

"I always assumed that you were part of that group, like you were sort of . . . tolerating me."

He laughs a little too loud.

I nudge him. "Shh! Someone will come!"

"Edyth," he says more softly, "you and me, we couldn't be like them if we tried. You're a wanderer, like me, and you know it. That's why"—he pauses and takes a breath—"that's why you should come with me when this is over."

"When what's over?"

"When we finish building the chapel."

All this time, that had never dawned on me. Leaving the priory had never seemed like an option.

"When"—my mouth feels like dust—"when will the chapel be finished?"

"This fall, I reckon. With the lot of us on the crew, it goes fast. The building wasn't in as bad shape as they let on."

I hesitate. "That's soon. . . . I only just started at the scriptorium." What I don't want to say is that I can't imagine leaving there. I love the work, watching stones become pictures.

"Edie, by the time we'd leave, you'd have a fine skill—you could work in any town I do. Scribe work's always in demand."

"I have to think about it, Mason. You say I'm a wanderer—I don't know if that's true."

"It's true enough, isn't it?" he presses. "A misfit, maybe."

"Well, I fit there," I protest. "In the scriptorium."

Silence hangs in the night air.

"I should get to bed," I say at last, rising.

"You will think about it, though?" He takes hold of my hand and kisses it. "Coming with me?"

"I will," I promise. Conflicted as I am, I lean over and kiss his soft lips.

"That's all I ask," says Mason. "Good night, Edyth."

As I gingerly round the corner, I hear the gravel crunch on the other side of the chapel, and I press myself into the side of the building until I see who it is. It's hard to tell, but as the veiled figure gets closer, I can make out mutterings, as though the person is having a conversation with an invisible partner.

The Dragon Nun. Felisia.

My heart pounds in my throat. Felisia has no discretion whatsoever. If she sees me, my secret is out. But what is she doing out here herself? Everyone's supposed to be in bed.

Mason comes around the building and passes right by me on his way to the stonemasons' shed. He almost bumps into Felisia, and she gives a little shriek.

"God be with you, sister. Should you be out like this in the dark?"

"Thank you, sir," she fumbles. "I came out to . . . look at the moon. . . ."

"That's all right," Mason laughs. "I won't give you any trouble. Night, then."

"Good night," she says, sounding faraway and strange. I hear Mason go into the stonemasons' shed and shut the creaky wooden door, so I finally emerge from the shadows.

But the Dragon Nun is still standing in the path, looking at the moon, and as I step out, our eyes meet. She stares at me and breaks into a slow grin, then continues on her way to wherever she was going.

Summer
1349

— 14 —

Weeks of our Sunday night meetings have passed, and Mason hasn't pressed me for an answer again. I guess it's because growing season's under way, and all hands are required for haying and planting, weeding and watering. Sunup to sundown, there's no time for leisure or thoughts of a future beyond harvest. Even work at the scriptorium has to slow down—you've got to think of winter in summer, summer in winter, if you don't want to starve.

Out through the rear gate, arm in arm, Alice and I almost skip with grati-tude for the freedom. The woods rising at the edge of the open fields tantalize me with their cool darkness, the hot breeze waving the treetops like a thousand beckoning hands.

As frigid as winter was, summer's already every bit as unrelenting. I get to wear Mam's weld-green linen dress and a straw hat without a veil, without even the linen coif—and I don't have to wear hose under my gown. Bare feet, clean sweat—and seeing Mason there across the field makes me feel my body mov-ing inside my clothes. At home, I would work in nothing but my linen tunic, as long as I had an apron over it. But this is as much of a concession to the heat as modesty will allow, so says Agnes de Guile.

Lately the sub-prioress has been stern with me, short-tempered with my mistakes, dropping cutting little remarks about my family, my poverty, the com-promsies made to allow me here. I can't help but wonder about Felisia and that

night near Easter. She must have known I was with Mason, but maybe she hasn't said anything about it. Still, the change in Agnes has me thinking that either it's about Mason or she's gotten wind of my trance in the scriptorium.

"She's not supposed to treat you that way," Alice says, rebraiding her hair.

"What way?" I shrug and keep on raking. "I'm not a nun. I can't expect to be treated like one."

"Why, because you're poor? The *Rule* says that you're not supposed to show favoritism to anyone because of their estate. It's supposed to be different here."

"It only says that the abbot or prioress can't play favorites."

"Right," chides Alice, like a teacher. "So I guess if you're not *officially* running things, you get a pass? Because she's not *prioress?*"

"*Yet,*" we say together.

"You'd think—we spend all day and night praying, studying the *Rule* . . ." I ponder. "And she's the one teaching everyone. I guess I assumed people got better as they got older."

"It doesn't work that way," says Bridgit, tying a bundle from the hay we've just gathered. Her strong forearms protrude from the sleeves of her wheat-colored linen gown. "People simply get more concentrated, like boiling down a sauce."

Alice and I both laugh.

"You're lucky, though, being young," says Bridgit. "If you put the right ingredients in the sauce now, you'll thicken properly. And the most important ingredient is forgiveness."

Da's face flashes in my mind. The glee on his killer's face. The fight we had right before he died. Henry sending me away.

"Yes," I say, "but some things can't be forgiven."

"They can," says Bridgit. "They must."

The three of us fall into an unspoken symbiosis as we bundle and tie the sheaves.

"De Guile," says Bridgit after a while. "She was a gifted young girl when she came here, like yourselves. Only . . ." She stops herself.

"Too much salt in the sauce?" I suggest.

"Yes," says the woman, smirking. "Too much salt in the sauce."

When you're starved of sleep from middle-of-the-night prayers, there's nothing more defeating than losing even a few minutes. Wednesday morning, I wake to the song of robins and the blue wash of dawn at the window. I lie in bed, thinking of Mason, enjoying the warmth of this cocoon, the warmth of my own body under the thinnish covers.

Just *then*, the bell rings for prime. I slink into the pale green gown, reach over to the bedpost and put on the veil. My hose lie on the floor, and I pull them on and fasten them around my knees. Already I can't wait to kick them off and head to the fields, but first, the scriptorium calls.

As I'm halfway through reviewing my pigment list, I hear the hammers starting, and I sigh. It's too distracting.

"I'm going to get a drink of water," I tell Bridgit, and head downstairs in the direction of the cloister fountain, but I divert my path toward the builders' shed. Mason brightens when he sees me.

"Sister," he says with a wink. He hands me a handkerchief and motions to his cheek. I wipe a smear of pigment from my own.

"Hello, stonemason," I say. "The sun's warm today. Cool under here, though." I can't help but flirt a bit.

"I suppose, unless you're swinging a hammer," Mason laughs. Sweat drips out from under his cap. He's chiseling a rough, dark stone. The man across from him carves a vine into a piece of white limestone.

"I have something for you," says Mason. He rummages through his satchel and takes out a little house made of polished marble, with tiny arched windows and doors. The sunlight catches it and makes it glow as he places it in my hand.

"This is for you," he says.

"Oh, it's heavier than I thought! It's so fine, Mason. It looks like a proper *home*." I smile and brush his arm. "Thank you." The stone is cool. I turn it over in my hands. How I would love to shrink to the size of an ant and crawl into a place like this with him.

And with these thoughts of *home*, I wonder how Henry made it through winter. My heart feels somehow softer toward my big brother, now that I'm settled in here. I hope he's found a way forward.

"Speaking of," I say, "do you have any news from Hartley Cross? About . . . Henry?"

Mason looks uncomfortable. "Well, let me see," he says. "On my way up here, I passed this village—so strange—they'd set up a guard and wouldn't let us in. Said there was a pestilence in that place." He points to another laborer. "Gilbert Carpenter over there said he heard the whole place is dead."

"I wonder if it was the same town we passed," I say. "Nothing but ghosts."

"Might be. Strange, isn't it? Oh, and guess what? Right before I left, Methilde Potter was betrothed!"

I'm scandalized. "No! To *who*?"

"That scabby-faced boy, the wainwright's—"

"John, break's over!" gruffs his foreman, looking at me. Mason gives an alarmed glance past my shoulder. I turn to see Agnes de Guile standing behind me. I hand Mason his handkerchief. He looks frozen.

"Edyth," she says. "Go back to work."

I slip the little stone house into my pocket and drag myself back to the scriptorium tower, without having gotten my drink of water.

— 15 —

Thousands of hay sheaves stand in the ochre field late that afternoon. I'm tying up my last bundle before I have to clean up when I hear the sharp crunch of someone approaching over the stubble.

"I'd like to speak with you, Edyth," says Sub-Prioress Agnes. "Come with me."

I try to finish tying the bundle.

"Leave it," Agnes barks.

"But—"

Agnes grabs me by the wrist so hard, my fingers curl. I drop the bundle and the hay explodes everywhere. We trudge through the field and back in through the rear gate, past the infirmary and the stonemasons' shelter, where Mason will be chiseling to the very last light of day. He gives me a careful glance.

The sub-prioress pulls me through the cloister toward the door of the prioress's study. Agnes's assistant, Felisia, is reading on a bench by the door. I haven't seen her this close before. Her veil shifts, and I don't mean to flinch, but I can see that the whole left side of her face is horribly disfigured from old burns. She smooths the veil into place and closes her book.

"Prioress Margaret is visiting the bishop," says Agnes. "We'll meet in here." She dismisses the Dragon Nun, who retreats to light the lily-shaped candelabra in the cloister walk. The golden hour illuminates the study walls in that indescribable hue.

"Edyth of Hartley Cross," Agnes says, sitting in the prioress's chair. She brushes her palm across the blossoms of a potted lavender. "Speak, child."

What should I say? Have I done something wrong? I rub my still-smarting wrist.

"I don't think you're a fish, are you?" Agnes chuckles, imitating the noiseless movements of my lips. I smile a little; I don't know if she's mocking me—but then, I never do know where I stand with her. She sees me rubbing my wrist. "I've been told I don't know my own strength," she says. "But tell me: Why do you think I wanted to talk to you?"

"Because . . . of the stonemason?"

"Should I have a reason to speak to you about that?"

I downplay our connection. "He's just a friend from my village."

"That may be," says Agnes, "but the priory is a different world from your village."

That's the truth.

"Do you like it here, Edyth? You've been here, what, six, seven months now?"

"Yes, Sub-Prioress. I like it here—it's very pretty."

"*Pretty.* Hmm. What did you do at home? I understand your father was reeve."

I wish he had never been given that job. Everything would have been different if he had stayed a sheepman.

"I did all sorts of things. Da ran the wool business for Saint Gabriel's and for Lord Geoffrey. I helped him with shearing and dyeing. And my mam—she was a weaver."

"Of course." Agnes ponders. "People of the *land.* Tell me, was your mother a forgiving woman?"

I look down at my hands. "She always gave me another chance when I made mistakes. If she hadn't, nothing would have gotten done."

"Well said, my dear. Tell me, it's painful for you to be here, isn't it? I know some of your story. How alone you must feel." I wonder how much of my story the sub-prioress really knows. I wonder why she's bringing it up now, because something in me guesses that the look on her face isn't exactly pity.

I turn my face away toward the dying light.

"Whatever your emotions, though, there can be no allowances for speaking to men, except the priest at confession, and Brother Timothy at work. This is a women's sanctuary, Edyth. Should you be found with the stonemason again, the discipline will be swift. Do you understand?"

I nod, but inside I'm all sharp green needles of panic at the thought of not seeing Mason. Already I'm contriving a way to get around this.

"There are, however, two points of concern for which I brought you here, Edyth. The boy is only one of those concerns. My assistant, Felisia, has a . . . nervous disposition. You have seen her outbursts—her mutterings about dragons and things, yes?"

"Yes, Sub-Prioress."

"Felisia has been our ward since she was a child. Her parents indulged her visions and did not discipline her. Once, in a frenzy, she chased one of these demons straight into the great fire in her family's hall, right in the middle of a feast. She was badly burned. Her mother and father knew she had no future prospects, so they brought her here. She was only seven years old."

Tears well in my eyes. That poor girl, her face disfigured and her mind broken. I feel bad for her. But I don't know what her story has to do with me.

"Some people have that same . . . openness to the things they perceive. Felisia's scars are a visible sign to all of us: that is what happens to anyone who does not tightly seal the door to anything beyond what we *all* see and agree on."

She stares at me.

"I know about your trance in the scriptorium."

A shock goes through me. "How?" Could Alice have told her? Joan?

"This priory is a small place."

I prepare for the worst. "What are you going to do?"

"I want you to come work for me. Felisia needs some time of solitude and penance, and I can teach you to discipline your unruly mind. I will instruct you in the rules of our priory more closely, since our ways still seem so . . . new to you."

A billow of peach-colored fear blurs my vision for an instant. "Do I have to leave the scriptorium?"

"No," Agnes says. "That will still be your general assignment. You will assist me in the mornings at chapter. And, Edyth, you'll wear the novice's habit now. It's only proper if you will be serving me, and who knows, you may grow accustomed to it."

I feel Mam's linen dress clinging to the day's sweat and see how threadbare it's become. Still, nothing in me wants to wear that habit. But I know I have no choice.

"You may go, Edyth. I will expect you five minutes early to chapter tomorrow."

As I walk into the chapter house right behind the sub-prioress the next morning, I glimpse the jealousy in Felisia's expression, and see clearly that a "time of solitude and penance" was not her idea. And as I see the din of voices in their usual colors, I feel like I'm in the wrong body, with the wrong eyes, more disjointed than ever before. Maybe Agnes is right: maybe she'll help me close the door to my difference, and things won't be so confusing.

I sit, as I've been instructed, on a stool to the right of the large oaken seat where Agnes takes her place. I hate being so conspicuous. As soon as I wipe my sweaty hands on my gray dress, they're damp again. I have one job to do at the morning meeting: to hold the sub-prioress's books and hand each to her at the proper time. I can feel Felisia's eyes on me. I'm sure this was the last thing she expected. But that's not for me to worry about. I'm working for Agnes de Guile now, and I make sure to steer clear of the Dragon.

$$-\;16\;-$$

Dusk, that moment between light and dark, when the whole world takes a breath at once, is always my favorite time of day. There's a place there, in that gray-blue light, where all the memories are kept, as though you could go to the cupboard and take out the jar of them. I volunteer for lamp lighting, singing softly with the other women as the candelabra light fills the halls—

> *Fulgor diei lucidus solisque lumen occidit,*
> *et nos ad horam vesperam te confitemur cantico.*
>
> *We have come to the setting of the sun*
> *And we have gathered to sing our evening praise.*

It's Saint John's Eve, midsummer. After compline, when we would be going to bed, the whole community of women goes out to the medicine garden. Tonight's the optimal night to pick the Saint John flowers, when they'll be at their most potent. Warmth radiates from the grass, and we have our shoes off, running our toes over it, letting the earth come up into our bodies. It's a beautiful night: the perfume in the air, the crackle of the fires being lit.

The sisters sit around the big bonfire by the gatehouse and weave flower crowns for each other, and posies to hang above their cell doors to keep the demons away. I sit apart from everyone. I prefer it that way.

"Saint John's wort is for melancholy," Joan instructs a group of students, never missing an opportunity to teach—even at a party. "Fennel for the stomach, vervain for the throat, and yarrow for womanly pains. The plants will yield more by autumn, so leave enough at the heart to let them recover, but tonight, take all you can."

Alice follows Joan closely, writing everything on a wax tablet. As she passes by me, she points and whispers, "Look who's home."

Prioress Margaret is back from one of her many diplomatic visits to this or that bishop, and she's seated on the throne-like chair from her study, leaning back and talking to Agnes, who sits next to her on a plain stool. Even seated, the prioress is like a poplar tree, more upright than even Lady Caxton. She doesn't need fine silks or elaborately braided hair. She's another kind of beauty—as though she's distilled womanhood, slowly boiling out all the dross until she's a column of grace.

A glowworm crawls across my knee as I make a posy for the prioress, of rosemary and elderflower. I like the combination of their different shapes, both of their leaves and of their scents, the piney midnight blue of rosemary and the brick-red circles of the elder.

I approach the two women and bow. "Mother," says Agnes, "this is my new assistant, Edyth le Sherman. She's from Saint Gabriel's Abbey, which donated for the chapel restoration."

"Thank you, daughter," says Prioress Margaret, taking the posy and smelling it. "This is lovely."

"Venerable Mother," I say, "this is to say thank you for taking me in after my parents died."

"Well, Edyth," she says, smiling. "I hope you feel at home here at Saint Christopher's."

"Thank you very much." I bow to them both and stroll along the gravel paths of the priory grounds. Over the wall in Thornchester, the hollers of the locals go up as they light their own bonfires. I wonder about Henry; he's probably doing the same thing in Hartley Cross right now. In the square, the boys'll be taking off their shirts and showing off their acrobatic leaps over the flames as the girls cheer them on. I remember the deep laughter of those nights. Now it seems like another life.

Mason's probably down in Thornchester, too. The priory has ale and bread at the gatehouse, for pilgrims or drunkards. Better to have the sinners within these gates than out wandering the streets. But Mason wouldn't stay here to fete with a bunch of nuns. I picture him, under the May sky in Hartley Cross, on a night just like this, only last year.

After a bitter and lengthy winter, Hartley Cross needed warmth and color, and as the new reeve, Da proposed that the town throw a riotous May Day celebration, damn the expense. Lord Geoffrey happily handed over the money. Every household did an extra brewing, and on May Eve, Lord Caxton's servants brought two cartloads of wood and built them up into an enormous pyre near the market cross.

"If the weather won't heat up, Hartley Cross will heat up the weather!" Da proclaimed.

Before dawn, the whole town gathered at Saint Andrew's. There were pork pies and candied fruits, spiced ale and cider, and even a great pig being put on a spit to roast all day.

Fathers held their little children on their shoulders, and families huddled together against the chill as the prime bell rang. The stars began to fade as the sky turned dark blue, the clouds becoming the color of salmon against a backdrop like a robin's egg. The town was washed in rosy light.

The girls gathered at the steps of the market cross, all of us dressed in our undergowns, with woolens underneath to keep out the chill. Mam waddled over, hugely pregnant. My hair was everywhere. She smoothed it and straightened my flower crown, taking in how I'd changed since the last year.

"Bite your lips a bit and get some color in them," she said. "My beautiful girl. Where have the years gone!"

"Mam, stop," I said, nudging my mother's hands away. Only she would call this mess beautiful. "Enough fussing!"

She patted my shoulders and retreated into the crowd to watch with Da.

The Other Girls bickered and teased and laughed to see each other in their chemises. The younger boys sneaked pinches and taps and tugs on unveiled braids. I stood alone on the edge, exposed and dizzy, overwhelmed at the multitude of people and sounds. I inhaled and exhaled slowly to calm myself. Then the older boys emerged.

And there was Mason, with new green oak leaves in his hair like Oberon, like the wild Merlin. I couldn't take my eyes off of him. I hoped he'd look my way, but all the boys in town had eyes only for Methilde, who was obviously going to be chosen as May queen.

I resigned myself to the truth: Edyth Round and Red could never be May queen.

Brother Robert wound the hurdy-gurdy, the rough, oaky shawm and pipes started up, making me see all shimmers and little silver spikes, and the people began to hum along as we processed to the market cross—

> Tempus adest floridum, surgunt namque flores
> Vernales in omnibus, imitantur mores
> Hoc quod frigus laeserat, reparant calores
> Cernimus hoc fieri, per multos labores.
>
> Spring has now unwrapped the flowers, day is fast reviving
> Life in all her growing powers toward the light is striving
> Gone the iron touch of cold, winter time and frost time
> Seedlings, working through the mould, now make up for lost time.

We took our places around the tall birch maypole, picked up our long ribbons of dyed cloth and turned to face our partners. The crowd sang along softly, the ode to spring, to heavenly love.

In toward the pole we girls stepped, the boys weaving around us. The dance was slow at first, with courteous bows, partners constantly changing, long looks and blushing smiles. The ribbons wove and unwove; the circles splitting into inner and outer rings. Then the musicians picked up the tempo, and the dancers twirled, trying to keep the steps in order, breaking into smiles, then laughter. Around and around the maypole we ran, until all of a sudden the musicians stopped the song—

—and Mason and I were face to face. Out of breath, red-cheeked, smiling first at the mayhem, and then a different kind of smile, something like knowing.

The day progressed, with its games and drinks, the first true feast of the year. Mothers and fathers pretended not to notice their sons and daughters going off in pairs. There might, after all, be favorable matches made on May Day. Today, every answer was Yes.

I took a pork pie from the table and filled my cup with Mam's gruit ale. Behind me, I could feel someone standing a bit too close inside the boundary of my own space. I turned my head slowly, hoping it was him, sure it couldn't be.

It was.

"Mary atte Brook's pork pies are good," said Mason, "but try the egg-and-onion kind instead. Here, I'll take one, and we can share." He was next to me. His shaggy, ash-blond hair was tucked behind his ear.

I started to sweat and get dizzy. He was talking. To me.

The thought of eating in front of him was mortifying—so visible. In my mind I nodded, but really I just stared. Mason smiled at me, and I could see how vivid his eyes were. The only time people looked at me was when they were making fun of me.

But he wasn't.

Suddenly he turned and started walking away toward the churchyard. He looked back at me and jerked his head. "Aren't you coming?"

So I followed behind him like a clumsy little newborn lamb.

Mason wove through the graves under the gigantic yew tree and hopped up onto the stone wall without even putting down his cup and pie. I put my things on the ledge and hoisted myself up, praying that my round head wouldn't topple me over onto the other side.

"Did you like the dance?" asked Mason.

"It was fun." Suddenly I hated the way my mouth formed words. I stuffed in a piece of pork pie. It was intolerably dry. I swigged some gruit and almost choked.

"My favorite part is seeing everyone out there in their skivvies." Mason laughed, tugging on his woolen braies.

I smiled and looked at my chemise. "Good thing the dancing sped up—I was freezing!"

"Me too! It felt like the sun would never come up."

"Longest winter ever," I mused.

"I didn't mind it so much," said Mason. "With Henry and me trading work for our fathers, I got to see you every Sunday."

I whipped a look of shock at Mason.

"What?" He shrugged. "I looked forward to it."

"But we've never talked or anything."

"We're talking now, aren't we?" He tugged at my sleeve.

"Y-you're not playing a trick on me, right?" I leaned back and looked over the wall to be sure no one was lying in wait. I sat up quickly and brushed his arm—he seemed closer than before.

"A trick?" He looked confused.

Between us was the spring air, the fading perfume of my flower crown and the gruit, and I let myself look at him, like we did at the dance—like I was supposed to be there, like I was meant to memorize the deep blue of his eyes.

Mason broke his egg-and-onion pie in half and handed me the larger piece, and I did the same with mine. We talked, and joked, way into the night by the bonfire, and every scrap of my awkwardness blew away in the fresh air.

I wasn't sure what was happening, only that things were different, and that all things were possible.

— 17 —

"I was hoping you'd be out here." A voice shakes me back into the present. I look over my shoulder—Mason is walking toward me. The Saint John bonfires throw gold all over his skin, the flames wavering in his eyes as he looks at me.

"I thought you'd be in town, Mason. Decided to celebrate with the frozen chosen instead?"

"Nice dress," he chuckles. "Is that new?"

"I got dressed up in cloth of gold for the event," I say, mocking the gray habit I have to wear now.

"Come with me," he says. I eye him nervously. "Don't worry. They won't see us." We keep to the perimeter of the walls until we get to the field gate and push through into the free dark.

The midsummer fires are burning in the fields, kindled from hay stubble and great logs donated to the priory. The farmworkers wave torches above the grainfields to dispel any bad air. The bonfires build up until the whole field is under a glowing, smoking tent of protection. We lean against the outside of the wall and watch the smoke rise. Things feel clean and changing.

"You sure you don't want to be down in Thornchester with the town girls?" I ask.

"Never thought about it," he says. "In fact, I made you something."

"Really?" I smile.

He removes my veil pin and lets the linen fall into his hand. From under his tunic, Mason produces a crown of Saint John flowers. He lifts it and places it on my head.

"A diadem for the queen," he says, doffing his cap, bowing ridiculously. I know how to laugh along with a joke at my own expense. But Mason has another kind of smile playing on his lips. "Different flowers than you had on at that maypole, but the face makes the flowers, not the other way around."

"This face?" I point. "Don't you know what they called me back home? *Edyth, Edyth, Round and Red?*"

"Pig muckers and leech collectors, all of 'em," he says, plopping down next to me. "To me, you're *Lady Edyth of Flower and Fire.*"

And his fingers brush mine, there in the shadow where no one can see. He softly pinches my thumb and lets his fingers wander to my wrist, stroking its thin bones. A petal of my flowery crown is falling; he reaches up with his other hand and plucks it, and the rest of the petals fall away in a shower around my face. We laugh a little, just to see each other smile.

Mason begins to sing softly—

> *Douce dame jolie*
> *Pour Dieu ne pensés mie*
> *Que nulle ait signorie*
> *Seur moy fors vous seulement.*

> *Sweet, lovely lady*
> *For God's sake do not think*
> *That anyone has power*
> *Over me but you alone.*

I'm surprised—I've never heard him sing before. His voice is beautiful, blue like his eyes. It reminds me so much of Da's, lilting and sweet. I know the language is French.

"Where did you learn that?" I ask, enchanted.

"At Christchurch. You meet people from all over the world when you're on a job site like that."

"I'm jealous. I'd love to travel somewhere else—outside of England, I mean."

"Maybe you will."

"Like you said once, it's not that simple," I respond wistfully.

We haven't talked about the idea of leaving together since that one night by the chapel. I don't want to press him, and I don't want to know if he's changed his mind, but the prospect is so tempting. And yet, the thought of leaving the scriptorium makes my heart sink.

"Can you see it?" he asks abruptly.

"What?"

"A thousand nights like this, looking at you in the firelight." He still has a gentle grip on my fingers. My heart is in a whirlpool, but I can't let it lead me. I can't follow a fantasy, no matter how enticing.

"Do you mean that, John Mason?" I say seriously. "Don't say it unless you do."

His smile grows wider and his grin turns into words playing at the edge of his mouth. There's something he wants to say, and I wish he would—but instead he grabs both of my hands and pulls me to stand. We run hand in hand, through the field, around the fires. He plays at thrusting me toward the fire, pulling me back just in time. Our bellies hurt with laughter.

Exhausted and happy, we watch the bonfires begin to dwindle; the nuns have gone up to the dormitory to sleep. I'm not one of them. Instead, I fall asleep in Mason's arms, close to him, but no closer to an answer about what's next.

I wake alone against the outside wall with the fields still smoking, the wilted flower crown still on my head, Mason's woolen hood as a pillow. It's morning, Saint John's Day, and by the time the bell rings for terce, it's already warming up. I hear footsteps on the gravel path coming toward the field gate and know at once that I'm in deep trouble.

"Get those flowers out of your hair and put your veil back on, you *savage thing.*" Agnes de Guile stands inside the half-open gate, with Felisia right beside her, waiting for me to come. I try to crumple up Mason's hood inconspicuously.

"I've been looking everywhere for you," says Agnes. "Do *not* make me late. We will speak about this later." Agnes grabs the hood and gives me the stack of books for chapter, storming ahead in disgust. Felisia smiles at me over her shoulder.

By the dormitory entrance is a large bowl of water steeped with the night's flowers and dew. The nuns cup handfuls and splash their faces with the flower water to keep cool. The sisters dare to laugh and chat in the greening cloister, but I can't shake the melancholy I feel, waking up alone outside the wall, without Mason. He never meant to stay, did he? Never meant to take me with him when the chapel job is over, after all.

Am I a fool?

As soon as I get to my cell, I crawl onto the bed and grip the blanket, gathering it around me and pressing it to my eyes. Facing the wall, I let the tears come, my heaving sobs dropping into the dry, empty well at the center of my belly.

Who was I to think I could have it both ways?

— 18 —

I long to throw myself into work at the scriptorium, back into the cool of the stone tower, and forget about Mason's noncommitment. But last night's bonfires mean today's cleanup, and we all trudge out to the hayfield to rake up the burnt stubble and get the soil ready for the winter rye.

From the corner of my eye, I can see someone marching quickly and decisively toward me. Alice shoots me an alarmed look.

"It's the Anti-Pri," she mutters.

We bend over the straw, hoping she'll pass us by. Agnes instead strides right up to me, making me flinch.

"Edyth, I want to talk to you," she barks, loud enough that her words will be heard.

"Yes, Sub-Prioress?" I stand to face her.

"It's come to this so soon, has it? You could not wait to undermine me?"

My skin tenses. "Excuse me, but . . . what did I do?"

Agnes's jaw clenches as she glares at me. She lowers her voice: "Did my eyes deceive me this morning by the field gate? You were with that boy."

"I was alone when you woke me, Sub-Prioress. I'm sorry I missed the office."

"Are you questioning my judgment? Haven't I been your teacher, your shepherd? As the *Rule* says, *Id est indisciplinatos et inquietos debet durius arguere.* 'He must sternly rebuke the undisciplined and restless.' I *must* order penance."

Bridgit pipes up, without lifting her eyes from her work. "Isn't it the prioress's job, actually, to exercise discipline? Like it says in the *Rule* and all."

I admire Bridgit's audacity. Agnes's eyes water and the fat of her neck quivers. I search the sub-prioress's face.

"That may be. But Prioress Margaret has gone away again, to see the archbishop. Until she returns, I will give you *mercy* and not what you really deserve. I am removing you from the scriptorium, Edyth. From now on you will . . . fetch things."

"You can't do that!" Bridgit protests.

"Can't I? I am in charge while Prioress Margaret is away."

"You're punishing *me* by taking my apprentice!" Suddenly I can see years of history in Bridgit's scowl. Agnes's departure from the scriptorium must not have been smooth.

"Be careful, Bridgit. Remember that you are a *conversa*, like Edyth." That makes Bridgit hold her tongue.

I feel like I'm being sliced open. So that's it, then?

Fetch.

Things.

What things? From whom?

I stare at Agnes, not knowing what to say, my mouth open slightly under my overbite. She glares at me. "Is there an issue with your assignment?" she asks coolly, as though *Fetcher of Things* is a normal job description.

"I'm sorry, Sub-Prioress, I'm just not sure what you mean by—"

"What is the sixth step of humility, Edyth?" Agnes puts a hand on my cheek, like Mam used to do when I was little.

I search my memory. "*To be content with the lowest position and most menial treatment.* But—"

"Remember that." Agnes turns toward the gate. "You are to take one week of silence. And should you break it . . ." She takes a breath. "Alice Palmer, would you please help your friend learn the value of silence? Thank you, Edyth. That is all."

I stand in the burnt field, holding the rake and staring. My new apprentice-ship, such as it is, will be to clean up after everyone else.

So that is that. I can't speak, and because I can't use words, all I have is anger, rising like bubbling, popping bread dough. My head is full of cobwebs and bursting pockets of sour air. I want to hit something, punch it hard.

These colors of rage are the worst, like the orange flames of Da's hanging, like waves along a clothesline. Most of the time, the vibrations are integrated, like the Sound—the washy blue of grass under my bare feet; the angular ochres when gravel crunches under my shoes. It's been like that from before I learned to speak. At home, they were a bit duller. *Safer*. But without speech, all I can *do* is feel.

Agnes has even forbidden singing the office during this silent punishment. Everything seems out of harmony. During nones, I look around the church, searching for something new to fixate on, something to distract me.

And suddenly there it is, in a panel of stained glass in the upper gallery.

I've seen this picture before.

After Da and Mam died, I barely slept. I had nightmares for months. But then I started having an old dream again from my childhood. It replaced the terrors, and now I have it all the time. I've become so used to it, I've barely given it any thought until now.

In the dream, I'm standing in a birch wood, but there in the middle is a great, ancient yew tree, like the one in the churchyard. And ever since I saw him by the river at Michaelmas, Mason's appeared, under its boughs. Ripples of color emanate from the crown of the tree, and Mason climbs right into its heart, like you can with yews, and from underneath ushers a deep stream of water. Then, out from the center of the tree, instead of Mason, climbs a great white stag. He leaps into the pool, disappearing completely. I get on my hands and knees and peer in, and what had looked at first like dark water is clear and bright blue, like a window, and somewhere on the other side of the world, the stag leaps away across a field. The water begins to ripple and obscure as dawn shakes me awake.

Whenever I'd have the dream at home, I'd go to the barn and pull out my hidden drawing board, trying to depict it, adding more and more detail each time. It was part of me, like it had been sleeping in my mind since I was born. I drew the elaborate yew tree, the stag, the pool. When I'd slide the board back behind the manger, I'd sigh with relief, like I fit a little more squarely in the world by drawing that dream.

And now there it is: a secret I thought was only in my head, in real brilliant blues and greens of stained glass. Why would I have dreamed of something in Hartley Cross only to see it here in this northern priory church?

When the nones office ends, I can barely restrain myself from running to my cell. I open the wooden chest, but to my horror, I've used every one of Da's parchments, front and back. So I return to the church, in the summer evening light, and draw the image from the stained glass right in the endpapers of my psalter. Agnes can take away the scriptorium, but she can't take away my prayer book. And there's plenty of room in the margins.

The transept door opens.

Footsteps—

I tuck the stylus under the book and try to pretend I've been praying. Agnes clears her throat, looks at me for a moment—but then she, too, looks up at the window. She climbs the chancel to the statue of Our Lady and changes the spent candles for new ones. I feel her watching me but I don't look up. She floats back out of the church and shuts the door. I relax, breathe, and keep drawing.

$$- 19 -$$

The curse of silence has become a kind of gift. I spend the afternoon hours in my cell, working on the dream drawing in my psalter. The sun shines through the keyhole window, lighting up the bright whitewash of the walls, and I realize that I've been surrounded by the biggest parchment of all.

It's been a while since I drew with the charcoal twigs from my drawing board at home, but I get out the linen bundle and unwrap it—and begin to draw on the wall. All the little bits from the psalter, every detail I can remember from the barn board. A huge yew tree spans the corner where my bed is, each branch radiating needles, the pool gushing forth from its roots in curlicues. It is glorious.

I'm in the middle of drawing a huge rack of antlers on a stag when there's a knock on the cell door. My hands are full of charcoal. What do I do?

Please be Alice. Please, please, please be Alice.

I get up and open the door a crack, but keep my head down and stay behind it. The guest sweeps in anyway. Without looking up, I know it's Agnes. I brace myself: whatever she'll do, it will be something I can't guess.

"I came to release you from your sil—" The sub-prioress looks around at the graffiti on the walls, at the desecrated prayer book, and I hear her breathing become deep, slow, deliberate.

"Come with me," says Agnes quietly, turning and exiting into the hallway.

My heart begins to race. How could I be so stupid as to think I could get away with vandalizing my cell? She reaches and grabs me by the wrist, dragging me through the calefactory, past the infirmary and orchard to the goat barn. One glance from Agnes is enough to clear the farmworkers out, and she flings me into one of the stalls.

"Take off your habit," says Agnes dryly while she searches the floor for something.

"What?" I scramble for a reason, knowing and not knowing what's coming. "Why?"

"Do it. And your tunic, off to the waist." Agnes returns to the stall with the broken handle of a willow basket. "Turn around."

I can't understand what's happening quickly enough to resist. I've barely gotten the second sleeve off my wrist—

One lash.

Two.

Ten.

Dark, jagged purple lines hurl through me, like being shot with arrows, clean through the face.

Agnes throws the bloody handle down in the manure and walks out.

I pull my tunic up, too numb to feel the fabric beginning to stick in my wounds.

My ears ring, the green Sound wild in my eyes, shaking and turning the barn upside down.

I vomit in the corner.

A cold tremble starts in my middle as I dress: the chill of the barn, the icy shock.

Once I can stand, I feel for the walls and push myself out into the daylight. I keep my head down, past the goatherds and stonemasons, and wander to the medicine garden, where I know Alice will be working.

"Edyth?"

I don't respond to Alice. I sniff back tears and instinctively reach into my fitchet pocket and feel for the little stone house.

"There's . . . ah, your veil's crooked. But there's blood— Oh God."

I look up woozily and swoon. Alice steadies me and accidentally touches my back. I cry out but then bite down hard on my bottom lip. I don't want to draw attention. I just want to disappear.

"Come on," Alice says discreetly. "We need Joan."

The infirmary's large central hall is flanked by open-front cells with heavy drapes instead of doors. In the dim, reddish cast, I can make out wall hangings painted with scenes of the Creation, Crucifixion and Resurrection. There are charts of the four humors—bile, blood, black bile, phlegm; and of the four elements—earth, air, fire, water. Anatomy scrolls and books of physic are strewn on the tables, along with remedies in all stages of concoction. Racks suspended from the large oaken beams are hung with bunches of drying medicinal herbs. Rows of glass bottles line the shelves filled with tinctures and powders. Jars and bowls of all sizes are interspersed with more books, and braziers are lit, with small, three-legged iron pots above them.

It's the kind of inventory you take when you're out of your body.

Eighteen bottles on the top shelf. Five different sizes of mortar and pestle.

"You weren't beaten at home, were you, Edyth?" Joan asks plainly as she examines my bloody back.

No answer. Not a turn of my head. Silence.

Forty-two bunches of herbs hanging up. Three insects trapped in that chunk of amber.

"I can tell most things without words, dear. Skin around the lash marks is like silk. The only rough thing about you is your hands." Joan unlocks a cabinet and hands me an amber jar. "Have Alice put this on the wounds twice a day until they're gone. You don't need much—a drop at a time. Return the jar when you're done with it."

I take the top off of the jar and smell the salve, a burst of warm yellow, the scent going through me, already healing me from the inside, stilling the need to count the contents of the room.

Joan confines me to my cell under cover of a bad cold. I overhear her whisper to Alice. "Agnes—*that woman,*" she huffs. "It's time for Mother Margaret to come home."

When Alice escorts me to my cell, it's been wiped down, but the ghosts of my drawings remain. All I can think of is drawing, and color, and drawing and color, and another tremble begins—but this time, it's resolve. Agnes can beat me, but as soon as I get the strength to lift my arms, I'm going to do it all again.

— 20 —

The rest and quiet are just what I need to really think about all that's happened to me. My back heals enough in a few days that I can move without my clothes torturing me. I'm still stunned and jumpy and can't say much more than *yes* and *no*. Even the sound of my own voice is abrasive. But defiance grows like a seed within me. This is the last day before I go back to my duties, and I don't know how, but something is changing. I feel it.

While everyone else is in the refectory for supper, Alice brings me a simple meal in my cell. I'm not hungry. I sit on the bed, turning the little stone house over in my hand. She tells me the latest news as she applies the salve to my back.

"I'm to give my first teaching at chapter soon," she says. "I can recite it for you if you want."

I'm not really listening. "Do you think Mason knows?" I ask blankly. "About the beating?"

"I don't know. I can try to find out, get him a message," Alice suggests, "but probably best to keep your distance until things feel normal ag—"

"Did you ever feel like you're part of something bigger, Alice?" I interrupt her. "First Mason shows up here, then I see that window with my dream in it. I can't explain it, but I feel it, like something's unfolding itself to me."

She's taken aback at my vehemence. "I've always known what I wanted, since I was a little girl. There's not a doubt in my mind that I'm where I'm supposed to be, whether I'm part of something bigger or not."

"I've never had that certainty a day in my life. But I'm beginning to. And Agnes can't stop me figuring it out."

Alice changes the subject. "Why don't I see if I can get you some scraps of parchment to draw on? Who knows, if you're more careful, maybe the scribes will put in a good word and you'll be allowed to work in the scriptorium again."

I nod and smile. She gives me a cautious embrace and leaves me.

My confinement nearing its end, I go out the rear entrance of the dormitory and head toward the chapel. I'm not sure I want to see Mason after he didn't even try to get word to me. But there he is, standing in the doorway, his figure sculpted by the fading afternoon light.

"Edyth!" Mason whispers. "Come inside?"

And should I? I stand stock-still, staring at him. Saint John's Eve seems so long ago. For a few days, I was mad at myself. Now I resent him. For getting my hopes up about leaving, then never mentioning it again. For leading me on in the firelight, then ditching me in the morning. For not fighting for me when I needed him. Still, something makes me step over the threshold into Saint Eustace's chapel for the first time.

I've never been inside an unfinished church before, and its roughness takes me by surprise. It's far bigger than Saint Andrew's, but not majestic like the priory church, either—more like a lord's hall than a sanctuary. A thick coating of stone dust lifts from the floor and floats in the air. Wooden scaffolding lines the walls, and rafters await a covering. Shapes are drawn on the floor, and cubes of dressed stone lie waiting to be placed.

He points out the chapel's features. "There'll be arches to match the priory church. And stained glass, and a roof, of course," he chuckles.

We sit on the steps of the chancel, neither of us knowing where to begin. "Alice came to see me," he says at last. His voice is halting. "But I already knew—I saw you when you came out of the goat barn. It was hard to miss . . . the blood, you know . . . coming through your dress."

I grind a little pile of dust under my shoe. "You knew." He doesn't say anything, and I clench my jaw. "And you didn't try to get a message to me? Nothing?"

He looks genuinely surprised. "I was trying to protect you."

"Protect me? You left me there in the field, Mason. I woke up with Agnes standing over me. And you forgot your damn *hood*."

"What was I supposed to do?" he protests. "Wake up there with you? Wouldn't it have been a lot worse if we had *both* been found in the morning?"

"You don't protect someone by abandoning them," I chide. "You could have woken me up so I could go back to my cell. You could've spoken up for me when you knew I got beaten for a *drawing*. Asked how I was. *Anything*."

"I really thought if I stayed away—"

"Mason, one minute you say you're going to break me out of here, then you completely drop the subject. What is it that you really *want*?"

"I didn't want to pressure you. And I hoped the answer would be yes, anyway."

"But you can't assume that, because the fact is, aside from what's going on with the sub-prioress, I actually *like* it here. Being assigned to the scriptorium was the best thing that's ever happened to me, and I've lost that. Now? If I breathe sideways or, God forbid, I shit at the wrong time of day, I'll be punished. I'm trying to make it work here and I can't risk it all on a fantasy. What if I get kicked out because *you* can't make up your mind? I don't have other options. I'm here on Henry's arrangement. I doubt he can find me a better one."

"Edyth," he sighs, "I have to tell you something."

"What now?"

"It's about Henry. Remember when you asked me for news from home? I didn't tell you everything. I couldn't. But I have to now. Henry's . . . gone."

"Gone? What do you mean?"

"He's dead, Edyth. He took his own life."

That ringing in my ears comes back, the shaking green Sound, my head squeezing so hard that I need to squint to see.

"After you left," Mason continues, "I tried to keep helping him, but my father was dying. Henry got so thin . . . dirty . . . I don't think he was feeding the animals, either.

"When I went to fetch Brother Robert to give my father last rites, I saw

Henry standing on the bridge where they . . . where they killed your da . . . and when me and Brother passed by again, he was gone, and I saw that Flemish dagger your father gave him. And blood. I'm sorry. So sorry. I should have told you."

My stomach lurches at the thought that my last words with Henry were fighting. Just like with Da.

Any shred of anger I held against my brother is gone instantly. Poor, poor Henry. He wasn't lording it over me. Letting me go was a sacrifice. He needed me. He was alone, too.

It's you and me, Edie, I hear Henry say. *You and me.*

"Dead? All of us, dead?"

Mason hangs his head and stares at his hands. "Not your baby sister."

I close my eyes and remember. The red circle drawing itself round Mam's knees. Her sweat glowing in the rushlight, her muttering losing more and more sense. The smell in the room was dark purple, crawling like vines up the walls.

I held Mam from behind, and out slid my sister into my mother's waiting hands. We laid Mam down, and the midwife pulled Mam's tunic aside for the baby to take the breast; the newborn grasped with her tiny paw-like hands and found it immediately, suckling like an eager lamb. Mam laid her hand on her new daughter, whispered something in her ear, kissed the little head.

And then Mam's head lolled to the side, and I felt my mother's spirit walk past me and out the door.

The baby felt it, too, the whish of our mother, walking away.

"I never get to say goodbye," I weep. "To any of them. To anyone I love."

"You don't have to say goodbye to me. I won't leave."

"Don't say that. You can't stay here past the fall. You're lucky they haven't kicked you out already. Don't you understand? You're a freeman. I'm a peasant's daughter, and a criminal's daughter at that. I'm still bound to Lord Geoffrey, and I'll always be. I'm only here on his permission. If I run away and get caught, I'm dead."

He doesn't answer, but puts his arm around me and pulls me close as I weep. Of *course* I want him to stay. And of course I want to go. Sitting here against him, feeling the warmth of his body, I wish we really could run away. But it can't be. Goodbye will have to come.

"We can sort it," he says. "We'll figure something out."

The grief comes in waves, for what's gone, and for what we've not yet lost. Mason carves out a space, right there in the hollow of his arms, for me to both hold my family and to let them go. Sometimes I feel him tremble, too, for his own mam and da.

Blankets of soft green fall over our shoulders, like the two of us are an ancient sculpture of two lovers in the forest—an old, old love covered in moss.

We calm after a while, and he kisses my head as I lean on his shoulder. "Edyth? Can you draw me something?"

My face is swollen from crying. "I don't have anything to draw with."

"Here." He gets a long stick and points to the dirt. "This is how we do it when we make carving plans."

"What should I draw?"

"How about something from home?"

The first thing I think of is the market cross. I strain to recall it, though I'd seen it every day of my life. But then I remember how I'd step up to the cross and trace the knotwork with my finger, its rows of quatrefoils, its faded Latin letters, and it all comes back. I draw it on the dirt floor, and to finish it off, I draw Pounce and Juniper sitting obediently on either side, and we laugh a little. I sit beside Mason again, and he puts his arm around me.

"You know what I can imagine?" he asks, his words soft against my forehead.

"What?"

He pulls me closer. "You drawing the scheme for this chapel," he says. "You design, I'll carve."

"Don't get ahead of yourself," I laugh. "That was one drawing in the dust."

"Edyth, don't sell yourself short. Look around. We could do anything in here. And I hear you have a fondness for drawing on walls."

"All right, Mason." I nod, going along with the idea. "Let's see what you can really do with that chisel."

"I am grateful for your blessing," he teases me. "I shall endeavor to be worthy."

"To hell with the Anti-Pri," I say, sudden and plain. "I can do more than fetch things."

I lose that cockiness, though, when the bell rings—and I have to try to leave this chapel unseen.

— 21 —

When I stand before Agnes in her study, the scolding is intense.

The beating is worse.

"You have violated my trust again, Edyth," says Agnes de Guile, as she matter-of-factly wipes blood from the cane. "Being late to prayers—"

"But I—I don't remember ever hearing the warning bell." Gingerly I pull up my chemise and try to dress.

Agnes huffs and recomposes herself. "I can only *guess* why you were so distracted. Remember the steps of humility, Edyth. What is the seventh step?"

"Be convinced you are beneath everyone," I manage weakly.

"That's right. If you would only accept that you belong to the priory now. Why fight it?"

And suddenly, her tone becomes strangely soothing. She attempts to help me pull my sleeves on, but the cloth only catches in my wounds, and I shudder.

"Edyth, I understand your not finding a place here right away. I'm doing you a *favor*. You should be grateful. I'm protecting you from yourself. You could do a lot of damage here if you don't learn from me. You wouldn't want to hinder people's spiritual walks, would you?"

"No, Sub-Prioress." I wince, really wanting to shove her off me, but I'm just trying to get through the pain.

"I've been thinking a lot about your story, Edyth. No one asks for a curse—

murders, and suicides, and childbed deaths. Your whole family gone. But not lost. In fact, they wait in the fires of purgatory. Do you ever think of that?"

Of *course* I've thought of it. It's what I've been trying *not* to think about for a whole year. It obsesses me, waking or sleeping—nightmare images of Mam and Da, their faces contorted as they suffer in the smoky dark.

"But for some reason, God has let you live, Edyth. You can help your family now. Or at least, you can avoid making it worse for them. I can show you the way."

I get to my feet and look at her through disheveled hair. My anger at Agnes shifts to curiosity.

"I can help them? How?"

"Accept my training in penance. You will take their punishment on yourself, and shorten their time in the flames. But the more you transgress, the more you multiply not only their time, but your own."

It's confusing, but maybe she's right. I remind myself that as much pain as I'm in, theirs is far more severe. And in a strange way, it gives me hope—that somewhere, in some kind of eternity, they are still alive. If I can help them, it's almost like being closer to them. Maybe this is the reason I'm here.

"What do I have to do?" I ask soberly, lifting my chin, ready to do this for my family.

"Rule number one: detach yourself from sin, and do not see that boy again. Two: cease with your drawings. You are a manual laborer; reconcile yourself to that. Three: come to me daily after chapter for penance. Now go wash yourself, and then fetch feed to the hogs."

"Edyth!" Mason catches up with me in the alley between the goat and hog barns, but I hurry my pace, lugging this bucket of grain. If I go to him, I'll lose my resolve; I'll be pulled apart. If only I could steel myself against the desire to fall into him.

But he grabs my arm and turns me around, and I shut my eyes tight against the memory of the lash.

He doesn't need an explanation. "I'm going to kill her," Mason seethes. "She can't do this to you! You're not even supposed to *be* in this place!"

"Please, Mason, stop! Stop, please—" A torrent of sobs brings me to my knees.

"Whoa, Edie, it's all right. I'm not going to hurt you." He wraps his arms around my head and lets me burrow into his chest and cry, rocking there in the straw.

"I can't get out of this, Mason. I want to see you, but I can't hurt my family."

"Your family? Edyth, what are you talking about? Your family's gone."

"I'm helping them. I'm taking their suffering," I try to convince myself. "I can help Henry."

Mason sighs. "Did she tell you that?"

"I can shorten their time—"

"I know you don't believe that. She's a liar, Edyth. A damn liar."

The truth is as raw as my skin. Mason's eyes penetrate so deeply, I flood with tears again.

"Oh God, Mason," I sob. "I'm so stuck. I can't change this, can't change *anything*. It's like my life is being lived *for* me and I just want to end—"

I don't have the courage to say it.

"God," he whispers, pulling me closer. "God."

He strokes my veiled head until I quiet. At last I lift my face to his and he presses his lips to my cheek.

"Mason," I say, "I'm not used to the lash. I never got it at home. I don't know how to, you know, brace myself against it."

"What do you mean, *never*?"

"Well, I got roughed up by the other kids. But you know how my da was. Nothing but a look from him, a sharp word—would you want to give him a reason to punish you? And Mam was patient with me . . . and I kept my distance from anyone else."

Mason doesn't speak for a minute. He leans his head back against the wall and sighs. "My father hit me all the time," he says. "And then when I apprenticed, the master used to clock me on the head if I wasted stone. I guess this is the first time I *haven't* been hit."

Words fail me when I think of anyone hurting him.

He forces a smile. "I'd like to see these nuns try it on me, though!" Mason makes boxing fists, and we chuckle at the image of him and Agnes locking horns. And then we grow quiet again and stare at each other. He slowly rearranges wisps of my hair hanging out from the veil, and I think, *How remarkable this boy is, how good. After all he's endured, how his eyes can still sparkle with life.* And the terrible thoughts I had a few minutes earlier begin to dilute and wash away.

"It's like glittering gems," I muse—and I can't believe I said that out loud.

"What is?"

"Your laugh." I bend my knees up and hide my face. "I can . . . see it."

"See what?"

"You think I'm crazy."

"I don't think you're crazy, Edyth. Tell me what you mean."

I hesitate a long while.

"I used to think everyone saw things like I did," I begin. "Mam and Da and Henry played along, I guess. Different sounds and smells—well, they have different colors and shapes. Your laugh, it's like twinkling bright gemstones, yellow and sky blue and bright pink." I point in the air as though popping bubbles. "I feel the colors, too, like when I'm excited, or frightened—it fills part of my body with light. Sometimes it gets so intense, I almost faint. That's what happened in the scriptorium with the ultramarine. It almost happened today when Agnes—"

Mason puts his hand over mine and laces our fingers together.

"I wish I could see what you see," he says.

"No, you don't. I don't work like other people, Mason. There's something broken in me."

"That's not true."

"But I see things that aren't there. It's not *real*."

"What if what you see is *more* real? What if we're the ones who are blind?" His words stun me.

He grasps for his meaning. "My da taught me—he said to listen to the song of the stone and it would tell me how to cut. It's true; it really works. You put the wedges in a line where you want the crack to be, and you play the hammer down the line like an instrument—like bells. The stone sings what it wants to do."

"It sounds like banging a hammer to me," I admit. "Like red daggers, not music."

"And a laugh just sounds like a laugh to me," he concedes. "But it's obviously so much more."

I smile, astonished, *so* relieved. I wish I could see his laughter dancing in the air every day.

A wind rises up, tumbling a string of old leaves through the still alleyway, and on it, a voice carries. I hear my name being called. By Agnes. Another errand. My back's starting to smart against the fabric of my dress. I look intensely at Mason.

"Don't worry," he says. "I'll go around another way."

— 22 —

At chapter, Agnes tells me curtly that I'll be fetching for the prioress today, who's finally returned from a preaching tour. Something feels different in the atmosphere with Prioress Margaret here, like the air isn't as thick in my lungs somehow.

Alice is giving her first lesson this morning, the one she's been preparing for weeks. "*It is not the healthy who need a doctor, but the sick,*" she begins. "So says the Author of our faith. But who are the healthy, sisters, and who are the sick?"

She's nervous; it's plain by the way she keeps looking at the floor, trying to remember the next line she's memorized. I like it, though. Alice has a gentle yet authoritative way of teaching. She speaks like one of us, not someone trying to climb the priory ranks or show off how smart she is.

She concludes: "*And there is no health in us,* says the confession. But there is a remedy for our souls, and there is a Great Physician ready to give this medicine—only, however, to those who admit their need."

"Thank you, Alice," says the prioress. "Well done. We look forward to more from you in the future. And now Sub-Prioress Agnes de Guile will give our announcements."

After the meeting, Prioress Margaret approaches me. "Edyth le Sherman," she says, "follow me to my study, please."

She carefully puts her books away on the shelves, sits at her desk and shuffles through a stack of letters.

"Edyth, I see that some events have transpired in my absence."

I stare down at the floor, unsure of how much she knows. She picks up a note from her desk and begins to read.

Carelessness with precious materials in the scriptorium.

Insubordination.

Defacing of cell walls.

Flagrant defacing of a holy psalter.

Carousing with a young man from the work crew.

Habitual tardiness, and even absence from prayers.

She pauses, glaring at me. "Shall I continue? Speak, child."

I can't lift my eyes. I don't know anything about this woman or what she's capable of. Then I hear myself speaking.

"I am sorry, Venerable Mother."

I can feel the prioress looking at me, judging my very breath.

"Edyth, do you believe your punishment was sufficient for your sins?"

"Yes, Venerable Mother. I mean, I don't know."

The prioress stands up from her desk. "Have you learned your lesson?"

"Yes, Venerable Mother."

She slowly walks behind my chair where I can't see her. The room dims and falls silent to the rhythm of our breathing.

"I don't think you have."

My eyes fill with terror as the prioress walks over to another part of the room. I quickly glance up to see what implement she will use to beat me. She reaches up to the top of a large shelf, and I shut my eyes and brace myself. The light behind my eyes explodes into a hundred shards of gold, slicing the darkness into a shredded quilt of pink and orange. But I feel nothing in my body. That must mean I'm ready to take what's coming.

And then I hear the sound of pages turning; doubtless she's consulting some ancient text on how to make me hurt like hell.

"Edyth."

I open my eyes to see the prioress standing in front of me. In her hands is a huge Gospel book, larger than any I've ever seen, with a heavy wooden cover wrapped in calfskin.

"Open it," she says, placing it on a bookstand on her desk. "Come, child, open the book."

I unstick my hands from the chair and edge closer. The prioress points to the book with one hand and beckons me toward it with the other.

My heart beats fast as I open it. I've never handled a book this large. When I touch the cover, a warm sensation crawls up my fingers.

"Handle it carefully. It is centuries old, and fragile."

A wafting scent urges me to get closer. I lean into the book's gutter and inhale. For such a holy object, it smells earthy and low. The pages speak; I hear voices reading the words aloud to me from the great orbs of the uncial letters.

The parchment makes a soft crackle when I turn the page, and I'm drawn into another world. Animals in small drop capitals on opposite pages speak to each other across the parchment expanse. In the margins are winged creatures, some like regular animals in costume—rabbits, foxes. Some are unlike anything on earth: blue creatures with flared nostrils and wild hair, demons with gaping bright orange mouths. Things that tingle in my mouth like horseradish.

I turn page after glorious page.

"Stop at the next one," says the prioress. "There's recognition in your eyes. You've seen this image before."

I feel the blood drain from my face. I draw my hands away from the book, feeling repulsed by it, ashamed at its intrusion into my thoughts.

Prioress Margaret lets out a deep sigh. "Child, tell me what you see."

The only thing left to do is confess. "Yes, Venerable Mother, I've seen this before. It's from a dream I have. But I don't know what it means."

The prioress sits back at the desk and picks up a smooth stone. Tumbling it along her fingers, she stares at me. "Tell me everything."

There is no option but the truth. "I see things."

"Yes."

"Colors. All the time."

"Go on."

"The way that walking through leaves is light liquid blue, and the hammer on stone is bright red, brighter than blood. Ultramarine is . . . like going straight to heaven. No one sees it but me."

"And the world is not always kind to those of vision," she insists. "You know that."

She leans forward and addresses me directly.

"Daughter, I am not going to speak to you in symbols. Something terrible is coming, Edyth, and it is making itself known to you. Every generation has a defining moment, a crisis of decision. When I was your age, we faced *our* crisis: starvation and death on an unimaginable scale. Have you heard of this?"

I nod. "My grandparents died in the Great Famine. My da was eight years old. He said the cows bobbed in the floodwaters like apples."

"Many perished here as well. But they didn't need to. There was one person here who was called. She, too, was a visionary, Edyth, just like you. But she turned her back on the ancient way. Hardness of heart stole her gifts from us. Her life of praise became a song for the dead, a dirge that still echoes in these walls."

Rising from her desk, the prioress points to the open page of the book. In the margin is a list of names in impossibly thin letters, each in a different hand, and I recognize one: *Agnes de Guile.*

I look at the prioress in disbelief. "Sub-Prioress Agnes? I heard she saw things, like me, but I didn't know this." Suddenly I can see things from Agnes's perspective, that fear of her own sight. And people died because she chose to hide it all away.

Prioress Margaret takes the book from its stand and returns it to the shelf. She dips a quill in ink and writes my name below Agnes's.

Edyth le Sherman.

"You can no longer deny what you've seen, Edyth. You must be reassigned immediately."

"No, please!" I rise abruptly and reach out to the prioress. "Please let me go back to the scriptorium!"

"Why on earth would I send you anywhere else, Edyth?" The prioress lets out a laugh like silvery ribbons. "I'm promoting you. I mean to make you an illuminator. How else will you understand what you are seeing, unless you immerse yourself in your gift?"

I'm stunned. Illuminating is a *noble* art. I'm a peasant's daughter.

"You will start immediately," she continues. "Have your meal and change into your own clothes. I've already told Bridgit and the others. You will no longer be in the employ of the sub-prioress."

"Thank you, Venerable Mother." I'm breathless; my head swims.

"And, Edyth," she says, "this is no time for shame. Now you are *awake.*"

— 23 —

After the midday meal, I can't wait to get to the scriptorium. Muriel greets me at the door, and instead of turning left to the pigment room, we turn right to a table set up with the tools of the trade: a piece of parchment with a drawing lightly plotted on it. Brushes of all sizes and shapes. Feathers, some stiff, some fluffy. A penknife, a bulbous flask of water in a metal stand and some seashells. And two small pots of color that I recognize: terre verte and bone black.

"This is holy work," Muriel begins. "We never pick up the brush without a prayer."

"Bridgit taught me that," I respond.

Muriel recites:

> *Sint placentes sermones oris mei meditatio cordis mei*
> *In conspectu tuo Domine fortitudo mea et redemptor meus*
>
> *Let the words of my mouth and the meditation of my heart*
> *Be acceptable in your sight, O Lord, my rock and my redeemer*

I repeat it carefully. My Latin is still pretty lousy.

Muriel shows me each item in turn. I know about the pigments, of course, intimately.

"I've always wondered—what is this for?" I ask, touching the water flask.

Muriel takes it from its stand and holds it close to the parchment with the drawing on it. "Look through it," she says. The lines look magnified in the watery globe.

"Is that how you get such tiny details?"

"Exactly, so we don't ruin our eyes," says Muriel. I wonder what genius must have figured that out.

"First I will show you how brushes are made," she continues. "This kind is the most basic. Take a feather and cut off the top, like this. Cut a notch in it on one side. Then, from the bottom of the feather, cut a tube. Put the top piece inside the tube and . . . pull."

She glues the brush head into the tube with melted resin and adds a straight, peeled twig for a handle.

"It's a brush!" I gasp.

"We make many, many brushes and pens, as you can see!" Muriel gestures to the vessels full of feathers on each desk.

I finally burst. "What are we going to paint first?"

Muriel laughs. "Not so fast, Edyth! I know you're eager, but you're new. You won't be painting for a while."

"Oh." My face falls, and Brother Timothy chuckles from his desk. I know Muriel is right; all apprenticeships start with grunt work until you're ready to move to the next step. That's how students eventually become masters. I try to put a mature face on it.

"You'll start by ruling lines," she says. "Take this scrap and practice. Fill this page, then come to see me. And, Edyth—no mistakes."

Muriel leads me to the empty desk and gives me the few tools I'll need. She and Anne go for a walk, and I sit for a minute and run my hands over the slanted wooden work surface.

And then I see it: in the corner of the desk, a tiny carved drawing of a stag under a yew tree, swirls of water flowing beneath, a flying comet overhead.

It isn't fresh; the incised lines are now the same color as the desk. But the truth is unmistakable. Agnes de Guile worked here. As an artist—like me. Saw the vision, like me. Was tasked with a mission, just like me. I trace the carving with my finger as Brother Timothy limps over on his gouty foot and lays a stack of pages on my desk, the margins lightly outlined with vines and ready to be inked.

"I'll bet you can handle more than ruling straight lines," he says, looking at the carving, then at me. "Always remember this, little sister: It's not only about what you *see*. In the end, it's about what you *do*."

It's hard to believe all that's happened in one short day, but it's already the hour of the Angelus. The summer night sky glitters with a million stars as I step out, alone, into the cloister garden. Only the candelabra are lit in the corridors; no moon obscures the pinpricks of light. The silence is pierced, like the sky, by the barking of a dog. I watch the Angelus bells make blue ripples in the air, like fish coming to the surface of a pond, their little fish mouths opening, *pop pop pop*.

The Pri said this was a gift, the way I see things. Not a curse. For the first time, I truly open my mind to that possibility, and when the bell ripples stop, they make room for the stars, each one with a colored halo, like the holy people painted in the books—only these halos are violets and blues and magentas, brighter than the ochres or yellows or even the gold encircling saints' heads.

> *Angelus Domini nuntiavit Mariae*
> *Et concepit de Spiritu Sancto—*
>
> *The Angel of the LORD declared unto Mary*
> *And she conceived of the Holy Spirit—*

The taste of peppermint leaves. A prickle in my big toe.

I straighten my spine, close my eyes and let the minty prayer linger in my mouth until it fades, fully feeling, fully awake. I keep praying.

Ecce ancilla Domini
Fiat mihi secundum verbum tuum

Behold the servant girl of the LORD
Be it done unto me according to Your word

I lean my head back and unpin my veil, unwind my thick braids and shake my hair, enjoying the delicious relief of it coming down on my neck. The bells cease, and I look out toward the fields, where the constellations are brightest. Two planets almost kiss.

Just then, a fireball flashes in the western sky. It comes fast and then breaks into six pieces, all burning slowly in the dome of the night, a shower of sparks falling over the priory hill.

The comet from my dream, from the pictures.

It's beginning.

It's then I become aware of two others in the cloister with me, standing frozen in the warm night, with disbelief on their upturned faces, just like me.

Prioress Margaret.

And Agnes de Guile.

My heart pumps one question through my whole body:

What is coming?

— 24 —

Even through the hammering rain, the pounding on the gatehouse door is so loud, it travels over the roofs of the priory buildings to the dormitory. The last bell was lauds—that means it's the middle of Saturday night and now every one of us is up, vexed at missing out on our precious stretch of two hours' sleep. Five minutes go by, and I hear footsteps stomp up the stairs and throw open a cell door, the wood reverberating down the hallway.

"You're needed," Joan calls, clapping to wake her apprentice. I hear Alice get up and scuffle into her shoes.

"Sorry to trouble you all," the physician shouts as she walks out. "Enjoy your rest."

She slams the dormitory door shut.

A sick pilgrim must have arrived, traveling all night in search of a remedy. This is nothing new. With Saint Christopher's reputation for physic, and Saint Eustace's chapel nearly complete, we're always expecting visitors. But I think about that comet I saw tonight, and I'm uneasy.

The community has breakfast in our usual silence, made even more hushed by the torrent of rain pelting the wooden roof. We head to the chapter house, the humid air heavy with our curiosity about who arrived last night in such a panic. Agnes is unusually quiet and distracted. The Dragon Nun is obviously happy to have replaced me at her side, though her loyalty to Agnes bewilders me.

"I would like to ask our physician, Joan," says Prioress Margaret, "to give us a report on the visitors who came to our infirmary last night."

"Thank you," says Joan, coming to the center of the room. "A man and his son arrived late last night with fever. I'm sorry to report that the young boy has passed. He was only ten."

A sympathetic murmur goes through the room.

Lord, have mercy.

It's never easy to lose a child, never.

"The father, too, is affected," she continues. "He said that his son's illness began the same way, but he was not able to elaborate before he lost the ability to speak. I fear he is near death, also. I have asked Father Johannes to administer last rites, and for the chapel builders to begin digging a grave for them both. It is a sad situation. Let us all pray that the Lord ushers them into His gates quickly."

The prioress leads us in prayer and dismisses us to our work. Agnes throws a hard look my way, and Felisia wears a grin that chills me utterly.

Before I go to the scriptorium, I run through the downpour to the churchyard and stand under the yew for shelter, watching Mason and the other builders dig the grave. His clothes are drenched and his hair is dripping. I approach him, but he doesn't hear me over the sound of the shovels and the insistent rain. I'm just about to tap his shoulder when I see the bodies.

The father and son have both been wrapped hastily in bedsheets from the infirmary, which now serve as shrouds. Their bodies are rain-soaked, but blood still hangs on their lips. Their skin is purplish black and covered with sores.

But what stuns me more is *who* I'm looking at.

I recognize the boy and his father. They were my companions from the journey here to Saint Christopher's. It's the boy who offered me apricots, and the father who helped old Brother Timothy from the cart.

Suddenly Mason sees me. The fright on his face scares me.

"Get away from here, Edyth," he admonishes, looking over his shoulder. "Go!" And he turns back to his work, digging the muddy double grave.

I'm fixed to the spot. My heart pounds out of my chest, a catch in my throat, a whine in my ears.

Mason turns again quickly and our eyes meet again.

"Please, Edyth, go," he pleads. "Get away from this."

I bolt to the scriptorium tower, trying to shake the image of the diseased bodies from my mind. I work until the funeral bell rings. The priory mourns with a Mass that afternoon—

et lux perpetua luceat eis

—and the nuns all file out of the church. *How sad*, the sisters say. *Death is part of life, after all.*

But I can't move. Something lurches up from the recesses of my heart.

I relive the day of Da's murder again, his body looking too small to be real, lying on the muddy riverbank. The unbearable verity of putting my father into a hole in the ground. The hasty, no-top coffin made out of my drawing board. Brother Robert, pouring dirt over his death-distorted face. And Mam's. And Henry's—and all of a sudden, I can't breathe. Can't breathe through the smothering, swirling colors, the ringing vibration of the Sound.

The other novices in the row have to squeeze past me. Alice looks back from the transept door and sees me alone and frozen in the empty church, gasping for breath, tears streaming down my neck. She leaves the others and comes to me. She knows what's happening, that I'm being taken over again, and she smooths my face and gets me to focus through to her eyes.

"You're not going into a trance, Edyth. You're staying right here with me."

She gets me to breathe in rhythm with her until it passes. We sit side by side in the quiet for a good while, staring at the cross above the altar.

"You never get used to death, do you?" says Alice, her light hand on my back.

I wait a long time to respond. "It's not just that."

"What, then?"

"I knew those two who died."

"Really?" she asks. "Were they from your town?"

"No, from my journey here. But that's not it, either."

"Tell me," she insists.

"Alice, last night, I saw a star fall—a huge ball of fire. It came so close, I could see the flames licking off it. But right at the moment when it looked like it would land on the town, it broke into pieces and they went in every direction."

I point up at the window of the stag and tree, and there the comet soars above them. "Do you see that picture? I've been dreaming of that image since before I came here, and now I see it everywhere. I need to figure out what it means."

"You're thinking—"

"That boy and his da—I think it's bigger than them. Something's coming—for all of us."

— 25 —

The rain has passed, the air's fresh, but I take my Monday-morning walk with tension. I drift among the gardens and orchards, and climb the yew in the churchyard, perching on a branch and staring at the fresh grave.

Mason comes around the back of the infirmary and sees me. He sidles up and leans against the tree trunk, careful to make it seem like he's not talking to anyone.

"I'm sorry I shouted at you, Edyth," he says into the air.

"You did what you had to."

"I've missed you," he says. "I barely slept last night. I wished . . . you were with me."

Our eyes meet. We reach for each other, touch fingertips.

"Every time I fell asleep," I tell him, "I dreamed of that father and son, rolling out of their shrouds and tangling me with them, tumbling down into the grave, only to have the bottom disappear from the pit. It's the thought of all that weight and soil and rock on top of you. I can't shake that image away."

"But the body isn't the person," says Mason. "We both know that. That's just the shell. The hollow, empty shell."

"That's what Da would say."

A group of sisters walk by the churchyard, and Mason pretends to busy himself with tidying the ground around the grave.

Once they pass, "I heard you're back at the scriptorium," he changes the subject. "As an illuminator! It's about time they realized what you can do."

"That's right," I chuckle. "No more *fetching*. And no more Agnes—at least not as close."

"But less chance of seeing you." He looks up at me, a bit doleful.

"I know, but I think we can exhale a little now. Let's meet tonight."

"Only if you think you'll be safe."

"Without Agnes breathing down my neck, I think I will be. And I don't want to do this dance anymore. I want to make a plan with you. A real plan."

"I do, too, Edie," he says, reaching up, grasping my ankle. "I hate not seeing you. I don't want to be without you."

"Tonight, then?"

"Tonight."

It's hard to stay awake the next morning at chapter. I stayed up far too late with Mason, telling him about the comet, both of us speculating about what it all means.

Prioress Margaret announces that Saint Christopher's will be offering a meal for the poor this afternoon: a simple pottage, bread and ale for wanderers or peasants. She wants us to remember that the abundant life we live is not for ourselves only, but for others less fortunate.

"Remember," she says, "as those for whom God took on a suffering body, we must *comfort others with the comfort we have received.*"

Agnes speaks up. "Venerable Mother, shouldn't we protect our own first? We can send bread down to the parish churches and have them distribute it."

"Caring for our flock means getting our hands dirty, Sub-Prioress," she challenges. The community shuffles with the discomfort of their two leaders at opposite poles.

"Well, after all, we do *pray* for them every day . . . ," Agnes huffs.

"Good, Sister Agnes. I'm glad to hear of your commitment to the welfare of the stranger. Thank you. *You* will be in charge of laying hands on any sick who come to us."

We set up trestle tables inside the gatehouse arch. Alice spreads the tables with clean white linen cloths. Cook and her assistants bring out the big pots full of pease pottage with salt pork and barley, as well as a week's worth of bread. By the noon bell, people are lined up at the gatehouse all the way over the stone bridge crossing the river—the hungry, the sick, little babies as well as old men with crutches, but also young men simply having a tough year with this wet summer. Peasants come in a spectrum of fortune, but no one's above a bad harvest.

Joan and Cook serve pottage at one table; Muriel, Anne and Brother Timothy tear off hunks of bread at the next. Alice and I pour jugs of ale for the grateful guests, and Bridgit jokes it up with some of the regulars who come for Mass. The air is sweet and clean, and the warm summer sun feels good after all the damp of last week. Everyone spreads their cloaks on the great lawn and sets out their picnics. The builders gather with extra jugs of ale and sit around telling tall tales. Families laugh together, enjoying the weather and the company.

But out of the corner of my eye, I see that something isn't right.

Over in the shady nook of the gatehouse wall, one of the carpenters is crouched alone, clutching himself and rocking back and forth.

"I'm going to fill this pitcher," I tell Alice.

"Nice excuse." She winks at me. With a roll of my eyes, I leave with an empty jug, pretending to go to the brewhouse, but passing close enough to the man at the wall to get a good look.

He's sweating—no, drenched—trying to hold in a cough but letting it out into his sleeve. And on the cuff, there's blood. I veer away from him toward the group of builders. As I walk by Mason, I clear my throat. A minute later, he meets me at the entrance to the brewhouse.

"What's the matter?" he asks.

"One of your crew," I say. "By the wall."

"Oh, Gilbert. He wasn't feeling well—thought it might be something he ate."

"Did you go over to see if he was all right?"

"He said he needed some shade," Mason says dismissively.

"Mason. Someone needs to check on him. I saw blood."

No more needs to be said. He leaves immediately and pulls Joan aside. He takes her place serving the pottage while they bring Gilbert to the infirmary, and the rest of the day goes on with games and music and little babies crawling around, pulling up handfuls of fresh grass while their mothers let them wander.

The next day, Gilbert Carpenter is dead.

The day after that, one of Joan's assistants is, too.

The builders are at it again, digging two graves next to the father and son, this time for one of their own. The funeral bells ring and Mass is said for the carpenter and the healer. Father Johannes presses the round wafer into my grateful hand, this single item that grounds me in reality, in the here and now. This time, there isn't simply pity, but confusion. The priest chants the prayers a bit faster than usual.

Afterward, the custom of silent work is broken, as everyone wants to hash out their theories. Yes, Joan and Alice and Gilbert had all been near the sick father and son. But that was only a few days ago. And the carpenter died first, even though he wasn't around them as long as the assistant. And what of the physician herself? She was treating them directly, and she's fine. So is Alice.

At Friday's chapter meeting, nobody can keep order.

Joan speaks up. "The best thing to do right now is to eat and drink moderately. I believe the entire community should refrain from any meat or fish, and eat simple vegetable pottage."

Unusually for Joan, she concludes with a bright smile. "I see no one sick here. Perhaps it ran its course with the last two."

So it seems. For a week, we eat simply, and drink hot water steeped with fennel. The ale is diluted, and the ration of bread is halved. It must be working. During the whole week and more, no one falls ill, not even with a sniffle.

— 26 —

This morning, the bell at the largest parish church in Thornchester rings at an odd time. An hour later, it rings again.

Two more times, the bell tolls between offices.

The funeral bell.

During the Eucharist, Brother Timothy collapses to the floor. Joan fetches a stretcher, and it takes her, Agnes and two other robust women to carry Timothy to the infirmary. Mass continues until the end; it has to. Father Johannes can't very well leave the Body and Blood on the altar. He continues the service, glancing through the rood screen at the fray. The rest of the congregants say their prayers shakily, some with tears, some with stoic focus. Immediately after the *Amen*, I hurry to the scriptorium to escape to my work, and to think. Whatever this fever is, it's come close now, right through my own door.

Brother Timothy's got rather bad work habits. His desk is always cluttered. The quantities of paint he orders are never accurate; either he orders too little and Bridgit and I must hurriedly grind more, or he orders too much and it dries up and goes to waste. That's what I find as I stare at his work area now. Several pots of paint are already evaporating, and I know he won't be back to use them.

But as disorganized as he seems, Brother Timothy's work is masterfully precise. A lively illustration of *Bryonia dioica* is in progress, its vine snaking across the page and sprouting fuzzy flowers of the palest green. I recognize the steady verticals of Anne's letters, the title in red, the text in black. But this page will never be finished.

There's still paint left over, so I take a piece of fresh parchment and begin to draw. I re-create the comet, its beams radiating out in curvy waves, its inner circle opening like a flower, and I ink and paint over the lines of the drawing. I sit back and look at my work, and decide to go see Brother Timothy.

Flitting like an insect about the infirmary is Joan. She's all energy, shouting one-word commands at Alice, who's doing her best to keep up. Joan bounces from book to bowl, grinding powders, mixing them with liquid, pouring them on cloths and handing them to Alice to poultice Brother Timothy's skin. Joan's salt-and-pepper hair is bound up tightly but uncovered, her sleeves rolled up past her elbows.

Behind the curtain, the sounds coming from Brother Timothy are unbearable, like five men howling from within his one body. All I can do is stand in the doorway holding my painting, watching Alice and the physician trying in vain to comfort the old man.

"Give him this, and make him drink it down," says Joan, handing Alice a glazed cup. "*Make him!*" She notices me standing here. "What do you need?" she grunts, not looking at me.

"May I see him?" Hearing the question come out of my mouth makes me wish I had never asked it.

Joan barely looks up from the heavy leather-covered manual she's reading. "At your own risk," she says. "Just don't get in the way. And cover your nose and mouth."

Brother Timothy is calming a bit, by the sound of things. Whatever Alice gave him is taking effect. As she pulls aside the curtain, I duck in.

A single candle on the bedside table illuminates the tiny cell. The air is close in here, helped only by a small hinged window above. The stench is horrible. I know the smell of death; who doesn't? But Timothy isn't dead. He's tranquilized, but still aware. He struggles to breathe. He looks at me and begins to weep. The monk tries to speak, but his words tumble out of his flabby lips in gibberish.

Timothy's neck is covered with purple splotches rising to white, as though his ink pot exploded under his skin. He begins to cough and covers his mouth with the rag he's holding. Alice bursts in, almost pinning me to the wall. She lifts Timothy's head to make him drink. When he puts down the rag, it's covered with spots of blood. Alice holds out his bedside basin to collect the rag and gives him a clean one. She glares at me in alarm. Joan calls her and she leaves the cell.

Timothy reaches out his hand to me, his eyes pleading, like he wants me to simply embrace him, but I'm too afraid to come close.

"I made you something," I say instead. I feel stupid—what difference does a painting make to a dying man? I slip the picture of the fireball into his outstretched hand, and he draws it close to his face. His eyes open wide, and he nods, as though he knows exactly what the painting means, even if I don't. He parts his lips and mutters, the words barely intelligible—

> *O vivens sol,*
> *Porta nos in humeris tuis.*
>
> *O living sun,*
> *Carry us on Your shoulders.*

—and a trickle of blood forms in the corner of his mouth.

I back out of the cell and run from the infirmary as fast as I can, into the clean air of the night, as the heavens open again and begin to pour. I scramble to and fro, not knowing where to go, then race through the rain toward the chapel.

The new roof is finally on the chapel of Saint Eustace, protecting it from the elements, so the builders can live in here instead of the shed. I thrust the door open, breathless and soaked, my legs getting weak under me. The linen veil drips on my shoulders. My arms hang heavy, and I weep with a groaning from someplace inside of me that I can't name, dark violets and blues oozing like thick dough around me.

The builders are lying on pallets on the chancel, surrounding a fire built on the bare earth. Mason springs up and hurries to me.

"Come here," he says, surprised. He gathers me to his chest. "Are you all right?"

"I had to get away from there. Whatever that is, I don't want to be anywhere near it."

"Edie, what happened?" Mason leads me to a bed of unbound straw at the foot of the chancel. He puts a dry blanket over my shoulders and unpins my wet veil. I breathe and calm and sob again, and he holds me.

"Brother Timothy's dying," I finally manage. "He can barely speak. He's spitting blood."

"That's the end of it," says Mason. "That's how they all died. Once you see that blood, it's over."

"What is this, Mason? It's not like any other fever . . . it's different from sweating sickness or the flux."

"I don't know, but after Gilbert died, I couldn't help thinking—it's stupid . . . but what if it's punishment? What if we've made God angry?"

"But why would he punish Brother Timothy? A monk in a priory?"

His look is incredulous. "Not everyone here's a saint, Edyth. You know that better than anyone."

My tears stop—I think I know what he's getting at. "Are you saying you think *we've* made God angry?"

He gets up and paces, trying to formulate words for thoughts he's probably never had.

"I mean, I don't usually think about these things, God and rules and such—

that stuff's for old people, or nuns. But it's not like you're *supposed* to sneak around with a girl who lives in a convent . . . Maybe?"

It's a good question: what the rules are, when one of you is a vagabond and the other's bound to a life she hasn't made a promise to. Should you run from the rules if it'd save your life?

But that moment in the cloister with the Pri and the Anti-Pri returns to me, the comet streaking across my mind, trailing the prioress's words: *Every generation has a defining moment, a crisis of decision.* I wipe my face with the blanket, and the next words out of my mouth are the last ones I thought I'd ever say:

"Then you should leave, Mason. You should get out of this place before it gets worse."

"Leave?" he protests. "What about you?"

"I have to stay here. I have something I need to do."

"What do you need to do?"

"I don't know exactly what it is yet," I say. "But I will. It's not about me now."

He stares at the ground. "Forget what I said then—whether or not we're being punished, this chapel won't build itself. I need the full pay to get me through the winter, until I can find my next gig. And I'm not going anywhere without you, Edyth."

"But what if I could do something to stop it? Remember those towns each of us passed on the way here, the ones where everyone was dead? What if it was this same fever—what if we're next? Mason, if—" The words catch in my throat. "If we live, we can find each other. After."

Mason looks at me intently for a moment, then hunches over and methodically lays a handful of straw pieces in perfectly straight lines. At last he gets up and fetches an extra tunic, folds it and pats it like a pillow for me to lie down on. He pulls the cloak over me. It's a long time before he speaks again.

"Well, for now, I'm here," he says. "I have a job, and you have a place to lay your head. And whatever this sickness is, we're going to stare it back down to the pit of hell together."

— 27 —

Somehow I will myself to wake before dawn and leave the chapel to avoid suspicion. Cautiously I sweep over to the infirmary to check on Brother Timothy, and Bridgit's there, sitting vigil for her old friend. The hectic buzz from last night seems to have worn off a little, and Joan and Alice muddle through their exhaustion to find a treatment that will work.

"Alice," says Joan, "write this down: *Applied leeches for suspected profusion of blood. No improvement. Fever pestilential, not relieved by vinegar and rosewater. Will lance tumors to relieve phlegm.*"

Alice opens her wax tablet and takes notes in shorthand, but Joan is dictating faster than Alice can write. She spots me by the door, and my presence seems to give her an idea.

"Brother Timothy told you his herbal compendium was almost finished, right, Edyth?" Alice asks.

I nod. "Yes, it's still on his desk. I saw all the folios there last night."

"I think I remember something in there about treating pustules. May I go up to the scriptorium?"

"Fine," says Joan, taking out her lance and a bowl, "but hurry. He is declining."

"Sister Joan," I address the physician, "I don't know much about planets and stars and such, but did Prioress Margaret happen to tell you about the comet?"

"What comet?" She's instantly attentive. "Was there a comet?"

"Yes, the night the father and son arrived. I saw it, and so did she, and the sub-prioress, too."

"Tell me about it, Edyth—the size, shape, everything."

I get the painting from Brother Timothy's bedside table and show her. Joan is transfixed as I describe the fireball, its fragmentation—and I even tell her about the colors that came with it.

"I see" is all she says in response. She makes a note in her tablet, folds her hands and leans toward me. "You know what this means, don't you?"

"I think it was a warning about this disease," I guess.

"More than a warning, Edyth. A harbinger. Not every bout of fever gets a *comet* showing up. You were good to tell me."

Alice returns with the loose folios and looks for the passage.

Joan paces, biting her thumbnail. "Have you found it yet?"

"Just a moment," says Alice. She finds the entry and brings it to the physician. "Here it is: juniper tar."

"Right, let's prepare it and hope for the best." She crosses herself. "*In nomine Patris, et Filii, et Spiritus Sancti . . .*"

Joan delivers the blow at chapter.

"Brother Timothy has gone to his rest," she says. "I watched him all night. I am sorry to say, it was not a peaceful death. But our priest was there and administered last rites, and our dear brother suffers no more."

The older nuns take it the worst. They had known Brother Timothy since they were all young novices in the double monastery. Bridgit sits stoic, but her face is red, and she can't wipe the tears away fast enough with her drenched handkerchief.

"I must also tell you," Joan continues, even more soberly, "that this illness is like nothing I have seen. The planets are in a very bad alignment; thus a foul air is settling over the whole earth. We must combat it as best we can. I am seeking a remedy in all the books of physic I possess. Since we cannot control the air, we can at least bring *ourselves* into better balance. We must prepare for the worst, and commend ourselves to God's mercy."

"What of the pilgrims?" someone calls out. Murmuring spreads among the assembly.

"Of course they will be welcome here," says the prioress. "We have plenty of room, stores of food, and all is prepared."

"No, I mean, where *are* they?" the sister clarifies. "It's August. We should have had hundreds by now."

We don't have to wait long for an answer to that question.

The clamor wakes everyone up before morning. Agnes goes down to the gatehouse still tucking in her wimple, and we all run out to join her. Dozens of wailing women and shouting men beg to be let in, to be seen by the physician, to set their eyes on Eustace's relics for some little comfort.

"Right, yes, yes, everyone, peace to you all. Each person will be seen," says the sub-prioress.

But when I look out over the crowd, I'm utterly unprepared for the sight. I've never seen such panic, such total suffering. Men, women and children, rich and poor—dropping to the ground even as they wait to enter the gates.

The healthy are shown to the guesthouse. The sick are triaged in the churchyard before being sent to the infirmary. Now that Joan's seen several people through the stages of the disease, she knows what to expect, even if she doesn't know exactly how to treat them.

"First stage?" she quizzes Alice, while preparing a quantity of plantain ointment.

"Fever, confusion, staggering."

"And then?"

"The swellings, the bloody cough."

"And what comes after the lumps and the cough?"

"Speech is lost, the skin turns black, the heart races and fails. Death within three days—or less."

"Fine," says Joan. "So we can base our treatment on where the patient is on the time line. Get ready. I hear them coming."

The funeral bell tolls in town. Every church down in Thornchester is tolling them several times a day now.

Compline is tense that night. Right in the middle of singing the psalm, the Dragon Nun runs to the altar with a shriek, falls on her knees, then rolls to her back. The prioress stays in her choir seat, observing with narrowed eyes, but Agnes scoops her up and holds her.

"Felisia! God's mercy—what is it?" Agnes pleads.

"I have seen it," the Dragon Nun howls, wild-eyed and sweating. "I have seen the afflicting devil! He is here!" She convulses in Agnes's arms.

"What does he look like, this demon?"

She sits up and pulls Agnes close. "His body is a skeleton, covered in taut skin, green-gray like river mud. He has wings like a bat, and his mouth is hell itself, as huge as a city, flaming and devouring!"

"Devouring whom, sister?" Agnes presses. "Who is the demon consuming?"

She looks at Agnes, and her visage changes to a twisted smile. "Whoever he damn well wants," she says. "But he's starting with sinners like *her*."

She thrusts out her hand and points at me.

Suddenly Dragon's weakness returns and she melts in defeated tears. Compline devolves into a cacophony of gossip and accusation.

"Brother Timothy *was* shut up in the scriptorium day in, day out with all those *women*," says Agnes. She looks at me in disdain and turns to the rest of the nuns. "Why else would Timothy die the same way as a peasant traveler and his son, a laborer and a *conversa* medic? For Timothy to suffer directly from the hand of God like this? It must have been secret sin."

"*It is time for judgment to begin in the house of God*," wails the Dragon Nun.

Murmurs of assent go through the crowd of sisters.

"Sub-Prioress," says the Pri, her strong voice slicing through the chaos, "kindly tend to your ward and help her to bed. We must finish compline. Edyth le Sherman, since you have served the sub-prioress in the past, please assist them."

Agnes helps the Dragon to stand, and we leave through the transept. I hang back, not enthused to help, really hoping I won't be needed.

Agnes coddles the frightened seer, her arm around her shoulder as we head toward the dormitory. "Tell me, Sister Felisia, what else do you see?"

"You are going to lead this priory through the storm, Mother," says the Dragon.

"You mistake me, dear." She feigns humble amazement. "*Prioress Margaret* will see us through. I am only her servant."

"Saint Christopher's is about to go through a pruning, Mother," Felisia continues with inexplicable calm. "Stay the course, and steer the ship." And then she lowers her head to the side and refuses to say more.

Agnes pats the girl's shoulder as they peel off toward Felisia's cell. "A prophet," I hear the sub-prioress say. "God has sent us the comfort of a prophet."

— 28 —

"She's really rushing things this morning," I whisper to Alice in chapter. "That's not like the Pri."

"I know," says Alice. "Do you realize she skipped two whole pages of Bede's *Martyrs*?"

"Daughters," the prioress addresses the gathering, "I want to thank our sub-prioress for her faithful leadership while I was away. But I have been gone too long. I am ceasing my travels and will remain at the priory. It is time for our community to come together more than ever before, and each one of you has an important part to play. Saint Christopher's needs all of us, and so do the sick who are streaming to our gates."

"She and Agnes could not be more different," whispers Alice.

After dismissal, I gather the prioress's books, and Agnes sweeps into the space between me and Prioress Margaret.

"Venerable Mother," Agnes says with a reverent bow, "I feel that the Lord would have me renew my service to you at this difficult time. Please allow me the honor of carrying your books today."

Prioress Margaret looks surprised as Agnes takes the books from me. "I would like that, Sister Agnes."

"That's a change of character." I nudge Alice, watching the two women leave together. "What do you think that's about?"

"If I were to give her the benefit of the doubt," says Alice, "I'd say she was humbling herself. But . . . no. I think the Anti-Pri knows exactly what part she wants to play in all of this."

We stroll slowly through the cloister walk, trying to puzzle it out.

Suddenly I tug Alice's arm and we duck into an arched doorway. "Alice, I want to know what *my* part is. It's been two weeks since I saw that fireball fly across the sky, and there's no doubt now that it was an omen of this disease. The prioress said it would become clear why I was the one who saw the comet. But I'm lost. Am I supposed to hear a voice from heaven or something? I can't stop drawing comets, stags, yew trees and streams of water, and now I'm having Mason carve those things in the chapel, too. I'm trying to add it all up—it's so frustrating."

"You can't dwell on it so much. All you can do is stay open and patient until it becomes obvious. That's what Joan and I are doing with our treatments. Otherwise you're going to drive yourself mad, Edyth. How about this? When you finish at the scriptorium for the day, come help in the infirmary. If you haven't caught the fever yet, you're probably safe. We really need an extra set of hands, and it'll take your mind off of it for a while. It's impossible to think about anything else in there."

"Sure," I say. "I may as well do that as anything else."

That night, while Alice and Joan tend to patients, I pound herbs and prepare poultices. It's a miserable place to be, especially on a rainy night, with the utter darkness outside, the oppressive clay-red walls and soot-stained ceiling, the cries of the dying behind the curtains.

Then the door opens, and Agnes de Guile enters, rain dripping off her black veil into her face, like its own little tempest. Joan turns away and rolls her eyes.

"Good evening, Joan, Alice," says the sub-prioress, ignoring me while she scans the shelves. "I'm looking for something to help me sleep. All this excitement, you know. So many things to juggle. Might you have a bottle of something I can take before bed?"

"Certainly, Sub-Prioress," says Joan, feigning concern. "Alice, what should we recommend to help the sub-prioress have a restful slumber?"

"Tincture of melissa," says Alice, taking down a small glass jar from the shelf at the end of the infirmary hall.

"Good," says Joan. "Please prepare a dose."

"Make it extra strong, Alice," says Agnes. "I want it to work quickly. Oh, is that a new book?" she asks, looking through the folios on the table as Alice mixes the tincture with honey and distilled wine.

"Yes, Brother Timothy's herbal compendium," says Alice, handing Agnes the jar. She watches Agnes flip through the folios, and side-eyes me. "It has Dioscorides and *Bald's Leechbook*, both. And even some of Hildegard's *Physica*."

"Ah," says Agnes, distractedly examining the pages. "Good, good to have those."

Abruptly Agnes turns to leave, glimpsing a man in the first cell. He's lying catatonic and contorted on the bed in nothing but his braies. The sub-prioress shudders.

"Many thanks to you," she calls to Joan, and rushes out into the rain with the jar.

Alice shuffles pages back into a neat pile and gives me the ingredients for Joan's next concoction.

After the morning burial, which is becoming disturbingly routine, Alice catches up with me and grasps my elbow as we head to the church. "Slow down," she says. "We need to talk."

The sisters enter the calefactory door, and Alice and I slow our pace and fall behind.

"Something's not right, Edyth. The Anti-Pri—she's up to something."

I stop and look at her. "What are you thinking?"

"You know when she came to the infirmary asking for that sleep remedy? I thought I saw her put something under her scapular. It might've been a page

from Brother Timothy's herbal. I'm not sure which one. And, Edyth, she's been in three times this week asking for stupid little remedies, when we've got people there in their *death throes*."

"Are you sure she took it?" I ask.

"No," she says. "But wasn't she shifty?"

"She *was* in quite a hurry to leave."

"What about the nonsense with that insane Dragon Nun," Alice continues, "blabbering on about seeing demons? Did anything happen after you left with them?"

I shudder and recount Felisia's "prophecy" about Agnes "steering the ship."

"That makes horrible sense," Alice responds. "If any of us had pulled one of Felisia's stunts, it would have been ten switches," she muses sardonically. "Oh, Edyth, I'm sorry—I shouldn't have said that."

"It's all right, Alice. What do you want me to do?"

"You're going to see Mason tonight, right? Ask him to watch her, even follow her. She won't suspect him; workers are invisible to her. The three of us will keep an eye on the Anti-Pri and find out what's she's up to."

Between the prayer offices on Monday, we've got our paltry morning attempts at keeping the crops going, I've got my work at the scriptorium in the afternoon, and in the evenings, I help with the latest spate of sick pilgrims in the infirmary. When I'm exhausted like this, my colors get fuzzy and confusing, as though someone spilled all the paint on the scriptorium floor. I don't want to make any mistakes.

The sun lowers. I need a break and a good meal. Alice stabilizes her patients as much as she can, and we ask leave to go to the refectory.

"Just bring me a little something," calls Joan, who hasn't had a break in days.

Alice and I fall in step, and we hear footsteps following behind. I glance back to see Mason also going in our direction, probably hoping to sweet-talk Cook into yielding something extra for the builders to eat.

"*Ave*," Alice addresses him cautiously over her shoulder. He returns a quick greeting.

"How is the chapel coming along?" she asks.

"Slower, now that they've got us digging graves, too," he says. "There are only four of us now. I didn't come here for that kind of work."

"I didn't exactly come here to deal with pestilence myself," says Alice. "I wanted to write books and study physic. Edyth's told you what we're looking for?"

"Yes, and I've been keeping my eye on Agnes, anyway." Before Mason passes us to the kitchen door around back, he squeezes my hand. His eyes are lightless. "Whatever she's doing," he promises, "we'll find out."

Ahead of us, Agnes enters the refectory with the prioress.

"You know what's strange about that?" I mention. "The Pri usually takes her meals in her study."

"Let's sit apart on either end of the refectory so she doesn't suspect us," Alice suggests. "We're *going* to catch that fox."

Darkness finally falls. I sneak from the infirmary to the chapel and knock softly. Shrieks pierce through from next door, icy lightning bolts stabbing my eyes, my temples.

Mason opens the door. "This doesn't feel terribly romantic," I half joke.

"Come inside," he suggests. "Maybe we won't hear as much in here."

"What about the other builders?"

"They're drinking in the old shed," he says, leading me into the chapel. "They'll sleep where they are. Don't worry, we'll be alone."

Alone. That word suddenly feels different to me. We're alone together every Sunday night, but outside, sitting against the chapel wall, talking, kissing. *Alone* never had its own color until now, a new edge of magenta glowing against the background of all this fear. Mason lights a fire in the middle of the floor, and this empty chapel feels like home.

Instinctively we curl up in the bed of straw together and lie there, enjoying the quiet. I feel so safe in here, the rough stone and dust so familiar. I never was meant for sterile places or anodyne routines. I was meant for dirty hands and a homespun dress and a shaggy-haired boy who builds real fires.

You do something to me, Mason says, and that's not a bad thing, what I do to him.

You're different, he says, and not in ways that make him want to pull my hair or lash my back. Mason fills my mouth with white birds taking flight over the mists, over the feather spirits from the village river, with the taste of beating wings, the rhythm of my own heart.

I take off my veil and fold it under my cheek. Mason begins unbraiding my hair, and I can hear his breathing deepen. His fingers start to comb out my tangles, but I giggle at the useless effort. "Pretend I'm a wooly sheep instead, Mason," I say, and we laugh and he buries his face in my hair, pulling me closer, kissing my neck.

"Edyth, stay here with me. Bring your things from your cell. It's safe and dry, and I can protect you in here."

"What if someone finds out? The last thing we need is someone deciding to take a tour and finding me in here with you."

"You mean Agnes? She won't. I'll make sure of it."

"Well then, bar the door, Mason," I say, with unexpected boldness. "Something tells me we're about to find a reason for her not to say a word."

— 29 —

Prioress Margaret wasn't in chapter yesterday. Alice hasn't seen her, either.

"She usually helps in the infirmary after nones," says Alice. "I haven't heard anything—she said she wouldn't be leaving the priory again."

"Maybe she's had a visitor or something," I suggest, as Agnes de Guile takes the seat to preside over the chapter meeting.

"Prioress Margaret is feeling ill today," the sub-prioress announces as she waves me over and hands me her books. I hate assisting her, hate touching anything she's touched. But Felisia hasn't left the sanctuary in days.

Why doesn't Agnes make that damn Dragon come out of the church and do her job?

"Does Prioress Margaret have the fever?" Alice asks. Everyone dreads the answer.

"No, sisters, thankfully it's only a bit of stomach upset. For a rapid recovery, let us pray."

After dismissal, I take Alice aside. "Has anyone come to the infirmary for a stomach remedy for the Pri?"

"Not that I've seen. If the leader of our priory had a *hangnail*, Edyth, I would know," she whispers. "I think the Anti-Pri's lying. I'll go talk to Joan."

As I stack Agnes's books, I casually ask: "Excuse me, Sub-Prioress? I'm helping finish the illuminations for Brother Timothy's herbal, and a few pages seem to have gotten misplaced since it was brought to the infirmary. You wouldn't happen to know where they went, would you? I don't know exactly which ones they were; I've counted several times. I just thought I'd ask."

"Certainly not," says Agnes. "As though I keep track of loose papers. Isn't that a *conversa*'s job?"

"Thank you, Sub-Prioress." I bow, frustrated at not being able to find an answer that's surely right in front of us.

One book in Agnes's stack belongs in the prioress's study. There's no servant outside, so I walk in to return it.

The prioress is curled on a pallet on the floor, barely conscious, an imperfectly used bucket of vomit beside her.

"Mother! Prioress Margaret!" I rush over to her and want to cry for help, but something tells me to be as covert as possible. "I'll get Joan."

Making sure no one sees me leave, I quietly close the study door and feign nonchalance on my way to the infirmary. I tell Joan about the prioress and take the stack of Brother Timothy's folios.

Up in the scriptorium, I carefully collate the pages into alphabetical order. I can tell that something's out of place, but I need to look closer. I begin again, shuffling the pages and listing each herb.

Hart's tongue, I write. *Lavender. Licorice. Madder. Mandrake. Mugwort. Myrrh.*

Wait—there, between *Mandrake* and *Mugwort*—the missing entry is something under *M*.

Dragon won't leave the church; she sits there, endlessly moaning her "prophecies." Agnes has made her a pallet under the watchful gaze of Our Lady. Alice and I stay behind after vespers, duck into the shadows in a side chapel and watch, too. Agnes brings Felisia a small meal, and they whisper together, almost too softly for us to hear, except for a few unmistakable words that fill us with horror.

We have no choice but to wait there until compline with this secret mission churning our guts. We control our breathing, let tears stream without sobbing, turn our desire to scream into silent, pleading prayers.

The bell tolls, and Dragon breaks into loud prayers as the nuns file in. Agnes wipes away the nun's tears and sits by her at the end of the choir stall. Alice and I are going to have to sneak into our places. She goes first, a step at a time, then stops dead. From the dark, I see Agnes staring at Alice, red rage rising in her face.

It's safer if I don't go into the nave at all. I pad through the rear of the apse to the church's back door, and once I'm out, I run as fast as I can to the stone-masons' shed. Mason and I lock eyes. I don't need to say anything. He takes my hand, and we sprint to the chapel.

"What happened?" he pants.

"I think Agnes is onto us. Well, I don't think she saw me, but she spotted Alice coming out of our hiding spot. I'm positive that Agnes knows Alice was spying on her and Dragon."

"Are you sure she didn't see you?"

"Pretty sure. And, Mason, we know they're conspiring about something."

At that moment, we hear the gravel crunch outside. Mason and I look at the door with horror—we forgot to put the bar across.

"Behind that stone," he commands. "Hide. Whoever it is, I'll take care of it."

I huddle behind a half-carved capital up on the chancel and try not to breathe. The door creaks open, and I hear the familiar heavy footfall of the sub-prioress.

"Stonemason," she says. "I saw torchlight in here. I'm glad I found you."

"Good evening, Sub-Prioress," he greets her. Only I can detect a slight waver in his voice. "How can I help?"

"I will need a quantity of stone delivered to the church tonight. I have a project."

"How much do you need? What sizes?"

"Oh, ones that I can lift myself, though I'm stronger than you might suppose. And enough for an area as tall as you are, and again as wide—about one and a half times that. Bring it in the back door and leave it by the side chapel of Saint Christopher."

"Happy to," says Mason. "What is this for, again?"

"An . . . object lesson."

I hear her start to leave, and raise my head a little. That's when my foot slips out from under me. Agnes turns, but I see Mason shuffle his feet, trying to mimic the sound. She doesn't seem to see me.

"Quick as you can, stonemason," she says, and goes out into the night.

"We didn't bar the door!" I whisper, emerging from my hiding place, fear clouding my sight.

"I won't make that mistake again."

"I guess she didn't see me. I'm going to my cell—I can't risk her finding me in here." I kiss him quickly and duck out the door.

Just as I step out, a hand grabs my arm so hard, I see a flash of purple light in the night's dark. Agnes twists it behind my back and pushes me down the path to the barn where she first whipped me, spitting in my ear the whole way.

"You simply couldn't obey, could you?" she seethes. "I tried to help you fit here, but you insist on sneaking around with that boy. Have you learned *nothing* from me?"

"I never asked to fit here," I reply, trying to yank away from her, but *God*, she *is* strong.

"That's because you come from poor stock, and your family did not impress the proper things upon you. But that could be forgiven. You were simply—how do I say this?—*poorly formed*."

"Why are you doing this to me?" I grimace as she shoves me against the wall, still wrenching my arm. The goats in the barn wake up and start pacing in their pens, bleating like crying children. "I'm nobody to you."

"Why would you question me?" Agnes's calm voice doesn't rise a fraction, even as the flail comes down on me and sends me to my knees. She sighs, almost as though she's bored by having to do this again.

It's crazy, what you can be grateful for when you're being whipped in the dark. For one thing, I'm thankful she let me keep my dress on this time. And for another, it's getting late, and she seems to be running out of energy for the task.

Suddenly, unexpectedly, she stops.

"It's not real, you know," says Agnes. "That whole tree picture. It's a fantasy, made up by a dreamer a long time ago. It's meant to distract you from what *matters*."

Still bent over by the blows, I lift my head in disbelief. "But the comet—you saw it, too. And the carving on your desk."

"It was a dead end. People . . . people died anyway."

"But maybe they didn't have to."

The sub-prioress is silent. The animals calm in their pens.

"Can't you just *stop*?" she finally pleads. "Can't you simply follow the way we do things here? Don't see the stonemason. Don't indulge useless visions. It's simple enough."

"I have to find the truth."

"Haven't I been good to you?" she says earnestly, helping me to my feet. "I gave you a privilege, serving in the scriptorium. Girls like you aren't usually allowed to *touch* books."

My eyes have been clenched so tight, I can barely open them, but I stare her right in the face.

"Thank you for the privilege," I sneer.

She looks me up and down for a moment—and then strikes my jaw so hard, it's an explosion of violets as I fall into the hay.

When Mason finds me later, the bell is ringing for some middle-of-the-night office. I know my face looks bad, straw adhered to my skin and my tongue swollen in my mouth. Mason lifts me up from the floor and throws my arm over his shoulder. He helps me walk toward the chapel, but I don't want to go there. I just want to be alone, *alone*. As he fumbles with the door, I want to punch the stone wall in front of me, but know I'll regret it.

So I run.

I break away from Mason and throw open the calefactory door. The still air on top of my red anger makes me sweat instantly. I push along the wall of the spiral staircase, propelling myself faster to my cell, tears mingling with perspiration, trying not to swoon. The second bell rings, but I don't care if I miss prayer, even if I'm beaten for it *again. I don't care.*

I slam the door to my cell, and Henry's clay honey pot wobbles and spills water and field flowers across the desk. I rip off my veil; I hurl my shoes at the wall and roar.

Off comes this damned dress.

I tear my hair out of its braids.

I stand wild-haired in my linen tunic and throw myself, sobbing, against the stone wall.

Nothing is opening itself up to me. Nothing is in my control.

Back in my old life, I could talk to people who *knew* me. I could come and go as I pleased, in and out of the sheepfold, dance around the maypole with whoever I liked. I could pick pears and put a flower behind my ear or weave a whole crown of them and wear it all day. But in this priory, a world away from Hartley Cross, it's different—what it means to be a peasant's daughter, with a peasant's choices.

— 30 —

Five sisters are missing from chapter Monday, and everyone's restless. I show the prioress the wax tablet with the list of announcements. She tries to get through them, but her focus is wavering. She looks utterly exhausted.

"Why don't you sit, Mother?" I whisper, easing her into her chair.

"Thank you, daughter," she responds, weakly placing a hand on my bruised and lacerated jaw. I've put on a wimple to try to mask it, but it's obvious. Should I tell her, in her weakened state, what happened to me? Something tells me she's already guessed.

Prioress Margaret struggles through the agenda.

"Lastly," she concludes, "Agnes de Guile has something to say to us." She waves a hand at her sub-prioress. "Go ahead, sister."

Agnes rises and stands in the center of the room, surrounded by column capitals full of grotesque creatures, their eyes rolling and tongues sticking out. She takes her time before speaking, looking around the room at each sister, magnifying them like a scribe's water flask.

"Let us give thanks that our beloved prioress is feeling well enough to join us today."

"Amen," Bridgit chimes in, loudly.

"Sisters, in this confusing time, we must look for tokens of clarity," she continues. "And we have been shown mercy by the provision of two holy offices.

First, the revealing of our prophetess, who sits among us even now, enduring terrifying visions on *our* behalf." She gestures grandly toward Felisia, who, plucked from her nest in the sanctuary, sits backward on the bench, staring at the wall and moving her lips soundlessly. I glance at the prioress, but she's just trying hard to sit up straight. Agnes continues.

"Second, in this very priory, we are favored to be taking on an anchorite."

There was an anchorite back home, on the road from Hartley Cross to Saint Gabriel's Abbey. He lived alone in a roadside chapel, in a room with no doors, only a window where travelers passed food in, and a muddy hole where he dumped out his chamber pot. No companions, no sunshine. The very image makes it hard to breathe. Who would want to do that here?

"We will celebrate Mass for her today: our very own Alice Palmer."

"*Alice?*" the Pri asks, incredulous. Suddenly she leans forward in her chair, seized by a pain in her side. This can't be right. My head's all in a muddle—I jump up to help the prioress, but I want to run and find Alice.

No one can stay quiet. *The budding preacher? The promising scholar? The girl who'd rather live on gossip than food? Why would she shut herself away?*

"Alice has had an epiphany," says Agnes, ignoring the prioress. "Her life's calling is to pray for our community and for an end to this pestilence."

"Where is she?" says the prioress.

"She is even now keeping vigil in prayer. We are grateful for such a sacrifice. Someone of her talents, my, my."

Joan approaches Agnes and whispers against the din. "Sub-Prioress, you must be mistaken. My apprentice would have told me about—"

"Come to order, please," Agnes interrupts her, putting an arm around Joan. "Our most learned physician is only beginning to understand why this sickness has come to us. She does not have the *deeper* insight given to those of us who attend exclusively to prayer; she can only *consider the heavens*, as the psalmist says."

Joan sets her jaw and shrugs off Agnes's arm. "I've taken holy orders, same as you," says Joan. "Committed my path to the service of the Great Physician Himself, and studied in Salerno. Spare me your sermon, *Sub-Prioress*." She walks back to her bench, staring intently at Agnes as she sits.

"That is good enough in its *way*," Agnes continues, "but Alice will be doing the greater part by devoting her life to solitary prayer. You wouldn't deter your apprentice from her true calling, would you, Sister Joan?

"And let us look more closely at this illness, sisters, at how violent its end. The afflicted do not die peacefully in their beds, nor can they in any way be comforted, but are in wide-eyed horror to the last. Sin and compromise are in our midst. Remember—a bad end is a judgment!"

Several of the eldest sisters murmur—their ends are near, no matter what the cause.

"Sub-Prioress," Joan protests, "our priory has always been a place for the sick. That is who we *are*. We don't judge whether the patient is a sinner or saint—we *treat* them, like we would God Himself."

"What do you propose, Sister Joan?" asks the prioress, bracing herself, at that moment, against some unbearable pain. Instead of answering, Joan and I run to her side and help her to stand. Agnes nods permission for us to leave.

I hear Agnes's volume rise as we go: "This crisis demands a strong hand. God has ordained this for our benefit. We must deny ourselves every comfort—*give no sleep to our eyes, no slumber to our eyelids*. Submit ourselves to penance, night and day, until the pestilence is vanquished. If anyone is *truly* committed to a cure, she will be at prayer!"

"I'm bringing you to the infirmary, Mother," Joan whispers to the prioress. We help her take a few halting steps, but pain shudders through her body.

"No. It will arouse panic. The pallet is already laid in my study. I will be fine; it's merely a spasm."

Joan looks at me dubiously. "Go," she acquiesces. "Bring Mother there. I'll get my things and come examine her."

As we make our way across the cloister to her study, the prioress grabs me tightly. "Edyth," she whispers, "*find Alice.*"

I search in the infirmary, the medicine garden, even the chapel. In the priory church, I light a candle at the feet of the Virgin and pray for help, and as I kneel, I see, behind my eyes, silvery curls melting into the statue—a wailing cry.

"Amen." I cross myself hastily and follow the sound coming from the ambulatory. Past the altar, down the passage—I cannot believe the sight.

Where the chapel of Saint Christopher had been now stands a hastily erected wall. It doesn't reach the ceiling but is too high to climb. The kneeler and candle lean against the hodgepodge of architectural salvage. The bell tolls five minutes until terce.

The enclosure of Alice Palmer has already taken place.

"Alice?" I call, horrified. "Are you in there?"

I hear only whimpering.

There's a small opening in the wall, right at the floor. I lie on the ground and peer in: Alice sits in the corner of the empty niche with her knees pulled up. Her long, ash-blond hair is disheveled and knotted. She's in her linen shift with a blanket around her shoulders. Her mouth is swollen and bruised. The only thing with her in the enclosure is a chamber pot.

Her words are barely intelligible: "Edyth . . . she drugged me . . . the whole bottle . . ."

"Agnes did this to you?"

"And the Dragon," she mumbles.

The bell rings again as nuns enter the church from the large front doors, chanting—

> *Peccantem me quotidie, et non poenitentem*
> *Timor mortis conturbat me.*
>
> *Daily sinning, and not repenting*
> *The fear of death terrifies me.*

I recognize that prayer. It's the office for the dead.

People say this office for anchorites. They're saying it for Alice.

Agnes carries a tall candle of expensive beeswax as she leads two lines of sisters up the nave. Strangely, each of the sisters carries a bedroll. They really are planning to stay here, night and day, day and night.

Father Johannes begins the Mass. I scramble into the niche next to Alice's enclosure and stare out at the ceremony, tears falling from anger and frustration. The whole scene is surrounded and shot through with vermillion sparks.

Joan pulls Agnes toward the ambulatory, trying to contain her fury. I can barely make out the words she whispers to the sub-prioress:

"Don't do this. Don't do this, you wicked woman. This isn't how we do things."

Agnes ignores her. The priest administers the rites and serves communion.

"I'm going to get you out of there, Alice," I whisper into the window once the ceremony is under way. "I'll sort it, I promise you—I'm not leaving you."

No gate, no door; only that small window near the floor officially connects Alice to the world of the living.

So that's why the Anti-Pri needed Mason to bring the stone. The length to which Agnes went to silence Alice—she and Felisia must have thrown that wall up themselves, between night offices, when no one would have noticed the side chapel in the dim light. Mason was right—I'm safer in the chapel, with a door I can bar against her. But tonight, I don't want Alice to be alone.

I sneak to my cell, grab only a blanket to avoid arousing suspicion and tuck myself back into the niche next to Alice's enclosure, passing in and out of anxious sleep. I dream of being sealed in stone walls. I dream of drowning, of being buried alive. I'm woken at daybreak, sweating and startled, by the loudness of the Sound, that thin green vibration that's always in the corner of my vision. Nothing else crowds it out or suppresses it—there's no red *ping* of hammers, nor shimmering gray silk of birdsong. What's missing?

That's it—*no bells have rung.* I've woken with the sun, and not with the sound of a bell. There could only be two possibilities.

Either no one else is dying . . .

Or everyone is.

And the churches have given up ringing the bells.

Days pass, and there are no bells of any kind now. No funeral bells, no prayer bells. No weddings, or town meetings, or Masses. All becomes howling prayer, punctuated by the prophesying of the Dragon, the disgusting cooing of the Anti-Pri, and the hopeless wailing of Alice Palmer.

— 31 —

Never have I seen so much rain, and this is *England*.

Instead of walking in their usual twos or threes, half of the sisters circle the cloister perimeter alone, like spiritless husks, between refectory, dormitory and church.

The other half are dead.

If it's possible, Alice's enclosure last week has made my world even smaller. I no longer have free rein of the whole grounds, but I'm limited to a tiny circuit: scriptorium-infirmary-chapel-church. The stream of sick pilgrims hasn't slowed, despite the arduous task of a fevered person getting up the hill on impassable, muddy roads.

I know they need help in the infirmary, but I hide away in the scriptorium. There's solace up here, above the misery only a few yards from this tower. It's quieter and more somber without Brother Timothy to lift the atmosphere, but Muriel, Anne, Bridgit and I have a harmonious rhythm that works.

Joan finds me up here at my desk, painting drop capitals in red and azurite. "The rain's abating," she says, taking off her wet linen veil, the dark rings around her eyes showing her exhaustion. I feel guilty that I've avoided going to help her. "Edyth, I need you to go to town. Here's a list. Go see the druggist for the herbs and oils, and the jeweler for these stones—if they're still there. One of my patients told me the stores are being abandoned, and I can *not* run out of these things. I don't care if you have to steal them—God will forgive you for my sake."

"I'll go," I consent. "And, Joan—I know you're stretched, tending to the sick. I want you to know that I'm looking in on Alice. She's going to be all right."

"Thank you, Edyth," she says. "That means a lot." The physician puts her veil back on, but not before I see her eyes well with tears.

With the rain finally over, it's blazing hot. On my way down to the gatehouse, I stand at the north wall and peer down at the town encircling the priory hill. As far as I can tell, nothing moves but stray animals. Except for the trickle of pilgrims coming in through the gatehouse, the once-bustling town is eerily quiet.

Thornchester has a permanence that half-timbered, one-story Hartley Cross never did. Its bustling, dirty, colorful streets, its hundreds of stone buildings anchored in the land, give you the feeling that nothing was different before you, and nothing will change when you're gone.

What I see once I'm through the gates is completely different.

It is a cesspool. The ditches run over with filth, and I have to hop between one shit puddle and the next. Bodies are everywhere—cast outside of front doors, lying in the street, facedown in the rain-sodden alleys, piled in the churchyard. Doors swing open on their hinges. No one, alive at least, is out in the marketplace. Dogs bark or sniff at the dead and generally trot up and down the streets, loyal to no master.

The only sounds of human activity are muffled wails inside houses, muffled cries to God or the Virgin, gibberish like Brother Timothy's—like a patchwork quilt of old, fraying linens.

Joan's right: the shops are abandoned, somewhat looted, but not too badly—death comes so fast with this sickness that few people would care about grabbing baubles on the way out of life. I leave a couple of coins anyway, for honesty's sake.

I take shade from the heat at the closest of the two parish churches, Saint Mary's, under the stone archway into the churchyard. Voluminous sprays of white roses on the vine erupt their perfume, but it's mixed with another smell, the toxically sweet aroma of death. I round a holly bush toward the church door and stumble on three corpses, two women and a man, flies buzzing at their eyes. I gag and cover my nose and mouth, thanking God for the burst of white stars that at least gives me something else to see.

The side door of the church is open, and I walk right into the nave. It's intimate and cool, like Saint Andrew's back home. There's movement toward the front—a priest waddles out from the sacristy carrying the holy elements, a small glass pitcher of wine with a round glass stopper, a silver box containing the bread. I begin to walk toward the priest, startling him.

"Don't come any closer!" He puts out his hands to stop me, holding the box and pitcher out to me like an offering.

"Where is everyone?" I ask. "Why haven't you rung the bell for nones?"

"Rung the bell? For whom?" the priest scoffs as he begins laying his things on the altar.

Slowly I advance toward him. "But you're putting out the Eucharist," I protest.

"That's my duty," he says, nervous as a rat. "If anyone dares come, they can get it right from here. Come and take it if you want. It's consecrated. But I won't be here."

"Wait, where are you going?"

"Away. *Away!* Now get out!"

I know this priest. I've seen him before on feast days, eating and drinking with the prioress herself. Once or twice he served at the altar in the priory church when Father Johannes was traveling or ill. He always had a friendly piety— nothing like the sharp hostility coming from him now.

The whole way back to the priory, I'm dodging mud and muck in my stupid sandals. I can't believe how much Thornchester has broken down since I was there in spring, and I yearn for the safety of the priory confines.

Now I have a true sense of things. The state of the fields fills me with a sick churn. Barley lies broken and sodden. A wandering cow grazes on the stubble. A chicken shrieks from somewhere in the hayfield. The scent of baking grass is barely enough to push down the smell of decay rising from the churchyard, from the town, from everywhere.

I've seen crops fail a few times; probably one year out of every three is a bad year for someone. You find other ways to bolster the losses, stored goods to pull from, wool to weave and sell. There's the motivation to *not starve*, to push through the lean winter until another chance comes. And your neighbors recognize that their own bad year could be next—*someone* always steps in with mercy to get a struggling family through the winter.

But this? This is entirely different. In a normal year, at least people *fought* against hunger.

In a normal year, every other person was not dropping dead.

Thank God, it's cooler in the refectory. At least there's still food, and someone's cooking it. But a brazen mouse lugs a chunk of bread right across a shaft of sunlight, and no one flinches. Everything is filthy.

There are only a few people in the hall. A smattering of sisters huddle over bowls of thin gruel and hunks of bread. None of them sit together. On a table near the dais is a pot, a stack of wooden bowls and several large loaves. No one is here to serve or to clean up the piles of dirty dishes. Apparently Cook has taken the same approach as the priest.

I slip two loaves into my basket, one for Alice, one for me and Mason to share. Just then, the prioress comes in, with Agnes at her arm, and my back stings with memory, dashes of purple darting in the corners of my eyes. I'm glad to see the Pri walking, but she looks more tired than a body should be. She sits at the dais, and Agnes goes to the kitchen, bringing up the prioress's meal, more substantial than the common gruel.

It's strange to sit in this hall chewing bread while the world is ending all around me, not knowing what I'm supposed to do about it. I ladle some soup, tear off a piece of bread, pour some ale and watch.

Around the room, no one raises their head to acknowledge me, not even the prioress or Agnes. We all eat prayerlessly, clear our places to the dirty dish table and leave in haste, as though trying to occupy as little space as possible, breathe as little as possible, fearing to make one misstep and enter into a pocket of the bad air.

— 32 —

The only thing to do is throw myself into work. As I make my way down the cloister corridor toward the scriptorium, I see Bridgit walking ahead of me about twenty paces, staggering like a dancing drunkard, her skirts swaying. I've almost caught up with her when she falls hard to the stone pavement.

"Bridgit!" I call out. "Help! Somebody!" But my voice echoes off the stone vaults. I bend over her—she's unconscious, with a sheen of sweat over her face and neck. I'm about to shake her, to try to wake her up, but I stop myself. Something tells me not to touch her.

That's silly, though, isn't it? What's the harm? I reach out a finger and poke Bridgit in the shoulder. Her head lolls to the side, and on her outstretched neck, right near her collarbone, is a purple blotch with a white lump in the middle, like a ripe open plum and pit.

She stirs, and I startle.

"Edyth." Bridgit raises a weary hand. "Help me up. Help me to the infirmary."

Don't touch. Don't touch.

"I'll go get help," I fumble. "Stay there."

I know it's stupid. *What kind of friend am I?* I wonder as I stumble through the chilled calefactory and out the back door. *I couldn't at least help her to her feet?* I run with a pheasant's gait to the infirmary, throw open the iron latch and push in the door.

The first thing that hits me is the putrid smell, same as Brother Timothy, but multiplied by a dozen. So this is where everyone is. Every stall is filled, every curtain drawn open. Some cells have two people each, one in the bed, one on a pallet on the floor. Joan darts back and forth like a flummoxed sparrow. A cup of water here. A fresh rag there. Mopping up bloody spit. A poultice on a lump, or five lumps. It's impossible. The physician doesn't even notice me. And if she did, would she be able to help me? To leave these two dozen sickbeds to help one woman collapsed out in the cloister?

I have to find help somewhere else. I burst outside, and there's Bridgit, on all fours. In the absence of a friend, she's crawled here herself.

"Someone has to stop this," says Joan, laying Bridgit down on a pallet. "We're too full. I don't want to turn anyone away, but we're using every bit of space, and we'll have to start laying them on the table next. Do you have my supplies?"

"Here." I take out the bread and hand her the basket as the door opens, and Agnes comes into the infirmary with the prioress.

"Sister Joan," says Agnes, dripping with false sympathy, "our Venerable Mother is still unwell. I believe she needs to stay here. It must be the heat. Or something she ate."

Joan sighs. "This isn't the place for her, Sub-Prioress. There's too much contagion. Edyth, bring Prioress Margaret back to her study. I'll come by soon to check on her."

Agnes heads for the exit, satisfied to hand over the burden.

"But wait, Sister Agnes." Joan beckons her back. "I'm glad you're here, because I have to tell you, we cannot take any more pilgrims. Look at this place. Is there something we can do?"

"I agree with you, Joan," says Agnes. "This is quite the chaotic scene you have here."

"I was thinking that we could make space in another building. We did that before, during the famine."

"What, so we can become overrun by hell-bound sinners? We have to protect our own first, Sister Joan."

"Agnes, we *exist* to help the sick. It means certain death for them if we don't."

"I do have an idea, Joan. We'll talk about it in the morning." The sub-prioress turns on her heel and leaves.

"Take me to the sanctuary first, Edyth," says Prioress Margaret. "I want to pray." The prioress slings her arm across my shoulder, and I grip her around the waist.

"Here, Edyth," says Joan, handing me Alice's wax tablet and stylus. She looks like she wants to say more, but she's got too much chaos to deal with. "Take these to Alice. And give her my love."

The waning afternoon light hits the eastern wall of the stone church, giving its curved apse the look of a huge ship's prow. Before anyone here was born, this church stood in this place, sailing through centuries. Who knows what abyss it's speeding toward now?

The sundial on the outside of the infirmary tells me it's almost time for vespers, but since there are no bells, I determine to feign ignorance. As I bring the prioress in through the transept door, I hear a solitary sound bouncing off the soaring walls in the nave, a thin, white line, glowing with light, the echo returning to it like white stars.

It is Alice, singing from within her enclosure—

> *O aeterne Deus, nunc tibi placeat,*
> *Ut in amore illo ardeas—*
>
> *O eternal God, please now*
> *Burn us with that fiery love—*

The prioress stops, then walks on her own to stand right before the rood screen. She is so weak and thin, but she straightens like a basalt obelisk, her head tilted up toward the mosaic above the altar, with the bearded man in the center of everything, emanating love: the man in perfect control. She stretches out her hands—an offering, or a plea.

She joins Alice in the song—

Et perduc nos in laetitiam salutis.

And lead us to the joy of salvation.

The prioress isn't desperate, or frenzied, but she does weep, her tears running slowly down her neck like rain on a pillar. She sings like an innocent defendant in court, simply stating her case. The last note ricochets off the columns and showers down from the vaults.

Throughout the entire song, Dragon cowers in the corner, watching us from her straw pallet. It's hard to feel sorry for her now. Yes, she's one of the Pitiful, but so am I—and I don't think suffering has to beget her brand of mad malevolence.

And that raises an obvious question.

"Forgive me, Mother, but . . ." I falter.

She purses her lips and nods in understanding. "You want to know why I didn't stop Agnes and Felisia from imprisoning Alice."

"Yes."

She turns her head sharply. "I will ask you a question instead: In the Garden, why did God not close the mouth of the serpent, right from the beginning? He could have."

I consider this. "That's something that's confused me since I was a little girl."

"Everything God made is good, isn't it?" She breathes in slowly and turns her head toward Dragon. "He made snakes, too—*before* there was sin. But what is it that makes serpents bite?"

"Getting too close to them?"

She laughs at my naivete. "*Fear*, Edyth. That's what makes snakes bite, and gifted nuns, too. Fear can kill. But it does not have to win."

I still don't have my answer.

"Fear of what?"

"Keep asking that question. Of yourself most of all."

She takes another breath, slow and shuddering, but bears her pain with more ease.

"Edyth, I am sorry that my . . . present condition . . . prevented me from stopping Alice's enclosure. But it's done. So we must ask: What *now*?"

"Right." I nod. "What now?"

She smiles. "Shall we look in on your friend?"

I help her shuffle over to the wall, and the prioress lowers herself right down to the ground. We both look through the opening. Alice sits in the corner, her hair scraggly, feet bare, staring at the wall in front of her.

"Sister Alice," calls the prioress, "how do you fare today?"

Alice looks up and begins to shake her head.

"Is there anything I can get you?"

"A door," she responds in frustration, rubbing her eyes hard.

"*Patience wins all it seeks*, Alice. Do you trust me?"

Alice gets on all fours and creeps toward the opening, her eyes red-ringed, her pent-up anger palpable, exasperated at the prioress's quixotic leadership. "Mother, you could have saved me from this!" she insists.

"Let me take your chamber pot, daughter," Prioress Margaret responds. Alice stares at her, unsure, and slides the basin through the window. Suddenly she puts her face right up to ours.

"Mother, I figured out why you're sick. Agnes—"

"Alice!" the prioress rebukes her. "Not another word! We have this evening to get you what you need. Tell us."

"Parchment. Ink. And something to read, or I will lose my mind."

"Well, this is from Joan, with love," I tell her, sliding the wax tablet and stylus through.

The prioress winks at me. "Let us see if we can find Alice a good book to read in there."

I help Prioress Margaret up and bring her to the study. She weakly puts some books from the bookcase in a hemp sack.

"Give these to Alice," she says, lowering herself down to the pallet. "Bring her food. Empty her pot. Give her hope. You must promise to take care of your friend, no matter what it costs you. *There is no greater love than this.*"

I nod my head reverently. "I promise, Mother."

Back at the enclosure, Alice thanks me for the books and pulls the bag through the hole.

Then she slides me her wax tablet. She's scrawled one word on it, obviously something she doesn't want to say out loud, with Dragon only yards away.

Monkshood

What? I write back.

That's the page that's missing

Monkshood.

Oh God. Jesus.

Such a beautiful flower, monkshood. It really does look like its name. A rich, dark blue, like so few flowers can be, and not the dark, utilitarian blue of woad-dyed cloth.

Blue, almost like lapis lazuli.

I scratch one word into the wax, and Alice nods.

POISON.

— 33 —

A chill dawn glows the slightest blue through the chapel window, and I open my eyes to the piercing ring of a brass handbell surrounding my head in circles. Mason's not here with me.

That means the door's not barred.

Two sisters knock on every building of the priory and announce the closure of the gates.

"Healthy to the church, sick to the infirmary! Healthy to the church, sick to the infirmary, on orders of Sub-Prioress Agnes de Guile! No one out of doors, no one in the dormitory, no exceptions! The gates are shut and locked!"

Utter panic bursts forth. Nuns, guesthouse visitors and laborers all rush to the entrance, pounding to escape; desperate pilgrims in need of medicine beg to get in.

Pointless. Death is inevitable.

Who is sick? Who is healthy? What if I carry the curse in my body and don't know it, disease rotting me from the inside? No one knows until it's too late. And now we're trapped inside.

I dress and leave the chapel to find Mason. As I pass the calefactory, someone grabs my arm and pulls me inside. It's Muriel, and Anne's with her, too.

"We were hoping we'd find you right away," asks Muriel. "News? What's going on out there?"

"Bridgit" is all I can say.

"Does she have the marks?"

I hesitate, feeling the gall rise in my throat as I think of her falling in the cloister. "Yes."

Muriel drops her head in her hands. Anne leans heavily against the wall.

"And the prioress—" I begin.

"Mother has it, too?" Muriel starts to wail.

"No! Not the fever," I say. "She's ill, but it's not that."

"Then why isn't she stopping the sub-prioress?" Anne asks, bewildered.

"She—" I remember the Pri admonishing Alice not to let on. "She has her reasons."

"Is Prioress Margaret in any control whatsoever?" Anne demands.

"Yes," I fib. "She knows exactly what she's doing." The two of them don't seem to buy it.

"We can avoid this, you know," says Muriel. "We have a plan, even if the prioress doesn't."

"Go on," I say. "I'm listening."

"Let's hide in the scriptorium. We're healthy. It will only be the three of us; no one needs to know we're even there. They'll assume we're in the infirmary. The air in the tower is good, and it has a separate entrance and a lock. We can take turns going out to get food. Our work will keep our minds off the chaos."

"What about prayers?" I ask. But I've got bigger questions: *Where's Mason? Can the prioress be healed from the poison and stop the Anti-Pri? And how can I get Alice out?*

The handbells are still ringing, like shards of broken glass. "We can see the sundial from the window," says Muriel. "We'll hold our own offices."

"How will we get Father Johannes up there?" I add. "What will we do for Mass?"

Muriel turns to Anne. "She hasn't heard."

"Father Johannes is dead," says Anne. "Yesterday. They found him in his house."

"No priest?" It's like the ship has slipped one more of its moorings.

It doesn't seem like a great plan. But if I'm in the scriptorium, it could be convenient, maybe even safer than the chapel. I can get to Alice through the church's back door, get food to her, parchment, books from the library, and we can keep watch from the window. Mason will be right next door if I need him, and I can throw myself into drawing. It's as good an option as any other.

"All right," I relent. "I'll come."

"We'll have to trust the Divine Will," says Anne. "Let's go to our cells and gather our things, and meet up in the scriptorium in twenty minutes—discreetly. Don't talk to *anyone*. We'll lock the door from the inside."

Meanwhile, outside, panicked sisters and pilgrims zigzag with the crazy bells—

No! I was just leaving!

I never did want to be a nun! Let go of me!

I simply wanted to venerate Holy Eustace and go home!

—trying to figure where to breach the gates, how to get out, how to get in. The few remaining laborers, conscripted as guards, put their bodies between the crowds and the gates, but people try to scale the walls on both sides.

Most of the sisters, of course, go to the church. Everyone's scrupulously checked for signs of the illness and let into the sanctuary only after washing in cold water from the fountain. No one would admit their need for the infirmary. To be sent there is a death sentence; the bodies piled up in the churchyard are warning enough.

In my cell, I take a last look at the mural on the wall, shaking my head at my failure to decipher the vision. I put everything I can fit in Da's canvas satchel and shut the door with finality. I wait by the back door until all the nuns have vacated the dormitory, then hurry past the infirmary.

"Edyth!" comes a sharp whisper from behind the chapel.

"There you are!" I embrace Mason, relieved. "Where were you this morning?"

"I was packing," he says. He pulls away and looks at me urgently. "This is our chance, Edyth. We have to go now!"

"How? The gates are locked! Just stay in the chapel until the evacuation's over!"

He shakes his head. "I can only hide for so long. You're already packed, and I have food and some money. I can get us both out of here. We can go over the field wall. Come on. Let's go now, before they see us!"

"I can't, Mason—I can't leave Alice."

"Edyth, now's our chance. If we don't go, I'll be nothing but a gravedigger here until I fall into the pit myself."

"Mason, I can't. I'm sorry. I made a promise. I can't let Alice rot in there. God be with you . . . I'll pray for you." I start briskly toward the scriptorium, and Mason follows close.

"God's forgotten us," he says. "Maybe you should make a promise to me instead."

I stop walking and turn to meet his gaze. The bells have stopped, but a cacophony of lapis blue waves up my neck and over my head.

"Mason, please, don't make me do this." I thrust through the heavy door, and he follows me up the spiral staircase. I push the scriptorium door closed, turning the key just as Mason pounds on the other side.

"What is going on?" Anne springs toward me.

"Come out, Edie, please," Mason shouts. "I'm sorry. I should have done this all differently."

I sink to the floor against the door. "I know," I say. "Me too."

"I love you, Edyth." His voice breaks.

"Mason, don't," I plead. "We can't let anyone hear us. They can't know we're up here."

He stops knocking and lowers his voice. "I don't want to face this without you."

"Maybe we'll make it through," I offer. "Maybe God will be merciful."

I hear the ground-floor door creak open and heavy footsteps climbing the stairs.

"Who's there?" It's the voice of Agnes de Guile.

"I was just checking the locks," Mason lies. "The building is empty."

"Oh, good, stonemason. We'll need you to stand guard at the gates, and there are dead to be buried. Tell the other men, you'll each take two-hour shifts. Now get back to work!" She storms out and I hear the door slam.

"Mason," I say softly, my cheek pressed against the door, "you can leave. You have to. If you have a way out, take it."

"Edyth," he says, "this is our last chance. Who knows if either of us will survive?"

"We have to take that chance. We have to say goodbye."

"No." He's resolute. "I'll never say goodbye, Edyth."

A familiar softening returns to my body, the passive resign of childhood, when I'd let Mam and Da make hard decisions for me. With all my heart, I want to open this door, run into Mason's arms, let him carry me away from all this. Because he's strong. He hasn't gotten sick. And despite my chastisement, I *know* he loves me.

But he'll survive. His strength can save him, and mine can save me. I can't say the same for Alice. Mason may want me, but Alice needs me.

So I screw up my will, and turn myself to iron.

"Goodbye, Mason. God protect you."

Autumn
1349

— 34 —

Terce drags on forever this morning, breathing the endless psalm back and forth on a dull gray note. The three of us sit in the center of the scriptorium, our stools drawn together in a circle. It's been days since our confinement, and the air's getting so close, I feel like I'll lose my mind.

"Amen," we close.

"I'll go out for food," I volunteer. Alice will be needing more bread. Maybe I'll see Mason. Maybe we can figure out a better plan.

If he's still here, that is.

"Stay out of sight," says Anne. "Take the back way. Don't breathe too deeply. Oh, and remember to pick those medicinal herbs."

I grab a cloth bag and sneak down the staircase into the sunlight. The September heat blasts against my skin like a bread oven. The infirmary doors are usually kept closed to muffle the cries and moans, to keep out the bad air, but today is so stifling hot that they're flung open, and the full tableau of human misery is spread before me. I stand staring for a moment, forgetting myself.

A girl sits cross-legged against the shady infirmary wall, barefoot, in only a linen tunic. Her two brown braids hang limp and loose against her shoulders. The rest of her frizzled hair radiates from her head like sun's rays, and her down-cast, ashen face is covered in blotches, like purple clouds in a gray sky. Her lips are white, dry and cracked. She clenches her toes, muttering to herself. I feel

sorry for her, but there's nothing that can be done now. The disease is in her mind, and she'll be dead soon.

I take the long way to the kitchen. The grass is variously overgrown and patchy from the sun. In the frenzy to get into the church, pilgrims dropped things without caring; the paths are strewn with litter and weeds, and loose chickens run amok.

In the refectory kitchen, Cook sits on a stool, mindlessly stirring beans. On the worktable, a pile of greens is wilting badly. The kitchen doesn't have its usual smell of good things, but of an underlying scent of rotting cabbage. I clear my throat.

"*Ave*," I greet Cook. "I didn't think anyone would still be here. May I take bread for my sisters?"

"*Takewhatyouwant*," she mutters, without stopping or looking up.

"Do you need . . . help?"

"Ha," Cook gruffs. "Beyond help."

"I could chop these greens for you," I offer.

"Get to it, then."

I wash a dirty knife and dry it. Neither the wash water nor the towel look like they've been changed in days. I begin to chop the vegetables, half of which need to be discarded.

"Would you like these in the pot?" I ask. Cook shrugs. I scrape them from the board into the pot, fetch a clean spoon and taste the pottage. It's so bland as to be nonexistent. I take it upon myself to add some salt, dried herbs, ale. I find a covered vessel and ladle some soup into it, even as Cook keeps blindly stirring. I stuff my bag with two loaves of bread, half a small wheel of cheese and an armful of apples.

"Thank you," I say.

Cook keeps stirring.

With the hot pottage in one arm, the sack of food slung across my chest, and a finger through the handle of a jug of cool ale, I push back out into the autumn blaze. The girl is still outside the infirmary, still mumbling. I leave her an apple

I know she will never eat. As quietly as I can, I sneak up the scriptorium stairs and serve the stew to Muriel and Anne.

The workday passes, and it starts to darken outside, the still dusk reflected in the quiet of the scriptorium. I don't want to leave now, but dark means I can take the rest of the food to Alice.

I slip in the back door of the church. The sanctuary is full of fasting, crying nuns. Their chants are mixed with penitent sobs—

Have mercy!

Pass us by!

We are wretched!

Let your eye turn away!

Lift your hand from us!

—bursting in angular purple shapes that melt down the stone columns. The noise is hateful to me, but I can talk softly to Alice, undetected.

"How are you?" I ask.

"It could be worse," she says, pushing out the chamber pot. "I'm starting to think I'm lucky to be in here."

"Maybe you're right."

She takes the lid off the pottage and begins to eat. "Do you have something else for me?"

"Of course," I say, delivering a copy of *Poetica* through the opening.

"Oh, thank God," she says. "Aristotle."

She reads, and chews, and I lean my cheek on the cool stone wall and think.

So this is my life. No one told me this was how it could turn out.

My first real friend, behind an impenetrable wall.

The boy I love, probably gone, both of us likely doomed.

And now just waiting . . . waiting for the foulness to enter my body, waiting for the end of everything. The sick girl, Cook's eternal, automatic stirring—I cannot let that happen to me. I've got to push against this somehow.

Alice slides the pottage bowl back out to me. "Thank you," she says.

"You're welcome," I respond. "You've got to make that bread last a couple days, all right? I'll be back as soon as I can."

In the scriptorium, Anne calls us together, after vespers.

"Edyth, Muriel, let's talk," she says. We gather our stools closer. "We might as well admit what we've all been thinking. No matter how long we stay up here, it feels like we're only putting off the inevitable. The end is going to come for us, too. Let's face it: we're working on books no one will read."

"That's terribly *morbid*, Anne," says Muriel.

"Well, that's what I'm here for," says Anne. "A scribe's got to keep the artists' heads out of their arses." We dissolve into peals of laughter. What a relief to laugh.

"All right," I say, wiping tears away. "What do you suggest?"

"I think we three should make a book together."

Muriel and I exchange a glance. "Isn't that what we already do?" she asks.

"I mean something we do for *us*, not for a patron. We should stop whatever else we're working on and spend our last days creating our own book. About *death*. At least then, if we succumb, we'll have made our peace with it."

"But what if we survive?" Muriel counters. "We'll have a book but no patron. They'll have us for theft."

Anne ignores her. "I want to do the whole book in three colors: ultramarine, and gold, and silver."

"But those aren't *colors*; they're treasures!" Muriel protests. "Even a king wouldn't commission a book like that! They'd have our heads!"

"Oh, Muriel, you're so practical," says Anne. "Who'd have our heads if everyone's dead? For once, this isn't for anyone but *us*. Edyth, we're giving you a promotion."

"Fine," Muriel acquiesces. "But what do you mean, a book about death?"

"We're going to make fun of the bastard," Anne says with a dark smirk. "We'll mock death right back into hell."

"By making a book no one will read," I say.

"By making something *beautiful*," says Anne.

— 35 —

It's hard to express how these pictures are changing me. My soul's quieted, and my hand is free. I eat contentedly but just enough. Every night I fall asleep to the desperate cries of the nuns across the way in the church, feeling pity more than fear for Agnes and the Dragon. I sleep soundly and dream in colors from another world. Everything seems so much simpler, so much more profound.

My mind is on work; my mind is on death.

I'm less afraid of it somehow, as though I was bracing myself against life before. Now that the end seems so close, I can live free for however long I have left.

On the docket this morning is a very precious page: Muriel's miniature of Christ's anguish in the Garden of Gethsemane. The parchment sits on the slanted desk. It's one of the most exquisite designs Muriel has ever done. I imagine a reader, years in the future, turning to this image as they thumb through page after page in this collection.

Or maybe the world will never recover, and this book will turn to dust, as the grass grows tall as trees, and vines smash open these windows.

I've drawn an elaborate border around the piece. I'm going to work the margins with gold leaf today, and my skin tingles with anticipation. I've been perfecting my technique on a practice sheet, with small patches of the thin foil, like Muriel taught me. I get up and check that the doors are shut tightly. A draft of air would be a disaster.

"I'm doing the gold," I warn Muriel and Anne.

From the drawer marked *Aurum*, I carefully pull out an envelope containing small squares of gold leaf and lay it on my desk like a ritual. I hold my breath and take out a sheet of the gold with pincers, and then I lean my head all the way down to the page and breathe onto the gesso, the air from my very lungs making it come alive for an instant, enough to grab the gold like glue. I press the gold down into the moist gesso with a square of silk and burnish it with an agate stone, wiping away the excess leaf.

Piece by piece, I lay the gold around the border of the page, in the intricate border I've outlined. After the leafing goes down, I incise it with a sharpened stick, leaving the impression of stars in the sky surrounding the Man of Sorrows. And then it's time for the lapis.

My desk is arrayed with pots of ultramarine, and I lose myself in its current. I lick the end of my brush to get a finer point, giggling to think of the crushed gemstones getting stuck between my teeth, filling my body with blue. Even a queen wouldn't have such luxury.

When I wake up from my stupor, it's because Muriel is shaking me.

"What?" I murmur. Muriel gives me a fearful look.

Somehow—in another trance—I've nixed the ornate linework and laid down a border of gold skeletons instead, the whole of mankind's drama dancing around the nucleus of Christ.

Muriel nods slowly with pursed lips. "Now *that* is interesting."

"I need to see the prioress," I tell her.

I stand alone before the prioress in her study, turning my paint-splotched towel over and over in my hands. It's dangerous to be here. The wailing of the penitent nuns is close and loud, coming from right next door.

"Forgive me, Mother. I have something to tell you."

"Lock the door, Edyth. And speak softly." The aging woman wears her wimple but no veil. She leans back in her big oaken chair, sweating, pale, darkness encircling her eyes.

"Venerable Mother, we've been making a book, Anne, Muriel and me," I say. "We're using up all the lapis, the gold, the silver. I wanted to tell you, because it's right that you should know."

She's pensive for a minute. Talking is difficult for her, I can tell. "Continue," she manages.

"I was thinking about why things like gold and lapis stone are so valuable. At first I thought it was because—I don't know—the way they catch the light, or how bright they are. But then I thought, they're just colors chopped out of rocks, like any other."

The prioress smiles with interest, and I go on.

"I asked myself, how far do you have to go to find, let's say, yellow ochre? In Hartley Cross, it was everywhere. You'd find chunks of it in a field. I never put it together, but now I realize that the walls of Saint Andrew's were covered in ochre paintings."

"And how far do you have to go to find lapis lazuli?"

"To the edge of the faraway lands, as I understand."

"That's right, Edyth. It is because those elements are *rare*," says the prioress, with gravel in her throat.

"And that's why I know what I'm supposed to do."

The prioress leans forward and gazes at me intently. "Tell me."

"It was when I was using the ultramarine. I don't know why that color is so overwhelming, maybe because the world I came from was so drab, and that color's still so new to me. But I thought about the illumination in the Gospel book, my dream, the stained glass."

"Go on."

I take the Gospel book off the shelf and open to that page.

"This whole time, I thought the rest of the pieces of the puzzle were symbols

somehow. I knew the comet was real, because the three of us saw it, not just me. But I kept thinking that the rest of it was a symbol of something else, expecting to get the answer in my head, or in a dream. Now I really know: the tree is *real*, and the water is *real*. I think *that blue* is going to lead me to all of it, and I'm the only one who can find them."

"And that is why it had to be you," Prioress Margaret says, falling into a fit of coughing. She motions for the cup on her desk; I help her drink, then wipe the perspiration from her face. She finally calms and leans back with a contented smile.

"I'm dying, Edyth," she says. "But I'm satisfied, because you finally understand. Don't you see? Your whole life has been preparing you for this. Your dreams, your drawings, your colors—they're not an accident or a mistake. *You* are as rare as that beautiful color. You see more of reality than all of us put together."

"It's funny," I ponder. "It seems like when life makes the least sense, when I'm the most confused, the answer is right in front of me."

— 36 —

Leaving the prioress's study with the Gospel book in hand, I'm exceedingly careful not to be seen as I make my way to the chapel. I knock softly on the door, hoping Mason is still there, hoping he stayed for me.

"Mason," I call, "if you're there, please let me in."

When he opens the door and I see him, I want to die, the way my heart hurts. He looks tired, defeated, but he lets me enter. He bars the door.

"I was wrong to hide away," I whisper. "I want to live like I'm not afraid, of death or life or anything in between."

Mason says nothing, but leads me over to the pallet of straw and pulls me in so close, face to face. He brushes his lips and cheek against mine, and there's the barest space of soft air between us until he kisses me, and kisses me, and kisses me.

I've never had a feast of sensation like this, like each kiss is a bite of a soft, ripe fruit made of gold, silver—ultramarine. We grasp each other tightly, needfully. He slips off my gown and his tunic so we can feel that much closer, and we exhaust ourselves, and bruise our lips.

We lie quiet, really seeing each other for the first time.

"I love you, Edyth."

"I love you, too, John Mason."

He builds a little fire, hoping no one will notice the smoke. We hold each other again, watching the sparks rise.

"Mason, I need to show you something." I reach for the Gospel book and turn to the page with the yew tree.

"Is this the comet you saw?" he asks, sitting up.

"Yes. And this tree is out there somewhere for me to find. I don't know what I'm supposed to do when I get there, but I'm not worried about that. I can feel that it's true, that I'm living this unfolding story, and it's *my* story."

"I can help you look," he says. "Just meet me here in the chapel at midnight."

"Thank you, Mason. I want you to be part of this."

I close the book and begin putting on my green linen dress.

The sleeve of my linen chemise slides back.

Black spiders down my arm.

I look at Mason. We stare at each other for a long time, knowing what the other is thinking, the sickening horror that's just taken a bite out of our guts. He gingerly reaches for my arm and lifts it, looking into the sleeve. The black tendrils cover the whole length, from my armpit to my just-blackening fingertips.

Adrenaline floods my body like nettle stings. "Don't touch me!" I jump up away from him. "You're going to die!" I recoil, leaving the book on the straw, reflexively grabbing my painting towel.

"Edyth, it's going to be all right!" Mason's words are reassuring, but his tone betrays his panic. "I'll take you to the infirmary!"

"No. I'm not going in there!" I turn and run out of the chapel, I don't know where—just away.

With the towel, I wipe and wipe my hands, squeezing meaning out of the cloth—what is this all for, the malachite and terre verte staining my dress, the flecks of gold and ultramarine adhering to my fingertips, flurrying out of my hair? What is the rest of the picture—and how could it be the Divine Will that I should die before I find out?

And after all that, *is* this to be the end of my story?

Orphaned and dying forgotten in some cloister? Who will take care of Alice? And what will happen to Mason? We've shared more than each other's air now.

I may have just killed Mason. Judas, too, was killed with a kiss.

I run down the cloister walk, past the cold calefactory, the barns and stables and the vegetable garden struggling against the weeds. I feel it now, a painful swelling under my arm. I've got to get out. *Out.*

How I never noticed this weathered gray gate before, I don't know. The wall is a good eight feet high, tiled on top with lichen-spotted slates interposed with dark brown-orange mosses. I stare at the burgeoning golds of the trees just outside it. The gate is neglected and striped with ivy vines. If I thought I'd have trouble, I was wrong—the vines aren't holding it shut at all. I manage to shimmy it wide enough to fit through.

My heart heaves out grief and urgency.

I hurl myself through the gate into the clean, round air of the woods, and instantly I step into a different space altogether. Past layers of wet and rotting leaves, unfurling spirals of baby ferns and a pile of discarded pottery shards, it is pristine—different from the brushy woodland of home, like a carpet leading to the forest edge. I jump across the debris and enter the wood.

The forest floor is clear, with no fallen limbs, no brush, no coppiced trees. These are like the columns in the priory church, rising to meet at the upper canopy. There are elm and oak, all great, old giants, knobby and twisted. I can feel them connected under my feet in some vast web, something that's existed before me or my grandparents. Before the Normans and the Romans, even. Maybe these trees were here before there were any people at all, growing as saplings at the very birth of the world. If trees could be people, these would surely be elders.

I look overhead, where the sunlight flickers among the leaves. The colors are constantly changing, but there is a thread of sound pulling me in. I see it before my ears can even hear it, winding through limbs, dodging the falling leaves, wrapping around tree trunks. It floats and curls against the tawny reds and ambers, and the thread becomes a ribbon.

It is distinctly *lapis blue*.

I reach out to the rough bark of an elm in front of me, watching the color follow the contour of the ground into a darker space, like night. I'm deeper in the wood now than anyone should go. And there, in the inky distance, the ribbon widens into the sound of a boiling pot, or of rain on a roof.

I round another craggy oak, and there ahead, shrouded in color, is the most gigantic yew I have ever seen.

I approach the ancient tree; a split right down the middle of its vast trunk shows that the tree is hollow inside, like a cup, full of its own fallen needles. The soil around its base has eroded, exposing roots like flying buttresses anchoring their wooden cathedral. Beneath the roots, a spring bubbles away, clear and clean, a mist rising off its surface. It's *growing*, filling up a recess in the ground and becoming a pool.

The lapis ribbon dives into the pool and beckons me to come. I kneel at the edge and touch the water. It's *warm*. My hands are still covered in blue and gold, and as water meets skin, the colors begin to dissolve and run and meld with the black spidery splotch on my wrist.

I lie on my stomach and plunge my arms right down into the water. I just want to feel this on my skin before I die. I pull off my gown and hose and linen chemise and lower myself in. I only expected it to be as deep as my arms somehow, but I sink straight in like there's no bottom, and scramble up to the surface.

Blissfully I float in the warm water, thinking how strange it is that this place has been here all along, simply waiting for me to find it. I let myself sink to the chin, reach under my armpit and feel the lump. It's the size of an egg now, and I feel two more beside it, like broad beans. I massage the lumps, hoping the water is permeating my skin somehow. Nothing's happening. I don't know why I'm disappointed. I guess it seemed like something should. It's undeniable now: death is coming for me.

What does it all matter? I cup my hands and drink. Chamomile and honey branch out into my body, a sense of spring green unfurling inside me, like honeysuckle blooms juicing themselves through my veins.

Sleepiness overtakes me from treading water, and I climb clumsily out of the pool. The lumps smart terribly, but I tumble out feeling refreshed, warmth permeating my whole being. I find an Edyth-sized space among the roots and nestle silently against the tree to dry off, watching the sun set, dipping for sip after sip of the delicious, sweet, warm water.

— 37 —

It's a moment before twilight when I wake, lying among the roots of the tree. I pull the green gown back over my head and rebraid my hair in a disheveled mess.

But something is different.

I run out of the woods and burst through the gate, past a surprised, bleating goat desperate to be milked, and stop myself short on the threshold of the chapel. Its door is carelessly left open. Mason's on a scaffold working with a fine chisel, putting the finishing touches on a capital ringed with lions that I drew. Again and again he wipes his eyes with his sleeve. My heart breaks for what he must be thinking.

I stand in the doorway until he sees me in his periphery and stops chiseling. He turns his head, and I see tears making dark paths through his dusty cheeks.

"I tried to catch up to you!" he says. "I didn't know where you—"

I motion for him to be quiet and follow me. He grabs a torch, and I swipe a little bucket sitting outside the chapel door.

When we pass through the gate into the woods, I finally address him.

"Mason, I'm sorry I ran away. But it's all clear now. I have to—"

"Edyth, you're not well. You should be in bed. You know what's going to happen."

"I found it!" I grin, running to follow the color through the trees again, until at last we come to the yew tree.

"A spring!" Mason says. "I haven't seen clean water in . . ." He sticks his torch in a knot in the tree trunk, drops to his knees and starts scooping handfuls of water into his mouth.

"It's so *sweet*! And warm, like tea!" He splashes it over his dusty head and face, and laughs with relief.

"It's not just any spring, Mason. Look." I pull my sleeve down off my shoulder and lift my bare arm. "*Look.*"

Mason puts his face right up to my armpit, holds my arm and looks for any trace of the blotches. "But . . ."

"That's right."

"Your arm was turning as black as peat this afternoon."

"I know."

"No one survives this, Edyth. It spares *no one*. Are you sure you don't have the lumps anywhere else?"

"I'm sure," I laugh. "They're completely gone."

Mason stares as I pull my sleeve back on. "Are you telling me—"

"I'm healed, Mason. This is the spring from the book, from my dream. It was right here all along. And it wasn't just about *me* living or dying. It's going to heal everyone."

"I'm sorry," he says, nudging my cheek. "I thought you might be crazy, Edie. The end of the disease is like that." Mason hovers above me, his warm cedar breath surrounding me. Comfort waves off his body like tones of summer. I press into him with my whole body and put my arms around his neck.

"Help me bring this water to the sick," I say earnestly.

Beaming with excitement, we make our plan: Give the water first to Alice, Muriel and Anne, in hopes it might protect them from the disease. Return with larger vessels tomorrow—at midnight, to keep the spring secret. And let this place be *our* sanctuary.

We fill the little bucket to take back with us, and we talk, and drink, and kiss until the first tone of blue dawn reveals the shape of the trees.

The first thing I do is bring a cup to Alice. I write the story on her wax tablet, then tiptoe over to the scriptorium and tell Muriel and Anne about my healing. I don't know if the water will *protect* them from getting sick. They're skeptical, but they listen.

"It's all well and good to read about miracles," says Anne. "I'm just saying I've never seen one."

"Edyth's not the type to make things up," says Muriel.

"Well, I'm sick of warm ale in any case," says Anne. "Let's drink." They clink their cups of water together and drain them to the bottom.

The thrill of last night wears off, and I can't keep myself awake any longer. I know it's urgent that we get water to the infirmary, but we've got to wait until dark. A few hours of sleep in the scriptorium, and I go to the chapel to meet Mason.

"You gave them the water?" Mason confirms as we head back into the wood tonight, this time with bigger containers.

"Alice was all for it. Muriel and Anne didn't believe me at first. But they drank it anyway."

"Maybe there's a chance for them, then."

Through the columns of ash and elm, past the oaks, our pace picks up to a run. The leaves part alongside us like the Red Sea, sending smears of light blue and lilac along my periphery until we arrive at the grove where the yew tree's arms rise, embracing the sky. Out from the roots of the yew tree, the spring still effervesces. The pool has doubled in size from last night.

"Edyth, come see this!" Mason says from the other side of the yew. He climbs into the tree, and I follow. The expanse inside is as big as my dormitory cell, cool and sheltered.

"You could make a nice little home in here," he says.

"Maybe we'll have to," I respond, sitting on the bed of dry needles. It feels so safe in here. I scoot next to Mason, and he puts his cloak around both of our shoulders. I kiss him without fear. "It's time," I say. "Let's get the water and see what happens."

We kneel by the pool, our knees wet and muddy, filling our buckets. We sit at the edge of the spring and stare at the hazy reflection of the moon, feeling the warmth rising from the water, listening to the crickets and the sounds of the autumn night. But it's still, too still. We can't pretend people aren't dying while we stay here. I move his hand from my waist and squeeze it.

"Let's go."

We pick up our vessels and set off toward the infirmary, walking silently under the waxing moon.

— 38 —

So slowly our feet tread in the autumn leaves, under the woad sky, carrying the water we hope, believe, doubt, plead, will bring life to the dying. It was one thing to give it to Alice, Muriel and Anne—they're quarantined. I'm suddenly sober. This will be the real test.

We squeeze through the gate onto the gravel path, past barns of neglected and wandering livestock, the vegetable garden tangled with vines, the orchard dropping its fruits.

On our left is the doleful song of the nuns in the church, doors closed against corruption, breathing their psalms against the foul air of pestilence, hoping in that big boat of stone to get safely to the other shore with their souls intact.

On the right is the infirmary, emanating with the moans of those under the sentence of death, breathing their pleas to someone, anyone: the Blessed Mother; their earthly mothers; their spiritual Mother, the prioress.

We stand in the open pathway, in the space between.

"Mason," I say, slowing a little, "if this doesn't work, if my own healing was only a coincidence, then we're walking right into the mouth of death."

"Do you want to turn back?" says Mason. "Or maybe give it to the nuns instead?"

"They don't need it in there," I say. "*It's the sick who need a doctor,* remember?"

In the infirmary, every torch is lit down the long gallery of cells. The walls are the deep red of burnished clay, glowing against the beams of the timber roof. I hadn't noticed the row of blue-winged angels painted above the cells, cohorts of commanders, interceding for the sick below. The walls become sootier the closer they rise to the ceiling, but the angels peek glints of light out of deepening darkness.

We duck into the corner by the door and wait. In walks the last person I would have expected: Cook.

"I hear you're short on help, and I'm short on diners," says Cook. "Can you put me to work, Physician?"

Joan stops her ministrations. "It means certain death, Cook."

She sighs. "What choice do I have? I'm going to stand before my Judge one way or the other."

"If you insist," Joan sighs, but I can tell she's glad to have the help. "Now listen, Cook, back when Father Johannes found the first sign of disease on his own skin, he dispensed all of us to hear confession, even give communion to the dying. You do whatever these people need you to do."

"Right," says Cook, crossing herself. "Holy Saint Cook, at your service."

A curtain's pushed aside, and the prioress herself exits a cell. Weak as she is, of course she'd spend the last of her strength here serving the dying. She sees me and Mason standing frozen by the doorway, and draws a deep breath.

"You found what you were looking for," she says, smiling.

I return the smile, holding up a vessel. "It's healing water, Mother. And there's plenty more."

She takes two tin cups from a cabinet and hands them to us. "Draw some, and follow me."

We go with her into the very first cell on the left, the one where Brother

Timothy died. A man is there, naked to the waist, covered in black pustules, his skin purple against his whitish-yellow hair. He's clutching at his chest, gasping for breath and coughing out blood. His fingertips look like they've been dipped in liquid coal; his eyes are frenzied.

The prioress takes a clay cup from the table at his bedside and holds it out to me. I pour the water into it. She sits on the edge of the bed and fearlessly slides her arm under the bare, seeping shoulders of the sick man. She holds the cup to his cracked white mouth and says softly,

O omnes sitientes, venite ad aquas.

All you who are thirsty, come to the waters.

The man drinks and licks his lips. The wildness in his eyes softens into something more like frightened confusion; he looks at the prioress as she lays him back down, like a child being put to bed after a nightmare. She washes her hands in a basin of cloudy water and dries them as she walks over to the table in the middle of the room.

"Now you do it," she says to me, and walks away to tend to other responsibilities.

But I'm frozen to the spot. This is the moment where it all becomes real. Mason urges me on with a nod.

Somehow my feet pull me heavily on toward the next cell. I draw the curtain slowly and slip it into the bracket on the wall. There's an entire family in here. A husband sits on the bed with his wife's head in his lap. She's unconscious and in much the same state as the first man was. There on the floor lie two little ones on a pile of dirty straw, writhing and mewling like kittens. Their parents are powerless to help them. The father is only moderately better than the rest of his family. All he can do is watch them die, and wait for his own death to progress.

I reach over to the little side table and pick up their cup. Tin clatters against clay as I pour out the water with trembling hands. I offer it to the father, who's the only one capable of receiving it, but he points to his children, that they should drink first. I kneel on the ground, and as I saw the prioress do, I slide my arm underneath the shoulders of the younger child.

She can't be more than four—the age at which parents start breathing a little easier for a child having survived the perils of childhood. The girl's mouth gapes open. She has a row of perfect baby teeth. Her eyes are half shut. I put the cup to the girl's bottom lip and she instinctively closes her mouth around its rim.

O omnes sitientes, venite ad aquas.

And I relax into the compassion I feel for this child. Since the sick can't go to the waters, I'll bring the waters to them. All they have to do is drink.

Mason and I give water to the pilgrims until the containers are dry, and I feel buoyed by hope. By dawn, the infirmary has fallen silent. Cook slumps in her chair; Joan has her head down on the table, sleeping for perhaps the first time in days. The prioress is curled up on a pallet outside a cell.

Joan wakes up, rubbing her eyes with the heels of her hands, and immediately begins writing on her wax tablet as though jotting down a dream. Mason and I look in the cells, and most of the patients are either sleeping peacefully, their chests rising and falling in easy rhythms, or sitting up, stunned by the peace they feel.

Despite our own exhaustion, Mason and I make our way to the door with our now-empty buckets. We pass the first cell, where the man with the frenzied eyes had been so near death. He's sitting cross-legged on the bed with his back against the wall, staring up at the light beginning to come through the window. His skin still has the memory of purple, but the lumps have receded, and his hands, folded in his lap, are no longer tipped in black. His lips move in silent prayer as tears drip down his pale beard.

He's made it through the night, and must now face the day alone.

I awake to a soft knock on the scriptorium door sometime in the afternoon, after sleeping all day.

"It's me," says Mason's careful voice. I get up and open the door. My eyes are still puffy; I blink a few times to unblur Mason's face.

"You have to come."

"Where?" I ask, still shaking off my sleep.

"The infirmary. You have to see this." He takes my hand and we hurry noiselessly down the stairs. I haven't even put on my shoes.

When we get to the infirmary, it's bustling and noisy, but not with the death throes of the night before. People are laughing and crying. The couple with the two small children are unapologetically kissing in the middle of the gallery as their children play at their feet. Not a few are kneeling and weeping in loud prayers of gratitude.

They are all alive.

The prioress leaves the woman whose confession she's hearing and greets me and Mason at the door. Her face is gray and tired, but her smile is euphoric. She grasps me by the shoulders, wanting to say something but not finding the words. She simply nods her head in approval.

"*Ave!*" she shouts, and claps, turning to the crowd. "Your lives have been restored to you. Now you have a task to do. You must go down to the town and search for those who still live and tell them to come here. You all must leave this place and return to your own homes and towns and begin again. Gather your belongings and go!"

"But the gate—"

"Am I not still prioress here? I will unlock the gate myself. *Go home!*"

Some of the pilgrims don't seem to recognize me; they were too close to death, the disease having penetrated too far into their brains. But those who do recall me holding the cup of honeyed water to their lips come and kiss my hand as they leave.

The infirmary clears out. Joan and Cook and the Pri set about changing out the hay and bedclothes. We know what work awaits us tonight.

— 39 —

Autumn's coming in as dry as summer's been wet. The peas and beans should have been harvested weeks ago, but the vines lie shriveled in the field, foraged by pigs and goats that have quickly reverted to their feral natures. The nuns in the church refuse to come out to eat, but it's just as well with food this scarce, the water from the cloister fountain running in a cloudy trickle. Still, they fast, and they cry, and when I visit Alice, I watch them sitting in the sanctuary corners staring in despair.

But the water from the yew's roots is working, night after night delivering people from their slide into death.

We enter the woods under the curled russet parchments of the great oaks, listening to the acorns beat against one another like seashells, dense and hollowed. Mason lugs a leather sack on his back and a wooden bucket in each hand. I carry the wooden yoke across my shoulders.

"I have a surprise for you," says Mason as we round the corner to the yew tree.

"Mason!" I gasp. "What's this?"

Around the pool, Mason's put in a pavement of smoothly dressed stones, smuggled from the chapel, so we can sit without getting muddy. Four steps lead down into the pool. A small channel collects water in a stone basin for drinking or filling vessels before it runs off into a longer channel away from the spring.

"I took a break from the chapel and worked on this instead," he says. "And there's one finishing touch."

I stand in the water on the second step with my hands on my hips, watching Mason and enjoying the warmth seeping into my bare feet. He slings off the sack and reveals what's inside.

It is a small memorial stone, a pointed arch framing a carved re-creation of the page from the Gospel book. He slides it into place against the yew tree, opposite the steps where I'm standing.

I get out and embrace him. "You trusted me. Even in all this chaos."

"To think, this spring was here all along, but who else would have found it in time?"

"I just decided to listen and say yes, that's all."

"Maybe you're actually a saint," he teases. "Maybe you'll levitate next. You'll float up into the stars, and I'll have to hold your skirts to pull you back down to earth." We both laugh and trade legends of improbable saintly phenomena. We grow quiet, letting the after-laugh wash over us. We pray. We hold each other close before it's time to fill our buckets and go back. Here, in this nest on the top of a little Yorkshire mountain, we feel free.

"There's not much left to do in the chapel," he says. "Now that I'm not digging as many graves, I've been able to put up more wooden scaffolds. Once I'm done with the capitals, I can collect my pay—and probably haggle for the pay of the other builders, who . . . ah . . . didn't make it."

I turn to him, scandalized. "Mason, that's awful! You can't take money from dead people."

"I did the work of several men, and dug their graves, Edie. *A worker's worth his wages.*"

"You're right," I admit.

"After I get paid, though," he continues, "I want to leave. Together."

"I can't leave yet, Mason. I have to see this through. Not just the water, but I've got to get Alice out, somehow. That hasn't changed."

"There's nothing saying you have to be the one to give the water, though, is there? Can't you tell someone else where it is? Like Joan? Now that it's got a marker, they can find it easily."

"No. Absolutely not. Can you imagine *Agnes* finding it—or Felisia? If the prioress dies, Agnes will take over, and I don't know what she'd do with something like miraculous healing water."

He looks disheartened. I know what he's thinking—he's scared that I've entrenched myself here, that I won't leave the priory with him after all.

"Let's start back," he says as the shadows turn purple. "We've stayed too long."

We emerge through the last grove of trees, and the priory reappears downhill. Suddenly we hear the leaves *shush* some distance away.

It's the Anti-Pri. And there's nowhere for us to hide.

Agnes has been in the forest, too. She's thin and pale, her habit dusty and her veil disheveled. She advances quickly toward me and Mason, gripping a basket of long blue flower cuttings in one hand, a pair of shears in the other.

"Sub-Prioress," I greet her, bowing my head. "We were just—"

"You two," she says accusingly, pointing the shears at us. "*This* is the evil that has brought this holy house low. You and your secret sin. I knew it had to be you, wicked, vile creature." She puts down her basket and throws the shears on top.

"I don't know what you mean." I try to pass but Agnes blocks the way. Water sloshes in the buckets hanging from my yoke.

"We are dying in the church, and your infirmary is sending people dancing out of the priory gate," she says. "Why is that, do you think?"

"Maybe Joan found the right tincture," I lie.

"See how she speaks to authority," she says into the air. "This is why you don't let them rise above their estate. Probably not even *baptized*. But what's to be expected from the child of cursed parents?"

"Edyth, let's go," says Mason. He tries to lead me around her, toward the gate. "She's starved. She's delirious."

"You'd think you'd be loyal," says Agnes, her tone changing slightly to something like pity. "To the priory. To me. *I* helped you to rise. The prioress never would have known about you otherwise. I did everything I could to lift you out of your pathetic state. From a *conversa*, a nothing!"

"You didn't do anything for me," I fume. "You hated me from the moment you met me! You only wanted me in the scriptorium so you wouldn't feel so bad about leaving it yourself. You beat me like a *dog*!"

"You see! This! This is what comes from heresy," says Agnes, wagging her finger in my face, her breath sour. "Pushing the boundaries, until you're fornicating in the woods like pagans!"

Mason puts his body between us. "You hypocrite!" he rebukes Agnes. "You want to talk about secret sin? Let's talk about yours. The proof is right there in your basket. Monkshood. You're a *murderer*!"

He kicks the basket and sends the stems flying. Agnes stumbles back as though someone's shoved her, and now I see how thin she's become, how dark the bags under her eyes as she holds Mason's gaze. She knows that if she says anything about us, we will expose her.

"Ha," she finally sniffs, sizing up Mason from bottom to top. "What does a vagrant like *you* know about *me*?" She picks up the empty basket, fishes in the leaves for her shears and makes her way to the forest gate.

She'll never face justice for her slow murder of the prioress or Alice's entrapment. The image of my father flashes, hung from a bridge with no recourse to a trial, murdered by his own townspeople on a flimsy accusation. With the world in such turmoil, true justice is the first thing to go.

"She won't say a word about us," says Mason. "We're going to make this right. We're going to get Alice out."

The infirmary is filled with the agonized cries of the sick, who queue out the door and into the churchyard. The sound of a baby's anguished wail makes me instantly crumple and put down my yoke clumsily, splashing the healing water on the gravel. Mason puts his buckets down and leads me away, over toward the north wall of the priory enclosure.

"Give yourself a minute," he says. The moon shimmers in the river below, the water there anything but clear. He puts his arms around me and holds me as I weep.

All of a sudden, his head perks up and he lets go of me.

"Look down there," he says. "What is that?" He points toward the distance, to one of the churches in town.

I squint at the light glowing from the windows of Saint Mary's. It's hard to make it out all the way across the river, but we hear shouts, and they're definitely coming from the church.

"I wonder what's going on down there," he says as we walk back to get our buckets.

"Let's hope whatever it is stays in Thornchester." I take a deep breath and take up my yoke. "Right, I think I'm ready."

He kisses my shoulder. "Come on," he says. "We have a long night ahead of us."

We go to work, giving water to the sick. Three patients died before we arrived; nothing could be done for them. Mason wraps them and lays them in the churchyard. But we give the drink, listen to confessions, hold the crying, pray with the devastated.

There's one man, at the end of the gallery, whose voice rises above the din and suffering. He's shouting obscenities and shaking the furniture in the tiny cell. No one can come near him. We're only glad he doesn't rage through the whole room.

"I don't even know why I'm here!" he hollers. "It would have been better to die alone in my own bed!" The man paces, covered in sores, tearing at his own hair.

Mason takes a tin cup and fills it with the spring water. "Sir, drink this. It will help," he says, gesturing at the rest of the people. "See how the others are beginning to improve even now. Take—"

The man thrusts his hand out and hits the cup, sending it spiraling into the air. It lands on the ground, ringing like a bell, and the healing water absorbs into the porous brick floor.

The prioress gets up from her pallet and approaches the man to comfort him. He grabs her by the shoulders and shouts in her face: "Get out of here with your goddamned potions and let me be!"

He shoves her, hard, to the ground. Several pilgrims come to her aid and help her up as the man staggers down the long gallery, running his arm along the length of the table and knocking pottery and remedies to the floor on his way out.

In the morning, the man is found dead on the gatehouse threshold.

— 40 —

This man will need to be buried. So will the ones who died before they could get the water, and that'll mean digging a new trench, but Mason's the only builder left alive at the priory. He and I go down to Thornchester to see if he can persuade anyone to help him bury these poor people.

It's far worse than the last time I came down here, and I have to brace myself to keep from retching. Bodies are everywhere in various states of decay. Dogs drag limbs they've scavenged from the streets. Two pigs wrestle over a piece of flesh wrapped in cloth.

Stumbling down the deserted high street comes a band of seven men, singing bawdy songs, piss-drunk and filthy, seemingly oblivious to the death and stench all around them. So we force ourselves to play along.

"Hey!" says Mason. "Having a good time?"

They explode into uproarious laughter.

"A good time?" says the biggest man. "It's the end of the feckin' world, brother! We aim to fall right off the edge!"

"Apparently the taverns are still open. Do you fine lords want to earn some more drinking money?" Mason proposes.

"What do you have in mind?" slurs the ringleader. One of them trips and falls into the mud, smashing his cheek against the ground. He doesn't get up. No one helps him.

"Up at the priory, there's some digging to be done," Mason tells them.

"Bodies, you mean."

"Yes."

"We've done that kind of work. Not worth it."

"And you're not sick?" I say. "Must mean you're some of the lucky ones. You'll be able to *enjoy* your pay."

"And you know those nuns are rich." Mason has to say that, even though neither of us has any idea where the priory stores money, nor whether the Pri will give it to us. This stops them and makes them consider it, though.

"I'll come," says a thin fellow in a yellow shirt.

"Sure, me too," says a grizzled man with what looks like dried vomit on his sleeve. Finally the ringleader coaxes all six into coming, and they stumble up the hill to the priory with us.

Men like this would normally never see the inside of a priory. I convince them at least to splash their faces in the cloister fountain. They don't notice the scenery, in any case.

"Is it true?" says the yellow-shirted man. "About the healing waters? Fella came through from the East Riding talking of the young girl who's not afraid, like the Savior Himself, to touch poor lepers."

Mason gazes at me, eyebrows raised, and I laugh it away. "What," I say, "the girl with rabbit-skin glue under her fingernails and a bucket of water by the infirmary door?" It's funny, but strange, to think you exist to people outside of your own four walls.

While the men extend the trench in the churchyard, I go into the infirmary to talk to the Pri about getting them paid. At first I don't see her; another group of pilgrims have trickled in, seeking a cure, and it's busy. Maybe she's hearing confession or giving the Sacrament. Finally I find her, but not ministering.

She's in a bed all the way in back, drenched in sweat, no veil, wearing only her shift. She can't bear anything to touch her, not even a blanket. When she sees me, she waves me in.

"Mother," I say, "let me get you the water."

"No," she says. "It's not for me. This is not the pestilence; you know that."

"But who says it's only good for the pestilence?"

"No, Edyth. Let this unfold as it should. I've made provisions. Remember what I said—fear kills, but it won't win." She lays her head down again and falls asleep.

The prioress must see the frustration on my face. Why won't she drink the water? Doesn't she know that if she dies, Agnes will take over the priory?

After the men dig the trench, I get them paid and fed, and we show them to the gatehouse, with barely enough daylight left for them to find their way back to town. But as we step onto the main path, we hear a grisly sound.

It's all chaos and orange sparks and billows—a jumble of shouts and chants and howling. We had locked the gates when we returned from town, but the dull red pounding of bodies thrusting against them makes the lock give way, and the doors fling wide on a wild procession.

There is a boy of about twelve right at the front, carrying a cross made of hazel poles. Behind him, three other boys bear torches at full flame. Following them are *hundreds* of men, walking two by two. They are stripped half naked, their white robes rolled down around their waists and trailing down to the ground like upside-down lilies. They're yowling a pitiful song of penance—

> *Dilexisti malitiam super benignitatem*
> *Iniquitatem magis quam loqui aequitatem.*
>
> *Behold, I was brought forth in iniquity*
> *And in sin did my mother conceive me.*

—and in their hands they hold leather whips.

Thwop. Thwop.

They are beating their own backs bloody.

My head swims, and I shut my eyes against the nausea and shock. I've heard of monks doing things like this in secret, but everyone knows it's shameful.

A lot of fat men trying to make themselves feel better about their gluttony, Da would say.

The Lord already shed His own blood, Mam would say. *Why try to add to it?*

The men come in, tearing at their flesh with the whips—and then, as though they're given a signal, the whole line of them hits the ground prostrate and spreads their arms out wide on the ground like living crosses, still singing. From the rear of the line, the last two men stand, pick up their flails and begin stepping over each man in front of them, a whip to each back, and they become first in line.

The procession completely blocks the bridge, the only way out of the priory without going upriver. There's nothing to do but stand aside and try to slip past them once they all come in.

"Who are they?" Mason asks the diggers' ringleader. "Were they the ones in Saint Mary's the other night?"

"They took over that church all week."

"Why did they come to the priory?" I ask.

"Guess those bloodsuckers ran out of donations," says the man. "They pick up desperate stragglers in every town. I think there's double the number that came into Thornchester. Murdered the priest."

The priest—he didn't make it out after all.

The sight of two hundred men beating themselves to a pulp is shocking enough. But all along the edges are women, shrieking like fanatics. They reach out their hands to the grisly men, get a palmful of blood and call out while smearing it across their own faces—

O holy man of God, pray for me!
Just a touch of the hem of your garment will heal me!
Say the word, O anointed, and I will be healed!

—starving for someone to tell them how they might escape wrath. We lean against the high wall flanking the gatehouse, but there's no escaping the notice of the agitated crowd. Suddenly the men at the front of the throng turn their attention toward the gravediggers. The new leader points his flail at them.

"Sons of the devil," he says, "with drink on their breath in this holy place, at the very time they should be killing their flesh!"

Mason and I duck into a recess in the wall at just the right moment to avoid the fate of the hired diggers, watching with horror as the mob descends, and beats all six of them to death.

The men's hysterical shouts reach a crescendo and the church doors swing open. There stands Agnes de Guile and, right by her side, the Dragon. The blaze of the church candles and the torches in the procession turn the nuns into silhouettes and specters.

"*Ave*, favored ones," says Agnes, her voice loud and hoarse. "Our prophetess told us you would come. You honor us. You are most welcome. Come share your message with the faithful here. The dormitory and guesthouse are no longer occupied. You may spend as long as you wish."

"That's not hers to offer," I whisper to Mason, thinking of the prioress, still clinging to life in the infirmary.

The boys at the front of the procession part to the side, and the first two men approach, kneeling before Agnes on the church steps. She holds out a thin hand and lets them kiss it.

"Come and bless my humble flock. Come, come. And the holy women, too," she says. "I am Prioress Agnes de Guile."

— 41 —

*A*gnes de Guile—*the prioress of Saint Christopher's.*

The sick probability of that rolls around in my aching head as I wake in the chapel. As the real prioress fades, I know it will soon be true in more than just Agnes's imagination.

The weather's turned at last. It's been snowing and melting for days, and a veil of fog hangs so thick, I have to feel for the walls of the buildings. This damp air can't be good to breathe, and I think of sick travelers as I wrap my cloak tighter and blow in my hands, scrunching my toes in my shoes. When I get to the infirmary, I kick something on the doorstep. I look down—it's the foot of a dead man.

The man is covered in a light dusting of snow. His legs are bare, as is his chest, blood frozen into slush. Only a rolled-down linen tunic covers the rest of him. He's one of the penitents from the church—and he has the marks of the disease. Mason and I lug his body to the new trench in the back of the churchyard. Did someone dispose of him here? Or did he come seeking the water?

That night, as we're giving the drink, two men and a nun pound on the door. The nun is Mary, the library apprentice.

"We seek refuge, please," they tell me. "We want to see the physician, privately."

"If they're not sick, there's no room," calls Joan dispassionately from a cell.

"Not from the illness," they tell her. "From Agnes de Guile."

Joan comes to the door and leans in close. "What is going on in the church?"

"Chaos," says Mary. "We're starving to death from fasting. Men are losing blood from beating themselves, and the women are doing it, too."

Cook immediately tends to the emaciated visitors with bread and soup of wild leeks.

"But where are the bodies?" asks Mason.

"They've been putting the bodies down in the crypt," says a stout man with a thin swatch of blond hair. "Prioress Agnes says if they die, it's because they were sinners, and they're not worthy to be buried in consecrated ground. But we don't believe that anymore. And some've brought the pestilence with them, but they won't admit it."

Mary speaks. "That man you found on the doorstep—Agnes told us he was cursed because he left the church to come here for a cure. They're planning something against the infirmary because of Edyth and her 'magic water.' She says the infirmary is a haven for sorcery."

"Sorcery!" Joan erupts. "I'm the one in here up to my elbows in shit and piss, while they're over there beating each other to death to please some other god they created in their own image. Which one of those is more like *sorcery*?" She slams down her pestle and paces the floor.

Now I'm nervous. If Agnes is planning something against me, I want to be behind the barred door of the chapel with Mason and his collection of hammers.

The next morning, I awake to the sound of Joan screaming.

On the infirmary doorstep are two more victims.

Muriel and Anne.

Pages from our precious manuscript are pinned to their chests, blood converging with paint and obscuring the sacred words. Unbound pages flutter gold and silver and blue through the air, parchment scrolls torn and rolling across the snow and sticking to my paralyzed body.

Mason runs over. "No, no!" he moans. "Edyth! I thought they locked themselves in!"

The ringing in my ears drowns every other sound in a wash of gray. I don't know what to think or feel; their bodies seem unreal, like sculptures, their clothes nothing more than marble drapery.

"They weren't even sick," I mutter in shock. "They kept themselves hidden this whole time, living on grains of barley. They never missed prayers."

"Let us help," says one of the defectors. "We are also illuminators, from York Minster. We knew this scribe before she came to this priory."

We lay my friends down in the churchyard, and all I can do is stare at them. It's when we go up to the scriptorium that the stun wears off—something breaks in me and I begin to wail.

The whole room is torn apart. Muriel and Anne's food stores are ransacked. Blood-smeared parchments are strewn everywhere. The muslin sheet between the grinding room and scribes' room is torn down, and pigment dust floats and falls in puddles of water from the broken magnifying flasks. The bookcase doors are thrown open, but only a handful of books remain.

I look through the door into the library. "Where are all the books? I gave a few to Alice, but where are the rest?"

"Prioress de Guile has declared them heretical," says Mary. "That was the final straw for me. I knew I had to get out of there."

"Stop calling her *prioress*," I seethe. "The real one isn't even dead yet."

We gather a roll of loose parchments and the rest of the books. I cobble together my supplies and put what's left of the folios I did with Muriel and Anne into a leather folder. It's far thicker than I thought—this really was going to be a proper book.

I'll keep working on it, for you, Muriel and Anne, I vow.

"This will end," Mason says, "and then we'll find the books."

The risk to get to Alice is growing greater by the hour, but I need to tell her what's happening. It feels even more important now to make sure she's protected.

"Alice," I whisper, my face right against the wall opening, "I brought food, and a clean dress, and a sheepskin to lie on—it's getting cold. But you already know that in here, my God!"

Alice crawls toward the window on all fours. "You don't know what it means to me that you came, Edyth. When these new people started with their frenzies, I thought, *That's it, I'm dead.* I commended my soul and waited to die."

"I wouldn't have let that happen, my friend. We're working on a plan to get you out. We need more time, but we will."

Thwop. The sound of whipping begins again.

"I have to go, Alice. But I'm not leaving you," I promise, reaching my hand through the window.

"Thank you, Edyth. Thank you for everything." She presses my hand to her lips and can barely bring herself to let go.

"Wait for me, Alice. I won't fail you."

I close the back door just in time to hear the voices starting to shout.

— 42 —

All night, Mason and I have been kept up by the tumult coming from the church. The men's shouting, the singsong voice of a preacher, the wail of the Dragon. We try in vain to ignore it. Eventually we fall asleep, with the door barred, of course.

But then there's the steady *thwop. Thwop.* I keep biting my cheek in my half sleep, tasting blood. And all night, rigid yellow bars roll in time to the rhythm, from left to right across the inside of my eyelids.

Before dawn I startle awake, disoriented, to a sound that has become unfamiliar.

"Is that the bell for prime?" I ask. We get up and say our prayers but can't concentrate for the mournful singing and another bout of loud preaching. The rhythm starts again—

Thwop. Thwop.

I think of the prioress. If she were well, what would she want me to do?

"Mason."

"Yes."

"I want to go into the church. I want to take them the water."

"Edyth, you heard what Agnes said about you! And you saw what those men are capable of, with Anne and Muriel, the diggers—they won't even want what you have to offer. You want to walk right into the belly of that beast?"

I'm resolute. "It's one thing to help our neighbors. We did that. But what about our enemies? They're running out of water in the fountain, anyway. We can't let them die of thirst."

Mason shakes his head. "I don't like it. It's not safe!"

"Well, I'd rather be fearless than safe. We can't let people die without a chance, even if we're on opposite sides."

He sighs in frustration. "Tonight, then? After the infirmary?"

"We'll do it."

We fill the buckets to the brim with the steaming water. I hitch mine to the yoke, and Mason wraps burlap around each handle of his. We hoist them and walk back toward the priory gate. The bright moon's got just a sliver shaved off its side. We drink in the quiet as we walk, knowing what tumult awaits us inside the priory walls. When we get to the gate, I put down my yoke.

"Mason, I have to be honest. I know this was what I was supposed to do. I don't doubt that for a minute. But even with all those people who've been healed from this pestilence, I ask myself every night, *What if this time it doesn't work?*"

"Edyth," he says gently. "You were as good as dead, and now look at you."

"I know, but what if it only works for a time? Do you have to *keep* drinking it? We drink it every night, so we're all right. What if all those people leave healed, only to get sick again and die on the road home?"

"You're right," says Mason. "There's no denying that possibility. But we'll all die someday."

"You sound like my da," I say. "I think he believed there were things worse than dying."

"Do you think that's true? What's worse?"

"To die with regret. To know you could've done something good, and instead chose to say no." We don't speak for a minute. "How about you? What's the worst you can think of, Mason?"

"To die alone," he answers immediately. "Without you."

"You won't." I wrap my arms around his waist. "We won't miss our chance again."

"When we're done with this task, I think we'll know it, Edie. We're going to get this water into the church, and we're going to get Alice out. And then I want to leave. I want to get the hell out of this place."

"I do, too." I step closer until there is only a breath between us. "I only wish it hadn't taken us so long to figure it out."

Mason kisses me urgently. I shoulder the yoke again, and he follows me through the gate.

Joan is sitting at the long infirmary table, writing furiously on a tablet. She's not well. As I look closer, I see her neck is covered in lumps, like quail eggs under the skin. I slowly sit beside her—I don't want to cause panic.

"Not you!" I whisper to Joan. "Hasn't the water helped?"

"Edyth, I haven't drunk the water, and I won't. I need to see if there's a medicinal cure. My specialty is medicine, not miracles. So far, it's been eight days since I noticed the signs on me, and I'm still here. Remember what I always say? *It probably won't kill you—*"

"*—but holler if you see Saint Peter.*"

"Well, I'm close to understanding this," she insists. "Let the pilgrims have the water. Go on. Tend to them. Let me write."

Mason and I continue to the last cell. Cook is seated at the prioress's bedside with her back to us, dabbing a cold, wet cloth on the sick woman's forehead, but Cook yields her place to me. Prioress Margaret's black habit hangs on a peg on the wall, and her bony feet hang over the edge of the bed. They look abnormally large compared to her thin frame. She clutches a small wooden cross to her breast. She looks so little, like an elderly child, like I could pick her up and lift her above my head.

"Oh no, Venerable Mother!" I say. "I have fresh water—it will heal you!"

"Sometimes we are beyond healing of the body, Edyth. But I do not need that water." She puts a thin hand on my cheek. "I have been given the drink I need.

"Do you know how good a pomegranate tastes, Edyth?" says the dying woman. "Have you ever seen one?"

"No, Mother, only in paintings."

The prioress falls into a fit of coughing. I immediately hold the rag to her mouth until it subsides.

"I used to have lots of them when I was a child," she continues. "I could pluck one up from the bowl whenever I wanted, break it open, roll the seeds out to stain my fingers like blood and run after my little brother as though I was a murderer. He would shriek and hide behind my mother, and I would pop the seeds in my mouth and feign total ignorance."

The prioress chuckles and forgets her pain for a moment. But she grows quiet again.

"I know nothing of games and intrigue beyond that, Edyth. I wasn't always locked up here in this place, you know. It wasn't my first choice, just like it wasn't yours. I was destined to be a noble lady. I was one, long ago. I had children, a husband. I had long, golden hair," she says, reaching up and picking at the scraggly white ends.

"I think you're beautiful," I say. "Like my own mam."

"But I found myself alone, like you, Edyth. And then I, too, heard a call to be part of something bigger than I could have dreamed. Something far more ancient than simply being the leader of this great priory. No—what some call *power* is nothing more than a cheap bauble. It had to unfold like this, and I could not interfere. Mine was simply the call to clear the path. For *you*."

The prioress beckons me closer, and I lean in. She looks acutely at me, her eyes losing their blue intensity.

"I've heard about what's going on in the church," she says. "We are infected with much more than pestilence. Don't believe those *fools*. They'll beat themselves right into hell. But what good is that? Look *up* instead, and follow the call to *the most excellent way*."

Her voice rattles.

"The world is about to be shipwrecked, Edyth. Be strong. Trust your vision."

She braces herself hard against me and closes her eyes. All the air rushes from her lungs, and she is gone.

At dawn, Mason digs the prioress's grave under the yew in the churchyard, in a plot chosen years before when she made her final vows, lying on the cold stone before the altar, marrying herself to death and love.

Joan leads the office for the dead, with the infirmary nuns and pilgrims assembled. As we part, she calls me aside and presses something into my hand. It's Prioress Margaret's seal. Her name has been burnished out. And on it is inscribed a new name.

— 43 —

There's one last pilgrim needing the water before Mason and I attempt to bring it to the church. In this cell lies another of the whippers, delirious, pleading for clemency. I slide my arm under his neck, lift the cup to his lips and recite—

> *O omnes sitientes, venite ad aquas*

—just as a heavy fist pounds on the door, startling me into spilling the water down his neck.

Joan keeps working, stirring the juniper tar over a brazier. "No more pilgrims," she grouses. "Please, Lord, have *mercy*."

Mason opens the door, and before he can stop her, Agnes de Guile stumbles in, bedraggled and soaking, her hands black, her neck covered in sores.

Joan steps out from behind the table, shocked to see her. "Agnes." Her address is firm but soothing.

"I hear Margaret suffers no more," she says calmly, holding out her hand, as though expecting Joan to kiss her ring. "I am happy to assume my office as prioress."

Joan's face is a mixture of disgust and pity. "Agnes, you're dying. Come, take a bed. I don't think you'll be assuming any office today."

"No one has cared for Saint Christopher's like I have," she rambles. "Margaret could not steer the ship."

I can't hold my peace. "Is that why you poisoned her?"

"Poison?" says Agnes, seeming genuinely surprised, her voice even and soft. "Did someone poison the prioress? Is this true, Joan? Let that person be cursed!"

Is she lying? Or delirious? *Can it be that she doesn't remember her own crime?*

"God help her," Joan says, bewildered. "Agnes, look at you. You are about to succumb to the Judgment yourself. There's still time to repent. Here—take the waters." She procures a cup for Agnes and reaches out to give it to her. Agnes looks at it with disgust, and her tone changes completely.

"You might want to think about repenting, yourself," she hisses, her yellow tooth flashing. "And everyone else in here with you."

Agnes throws open the doors. A throng of men and women wait for her, flailing their backs and howling. She leads them away to the church.

"That's it, Mason," I say. "It's time!" I head toward the rear door of the infirmary.

"What about the water?" he calls.

"Not the water. Hammers. We're breaking Alice out *now*."

In the chapel, I grab two of his smaller hammers, and Mason shoulders his tool satchel and another full-sized sledge.

We crash through the church door and are immediately confronted with the odor of old death. This beautiful sanctuary is completely defiled. The floor is smeared and puddled with congealed blood. Benches are overturned. Nuns and whippers shout frenzied prayers. Rats scurry across the sanctuary, right at the feet of Agnes, who has slumped herself onto the prioress's oaken throne.

"What do you have to say for yourself, demon?" demands Agnes, wild-eyed and frothing at me. "What kind of sorcery were you working on those pilgrims?"

I stand silent in the doorway, and she rushes at me, undaunted by the two heavy hammers I carry, and strikes me on the mouth. "Answer me!" she yells.

I don't care. There is only one thing to be done.

I push past Agnes into the ambulatory, raise my hammer and smash it into the wall of Alice's enclosure. She screams.

"Stand back, Alice," Mason calls, not stopping his swing, "we're breaking you out of there!" No one dares come near us as we beat at the stone. Many of the whippers scatter, spilling out of the doors in terror.

"Is anyone with you?" Alice shouts. "Edyth?"

"I'm here, Alice. It's over. Everything's over." My face reddens and I rage against the wall, completely enveloped in the fire of my anger. The stone cracks and begins to crumble down, dust mixing with blood on the floor, on our scratched hands.

"Stand back," Mason repeats, reaching into the hole we've made. He pulls stones crashing to the marble floor, sending bits of mosaic in every direction. "This was easier than I thought," he says. "She never did ask for mortar."

He lifts the hammer and breaks off the most precarious pieces.

The wall is down.

Alice stands in the corner, clutching her blanket. Her skin is pale as skimmed milk, dark caverns under her eyes, lips almost disappeared. And surrounding her on every side, reaching up to the window, are books—the entire inventory of the priory library is in the cell with Alice Palmer.

"It's all here," she says. "Muriel and Anne—they brought them to me before they got caught."

"What about—" I start to ask.

She holds up the one book I was most concerned about. The Gospel book.

"I brought it to her," says Mason. "I knew she'd keep it safe."

I reach into my fitchet pocket and hand Alice the seal. "Prioress Margaret wanted you to have this."

Alice turns over the seal and reads the name.

Prioress Alice Palmer.

Suddenly Agnes bellows, pointing to the wall. "Look what you've done! What makes you think you can come to our priory, a nobody, and create all this chaos?"

"*Me?*" I'm astounded. "Open your eyes, Agnes! Your fear cost people their lives!"

"Fear? What could I possibly have to fear?"

Agnes staggers toward the prioress's throne, but I run and cut her off.

"Your name was in that book, too, Agnes!" I shout. "You saw that comet before the Great Famine. You knew something was coming, that you were being called, but you ignored the vision. And people died because of you!"

Agnes stumbles again and falls, crawling away toward the dragon's nest—and begins to weep.

"Yes, people died, Edyth! People I *loved*."

She's so weak, so sick, so small there on the floor. I walk slowly toward her with one question burning in my mind. "Who died, Sub-Prioress?"

"My little . . . my little boy," she murmurs.

I crouch beside her. "And what happened to your little boy?"

She looks me full in the face, like a confessor, as though there's no history between us, and for the first time I see something like life behind her eyes. And that life is in agony.

"I was young, so young," she manages. "A widow, with no recourse. I sent my baby away, to another family, and I came here and took my vows. But the famine came, and the family couldn't feed him, so they dumped him back here and left. He used to play in the chapel . . . he used to hide . . . under the altar. . . ."

"Agnes," I ask carefully, "did your little boy . . . die in the chapel fire?"

She pauses, then dissolves completely. Sobs rack her wasted body. Even after everything she's done to me, I don't want to see her suffer. I wish, for a moment, that I had been alive then to be a friend to her, to let the young Agnes cry in my arms.

"That's why you took Felisia under your wing," I say softly. "Because she was burned. You felt like you failed, didn't you? Your son, the vision, all those people who starved."

She sits suddenly upright. "*Failed?*" she fumes. "Tell that to God! He failed *me*. He left me to suffer with the trances, the visions, this *curse*." She beats herself on the head with both fists. "No, I didn't find 'the answer' in time. *I* had to fight the battle myself. And I prevailed."

"You *prevailed?*" I stand over her pitiful, diminished form. "But you cursed your own gift. You lost a son—and raised a Dragon."

Felisia rises indignant from the straw. "Is this how you speak to the prioress?" she demands.

"She's not the prioress," I challenge the Dragon, "and you are no prophet! You're frauds! Murderers!" The hair on my arms stands on end, the hot words steaming, echoing off the sanctuary walls. And then, except for the occasional crashing of loose stone, the sanctuary goes silent, and I follow the collective gaze of the penitents to Agnes's body.

She is lying across the confession stool, a freshly lit votive candle in her hand setting fire to the sleeve of her habit. The disease has taken her life at last.

The Dragon, covered with dust, blood oozing from the lash stripes under her gray dress, turns to me and begins to holler, joined by the shouts of men and the exhausted cries of women. She staggers toward me, eyes ablaze.

"She killed her! That girl killed the holy prioress!"

"Edyth," Alice says, "you and Mason have to run. *Now.*"

And we do, through the back door of the church and straight into the chapel. But before we can bar the door, the whippers thrust it open, and the chapel is overrun. Mason swings at the men in vain.

They have me.

They get me out of the chapel and throw me onto the ground. A dog starts barking fiercely in the distance, filling the air with yellow spikes.

I spot a gap between two weak sisters, scramble to my feet and crash through, running down the path as fast as I can. Mason catches up with me and we break through the forest gate. If we can make it to the yew tree ahead of them, we can hide in its heart.

The mob chases me into the forest, but I don't look back. I know this wood better than anyone, its twists and turns and pockets of shadow.

We duck into the darkness of the deep woods, praying our footsteps won't show in the patches of snow and slush. The yew is almost within reach. All we have to do is make it inside. Mason and I hide behind an oak and hold each other. The horde runs right past us. I feel the weight of the stone house in my pocket and think, *This is what we're fighting for.*

After what seems like a lifetime, it looks safe to come out. We silently creep away from the oak—

—and lock eyes with one of the whippers, just lifting his flail.

He raises a shout, and the mob comes rushing like a pack of dogs.

We tear across the forest again, but Mason slips in the slush, slamming his knee on a rock. He crashes through the crowd of half-cheering, half-wailing men and women—in time to see them grab me.

We're standing on the pavement, right at the edge of the healing water. Patches of snow retreat from the roots around the warm pool, steam releasing upward in a great cloud.

"Look, it's right here!" I insist. "Just take it! If you drink it, you'll be healed— it's all yours!" But they set upon me, tearing off my veil, my cloak, pulling up stones from the pavement.

I feel something scurrying around my feet and look down.

It's Dragon.

She's taken the rope from around her waist and tied it around my ankle. Before I can make sense of it, she ties the other end around a hefty stone—as I see Mason's fist give her a blow that ends her life.

But as she falls, she knocks me into the pool. I know what is happening, as the sweet, warm water fills my lungs. But I'm not scared.

My body flails, tries in vain to free itself, but that's only the shell. My heart remembers every good thing, every moment of being loved.

I feel the soft baby sister in my arms.

Mam's woad-blue fingertips braiding my hair; Da's firelight ballads.

Brother Timothy handing me a picture to trace.

Joan's amber healing balm; Henry giving me the little honey pot.

Alice's smile when she's drilling me in Latin.

I feel the fullness of Mason's lips on mine, and I'm sure this is what a pomegranate tastes like.

The colors darken into a cloud of outrageous blue.

And I hear Da calling:

You know, don't you? People don't really die. They're just changed, like seeds break into wheat.

And the phantom forms disappear into the dark water above me.

Epilogue

The crowd dispersed, chanting loud psalms of darkened praise, leaving the Stonemason alone in the steaming well, plunging down again and again to try to find his love. He would not believe she was gone, fought it until the frenzy in his mind and the tension in his stomach made him vomit on the roots of the tree. He and the Healer would have left the day before, if not for her promise to the Anchorite.

And then, by some instinct, he ran back toward the priory. The mob was in complete disarray. The once-unified penitents fought each other, some justifying the murder, some condemning it. They shoved, stepped on necks, landed blows. Several of the men fled to the chapel, clinging to the bare altar for amnesty.

"Spare us, please!" they cried. "We tried to stop them. We told them that wasn't the way!"

But the Stonemason had no use for their tears.

The men who were still loyal to their misguided penance grabbed their flails and fled to the next town. To them, Saint Christopher's was beyond saving. But those who stayed were broken, battered, and desperately in need of care. The Physician set up more beds in the chapel as she told the Anchorite about her discoveries in battling the pestilence.

The Stonemason carted out the stone from the Anchorite's enclosure. He and a handful of repentant men and sisters walked into the forest, all the way to the yew tree, and began pulling up the pavement. They slid large stones over it all and covered it thickly with leaves.

"I'll never say goodbye," said the Stonemason.

This was no longer a healing well, but a grave.

"Tell no one about this place," he said, wiping his eyes with his sleeve. "This is holy ground." He took his tools and his leather satchel and walked through the priory gatehouse alone.

The Anchorite stood outside the walls and surveyed the emptiness. *Barren* was the word that first came to mind, but that wasn't it. Not barren—just waiting. Things had grown; the fields were littered with dried-up crops. Animals roamed free and fat on the people's forage. There had simply been no one to bring in the harvest.

The pestilence continued to devour everyone it could. Men and women drifted through the silent countryside and empty towns, pulled up by the roots, tumbling toward a future with half as many souls.

At Saint Christopher's Priory, a handful of nuns survived, and together they cleansed the sanctuary from its desecration and completed the chapel of Saint Eustace at last. Bread and wine were served on the altar once more.

An aging Physician wrote a book of cures.

A Cook learned to be more liberal with her spices.

Pilgrims still came through the gates, seeking to touch the newly displayed relics of Saint Eustace and a book illuminated in richest blue and gold and silver by a miracle-working girl whose lost healing spring had become legend.

And when they arrived, they found a young Prioress at the church door, waiting to tell them a story.

Amen, amen I tell you,
unless a grain of wheat falls to the earth and dies,
it remains alone.
But if it dies, it produces much fruit.

—JOHN 12:24

Glossary

ale: an alcoholic beverage varying in strength, drunk by almost everyone at the time, as water could be unsafe to drink unless drawn from a pure spring

alexanders: an edible flowering plant grown in the medieval kitchen garden, the taste of which is described as a cross between celery and asparagus

ambulatory: a passageway in a church behind the altar, sometimes divided into small chapels

Angelus: an evening bell, signifying a time of prayer for reflection and giving thanks

apse: the area in a church behind the altar

armaria: a librarian in a monastery

bastarda, Anglicana, Textualis, uncial: various terms related to handwritten fonts

braies: an article of underclothing similar to shorts or breeches, made from linen or wool

calefactory: a warming room, sometimes heated by a system of under-floor ducts

chancel: the raised platform at the east end of a church on which the altar stands

coif: a close-fitting cloth cap, worn alone or under a veil or hat by both sexes

conversa (*f, plural: conversae*): a resident of a convent who works as a laborer and is not ordained as a nun

coppice: a sustainable method of wood gathering that takes shoots from ground level instead of felling the tree, resulting in a tree without a main trunk

croft: farm

daily office: prayers said at certain intervals every day (see "The Daily Offices" at the beginning of this book)

fitchet: a slit opening in the seam of a dress that allows access to a pocket. A medieval "pocket" was not sewn in, but a pouch attached to a belt, worn inside or outside the outer garment

fuller: a person who processes woven woolen fabric to make it thicker

gesso: a material that lies under paint or gold leaf, made with a binder (usually animal glue) mixed with chalk, clay or pigment

gruit: an ale made with herbs, spices or other additives

habit: a simple gown worn by a nun or monk

hurdy-gurdy: a stringed instrument played by turning a crank, which rubs a wheel against the strings

illuminated manuscript: any book containing handwritten text and paintings, typically with parchment pages, created for either secular or religious purposes

kneeler: a prayer desk with a surface for

kneeling and a ledge on which to place a prayer book

lady: the title of a noblewoman, typically the wife of a lord (see below)

lime: a mineral compound that can be used as an ingredient in paint, especially white paint

lord: a loose term denoting members of a high social class who had authority over others, whether as landowners or military leaders

madder: a plant-based dye ranging from peach to red, also used medicinally

mastic: an aromatic gum that is added to paint as a binder or varnish

miniature: any painting in an illuminated manuscript, regardless of size. "Miniature" refers to "minium," a red lead-based pigment

muller: a glass instrument with a flat bottom for grinding pigments

nave: the main and largest section of a church, where the congregation gathers

paternoster: the Christian prayer, often called the Lord's Prayer, which begins, *Our Father Who art in Heaven*

pattens: wooden overshoes meant to raise one's feet above wet or muddy ground

peasant: any member of society not of the nobility. Peasants could be poor or wealthy, free or bound to a lord

psalter: a prayer book containing the Book of Psalms

psaltery: a stringed musical instrument similiar to a small harp

quarter days: days beginning each quarter of the year, when rents were collected and town authorities appointed (see "The Quarter Days" at the beginning of this book)

reeve: an elected official who oversaw work on a lord's manor

rood: a cross

rood screen: in a church, a tall, openwork separation wall between the chancel and the nave

scapular: a long cloth with an opening in the center for the head that is worn as part of a religious habit

shawm: a medieval double-reed woodwind instrument similar to an oboe

terre verte, aka prason: a green pigment—literally, "green earth"

theriac: an ancient medicinal concoction that could serve as an antidote or a sedative

weld: a plant-based dye yielding a range of soft greens

wimple: a cloth worn under a veil, from beneath the chin upward to the top of the head

woad: a dark blue plant-based dye similiar to indigo

Medieval books referred to:

Bald's Leechbook (9th century AD)
De Materia Medica, by Dioscorides (50–70 AD)
De Poetica, by Aristotle (ca. 335 BC)
Martyrology, by Bede (8th century AD)
Physica, by Hildegard von Bingen (1150–58 AD)
The Rule of Saint Benedict, by Benedict of Nursia (516 AD)

Author's Note

Go ahead and picture me in full nerd form: wearing a linen gown and veil, with a pouch and cup hanging from my belt, watching twenty guys in homemade armor reenacting a battle. I've always been a medievophile, and it was a no-brainer that I'd eventually write a book about the Middle Ages. I devour books and movies about it, and yes, even belonged to a medieval reenactment society. My illustration work is directly influenced by medieval art, and I'm inspired by many of the great thinkers of the time like Hildegard of Bingen.

Yet here I was, writing a book on my favorite time period, and finding I knew almost nothing. I spent hours just trying to find out, for example, whether or not carts were used to transport groups of people across long distances. (The result: inconclusive. I plead artistic license for Edyth's journey in Chapter 1.) I couldn't take anything for granted, except human nature.

Then, about halfway through the writing of this book, something miraculous happened.

A team of researchers discovered, in the ruins of a German convent graveyard, the skull of a medieval nun.[1] They were looking at her teeth for evidence of her diet when they found something unusual embedded in the enamel: microscopic flecks of a bright blue mineral: *lapis lazuli*, a pigment as valuable as pure gold.

But she was a *woman*, some opined. Surely—in their caricatured view of women's options in the Middle Ages—a woman wouldn't have been illuminating manuscripts. Only men had that privilege. Surely she wouldn't have been entrusted with such precious materials. *She must have been the cleaning lady.*

But though women of the time had fewer rights, they weren't like the re-

---

1 "Medieval Women's Early Involvement in Manuscript Production Suggested by Lapis Lazuli Identification in Dental Calculus," (with A. Radini, M. Tromp, A. Beach, E. Tong, C. Speller, M. McCormick, J. V. Dudgeon, M. J. Collins, F. Rühli, R. Kröger, and C. Warinner), *Science Advances* 5 (1), January 2019.

pressed slaves of *The Handmaid's Tale*. Just read a bit of Chaucer or Margery Kempe and you'll quickly discover that, though society had a different structure than ours, medieval women were every bit as saucy and strong-willed as they are now (present company definitely, ahem, included). Women richly contributed to the artistic and intellectual spirit of the times, whether or not we know their names. And this forgotten nun, who likely got that otherworldly blue in her teeth by licking her paintbrushes to a fine point day after day, laughs at our stereotypes from beyond her grave.

❧

What is the value of a human life? Does it have to be epic to be meaningful?

❧

We don't know for sure how many people died from the Plague outbreak of 1347–1351, but safe estimates arrive at approximately *half* the population of Europe. For centuries, everyone was tightly interwoven within the hierarchy of the manorial system. Yes, kings and lords wielded power over their vassals, and social mobility was rare, but there was a certain cohesion within local communities. Barring catastrophic personal choices, and natural disasters and famines that caused everyone to suffer, people had a measure of assurance that meant their basic needs would be met, through work, or charity in some cases.

In the aftermath of the Plague, however, when every other person was dropping dead, labor became scarce, and workers were in demand. People began to leave their villages, to set their own prices and put a monetary value upon their skills. The fact that the nobility had died at the same rate as the peasantry was a huge leveler. One's birth or status mattered less than one's abilities. The manorial system eventually unraveled. Greater emphasis was placed on the individual, and people could move up—or down—the class ladder.

The legacy of the new era that followed is surely morally mixed, but the

Plague, and the adaptability of its survivors, was directly responsible for the world we know today, because people could, and were forced to, take societal and intellectual risks. The Protestant Reformation, the Renaissance, the Enlightenment, the Industrial Revolution, the development of empirical science and medicine—in short, the birth of the modern world—all owe their origins in large part to the catastrophe of the Plague. These changes were almost as rapid and far-reaching as the impact of technology today.

The nature of human life is essentially "nasty, brutish and short," and that's been the case for the vast majority of people, men *and* women, throughout history, until only the last hundred years or so. *Most* people suffered unimaginably from disease, poverty and loss. *Most* people led lives of utter obscurity.

But it doesn't mean their lives weren't meaningful or important. In fact, even with all our options today, we are in the throes of what philosophers have dubbed "the meaning crisis." We have more ability to connect with each other than ever before, but we don't know who we are, why we're here, or what our lives are even for. And that extends into a deep suspicion of others. If our own lives feel meaningless, then the lives of our neighbors do, too—except to serve as Likers of Posts.

Surely existence means more than that, and always has. But do we unconsciously see medieval people as less important, less *evolved*, because the vast majority of their lives were private and obscure? Do we see medieval *women* as exceptionally oppressed and devoid of choices? Wasn't it possible for them to have rich lives—inner lives, connections with family and friends—without being widely known, without having their names publicly written down? Did no one truly *live* until our generation?

A Cloud of Outrageous Blue is, in many ways, a book about history itself. History is only the story of human beings making choices, and of how those choices intersect. We're all making choices in real time, even as teenagers, that will impact the future for generations. But not because of what we post online or the status we achieve—rather, by how we think and act out what we believe, about our place in our families, towns, countries and the world.

What would our blue-toothed nun say about us, across the span of time?

Might she, in fact, judge us as having too many options, too much leisure, and thinking too highly of ourselves?

This woman lived, as many did, a hidden life with little influence. She loved the people within her own small community, with the daily monotony of a monastic schedule. She painted her pictures not to make a name for herself, but as an act of private devotion and service to whoever would read her books. We don't know her name, and yet her body was full of gemstones. She lived, and died, and the treasure within her was absorbed back into the soil.

Yet here we are today, talking about how she's blown open our understanding of medieval women, their lives and choices, the trust placed in their capable hands. Who knows how much we today are affected by millions of people like her—by all the small choices that make up one life?

As an author and artist, a family member and friend, I'm trying to retrain my mind to think this way. I'm an outward-facing extrovert with big dreams, yet I'm recommitting to the small, the personal, the human-scale, not just the epic, public, and world-changing. I'm trying to go deep rather than wide—to be a better neighbor, whoever my "neighbor" might be. The more I focus on who and what are right in front of me, the more peace I feel, and the less anxiety about things outside of my control.

Every generation has its challenges. In *A Cloud of Outrageous Blue*, Edyth discovers that her uniqueness is precisely what is needed to answer the call of her generation's crisis. Because of her gifts of perception, she's able to find a miraculous cure for the Plague. But not everyone accepts it. Only dozens partake of it. And because Edyth's life is hidden, difficult and short, access to the cure is ultimately limited because of suspicion, fear and offense. Yet her decision to say *yes*—to her gifts and calling, to sacrificial love for her friends, to hope—opens doors for the future, for rediscovery.

The past is the gift we've been given. The future is ours to give.

1. Town Gate
2. Church of Saint Mary
3. Church of Saint Nicholas
4. Town Square

THORNCHESTER

RIVER SWALE

to Hartley Cross

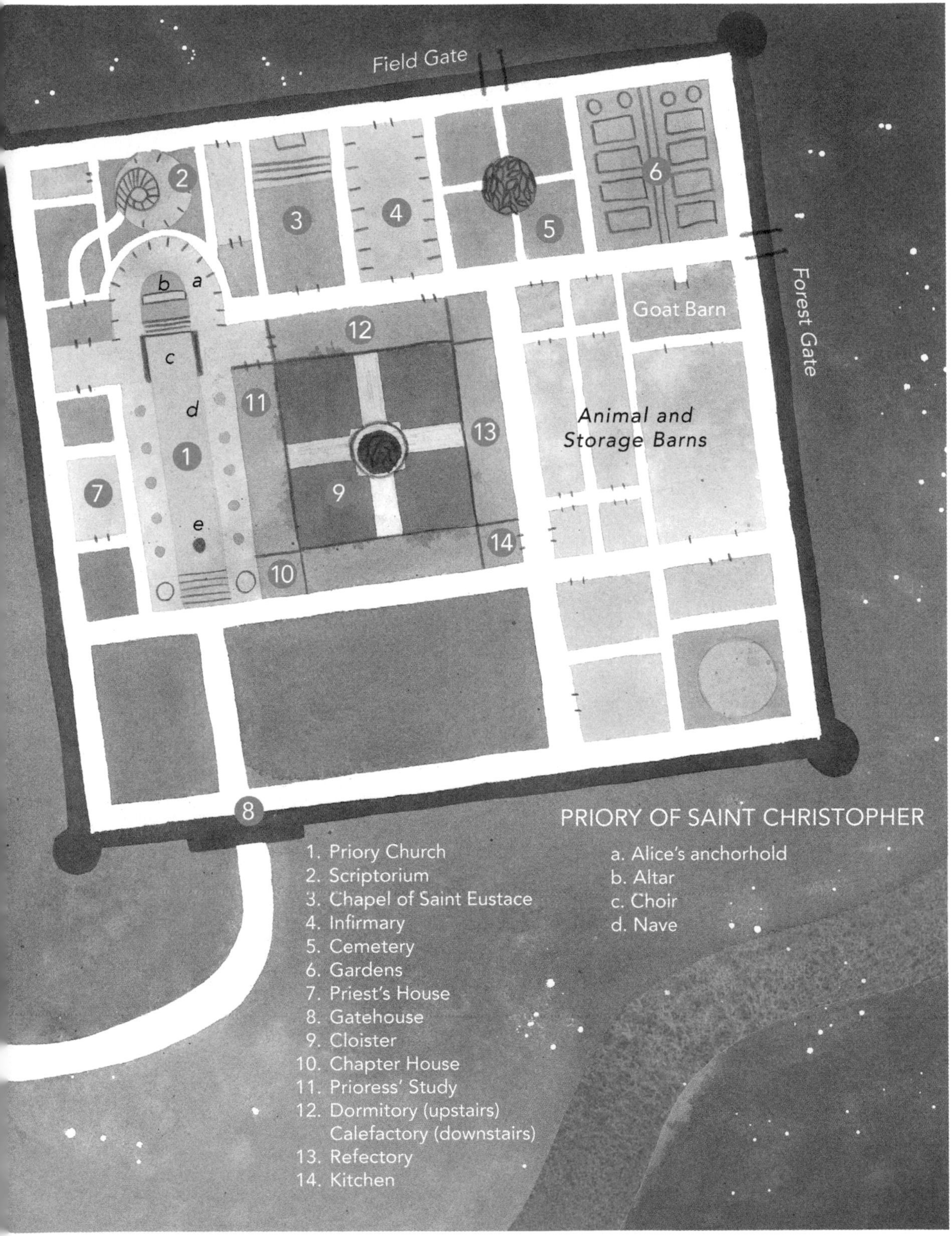

Field Gate

Forest Gate

2

3

4

5

6

Goat Barn

b a

c

12

11

d

13

1

9

Animal and
Storage Barns

7

e

14

10

8

PRIORY OF SAINT CHRISTOPHER

1. Priory Church
2. Scriptorium
3. Chapel of Saint Eustace
4. Infirmary
5. Cemetery
6. Gardens
7. Priest's House
8. Gatehouse
9. Cloister
10. Chapter House
11. Prioress' Study
12. Dormitory (upstairs)
     Calefactory (downstairs)
13. Refectory
14. Kitchen

a. Alice's anchorhold
b. Altar
c. Choir
d. Nave

Acknowledgments

The fourteenth century isn't an easy time to research. Source material is rich in some areas, obscure in others—particularly the lives of the peasantry, which constituted the vast majority of people until surprisingly recent times. So besides several ridiculously high stacks of books littering my house, I really depended on people who helped me to envision and embody Edyth's sensory experiences as much as possible.

I'm grateful for the librarians who enabled me to handle many ancient manuscripts at the British Library. Thanks to the Weald & Downland Living Museum and to the Hospital of St. Cross in Winchester, where I found my imagination made physically manifest.

A little closer to home, I'm always keen to lose myself in medieval art and space at the Cloisters, and pore over rare manuscripts at the Morgan Library. I'm very thankful to Father Vladimir Aleandro at Christ the Savior Orthodox Church in Southbury, Connecticut, for the hours-long tour he gave me of his sanctuary, where I felt the tangible holiness of a powerfully consecrated place, which was vital to capturing Edyth's multi-sensory experience.

A Cloud of Outrageous Blue is a book about many things, but one of those is perception: how we perceive the world, and how it perceives us. I wanted to explore a time in which perception was loaded with significance, both positive and negative. Synesthetes—people whose senses overlap, seeing sound as color or tasting words, for example—provide a fascinating glimpse into a kind of magic that most of us don't get to experience. Thanks to Molly Skaggs, Niki Tulk, Mikayla Butchart and Julia Denos, for letting me peer into your beautiful brains.

Thanks to Gary Moorehead for sleuthing, and for being one of the first to catch the vision for this book. Diane Calvert graciously loaned me her five-hundred-year-old home in Noyers-sur-Serein, France, for several months, where I learned the true necessity of a proper fire in the French winter and acquired a taste for very aged chèvre. But I digress. Since she's an accomplished manuscript illuminator and expert on medieval pigments, Diane's thorough reading of this story helped with many of the finer aspects of the craft.

My editor, Karen Greenberg, art directors Trish Parcell, Stephanie Moss and Alison Impey, and the whole team at Knopf Books for Young Readers and Random House Children's Books have given me a beautiful gift in being able to realize these illustrated novels. It's no small feat. I could not do what I do without my agent and friend, Lori Kilkelly, and I mean that.

I'm grateful to my readers: Dr. Mary Patterson, Bekah Sankey, Grace Andrejczek and Stephen Roach. Ray Hughes gave depth to my understanding of the UK's holy wells, and Corinne Sekinger-Clarke to the way land holds and reveals millennia of memory. You can't have those conversations with just anyone, you know. Orthodox icon carver Jonathan Pageau took time to help me with the subtle symbolism in this book. I'm sure I've missed the mark, but his guidance has been a gift.

Lea Fulton (also the model for Gerta in my first book, *What the Night Sings*) and Joshua Ramey modeled beautifully for the illustrations. And I've got to sing the praises of Dr. Alison I. Beach and the entire team who discovered the medieval German nun with lapis lazuli in her teeth. Knowing history, without revisionism, is critical to understanding ourselves as we live our own history in real time.

My grandmother Margaret and my mother, Eileen Margaret, are the namesakes for the prioress in this book, because with grace and a light hand, they've always done their level best to help me steer things in the right direction. So did my beloved graduate professor, Carl Titolo, whose memory, and wide-eyed pursuit of impermanent beauty, I honor with this book.

"The last shall be first," so the final thanks go to my dearest friends, Noelle Rhodes and Cassie Saquing, who have held up my weary arms in the sometimes long and lonely battle that was the creation of this book. And if I could give a blessing to the world, it would be for every parent to have kids of such quality as my two teenagers, and every person a life partner like my husband, Ben Stamper. Their tireless love—and their loyalty to me and to this messy art project called "family"—is truly holy.